WARRIORS

SHADOWS OF
THE CLANS

WARRIORS

THE PROPHECIES BEGIN

THE NEW PROPHECY

POWER OF THREE

OMEN OF THE STARS

DAWN OF THE CLANS

EXPLORE THE
WARRIORS
WORLD

MANGA

NOVELLAS

Also by Erin Hunter

SEEKERS

RETURN TO THE WILD

MANGA

SURVIVORS

WARRIORS

SHADOWS OF
THE CLANS

INCLUDES

Mapleshade's Vengeance
Goosefeather's Curse
Ravenpaw's Farewell

ERIN
HUNTER

HARPER
An Imprint of HarperCollinsPublishers

Special thanks to Victoria Holmes

Shadows of the Clans

Mapleshade's Vengeance, Goosefeather's Curse, Ravenpaw's Farewell

Copyright © 2016 by Working Partners Limited

Series created by Working Partners Limited

All rights reserved. Printed in the United States of America.

www.harpercollinschildrens.com

ISBN 978-0-06-234332-1

20   21   BRR   11

❖

First Edition

CONTENTS

❧

MAPLESHADE'S
VENGEANCE

ALLEGIANCES

THUNDERCLAN

LEADER OAKSTAR—sturdy brown tom with amber eyes

DEPUTY BEETAIL—dark brown striped tabby tom

MEDICINE CAT RAVENWING—small black tom with blue eyes

WARRIORS (toms and she-cats without kits)

MAPLESHADE—thick-furred orange-and-white she-cat with amber eyes

DEERDAPPLE—silver-and-black tabby she-cat
APPRENTICE, NETTLEPAW

FRECKLEWISH—speckled golden-furred she-cat with dark amber eyes

BLOOMHEART—gray tabby tom

SEEDPELT—light brown-and-white tom

THRUSHTALON—light brown tabby tom

APPRENTICE NETTLEPAW—ginger tom

ELDER (former warriors and queens, now retired)
RABBITFUR—gray tabby tom

RIVERCLAN

LEADER DARKSTAR—black she-cat

DEPUTY SPIKETAIL—dark gray tom

WARRIORS RAINFALL—skinny black tom

APPLEDUSK—pale brown tom with green eyes
APPRENTICE, PERCHPAW

REEDSHINE—dark orange she-cat

MILKFUR—white she-cat

SPLASHFOOT—pale gray tom

EELTAIL—gray-and-black tabby she-cat

APPRENTICE   PERCHPAW—thick-furred gray tom

SHADOWCLAN

MEDICINE CAT   SLOEFUR—black tom

WINDCLAN

MEDICINE CAT   LARKWING—gray tabby tom

WARRIORS   SWIFTFLIGHT—pale gray tabby tom

MIDGEPELT—patch-furred brown tom

CATS OUTSIDE CLANS

MYLER—black-and-white tom

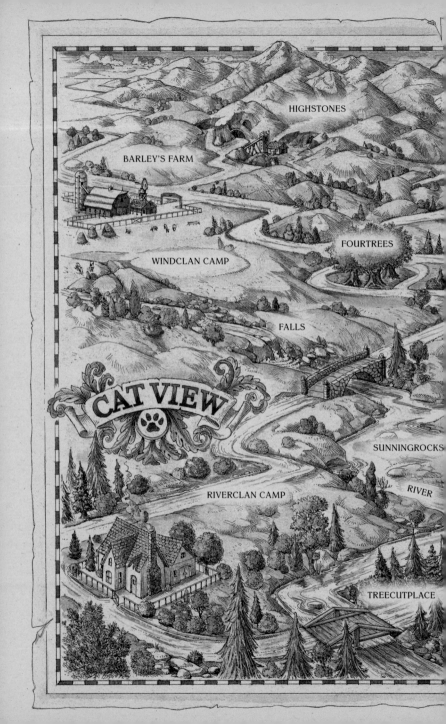

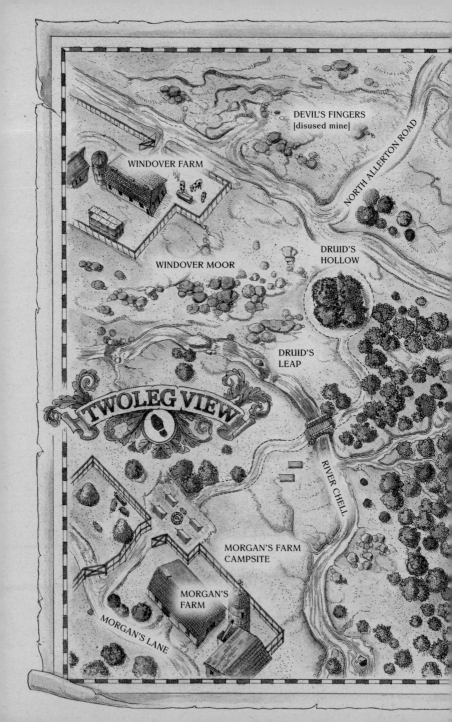

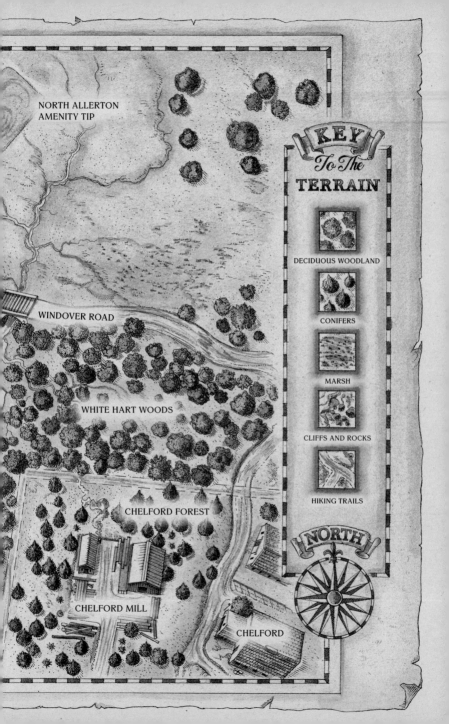

CHAPTER 1

♣

"Steady on, Mapleshade! You just trod on my tail!" The WindClan warrior jerked away with a hiss.

"Sorry, Swiftflight," Mapleshade apologized over her shoulder as she plunged deeper into the throng of cats. The light of the full moon turned all their pelts to silver, and fur tickled Mapleshade's nose. Above her, Oakstar's voice echoed around the trunks of the four gigantic oak trees.

"My warriors tracked the adders to their nest at Snakerocks and blocked the hole with stones," the ThunderClan leader reported. "Thanks to their courage, no adders have since been seen in our territory."

"They were lucky not to get bitten," grunted a ShadowClan elder near Mapleshade's ear.

"Too right," agreed her Clanmate. "Remember when Marshpaw trod on an adder on his first patrol? That was a bad way to die."

The first cat shrugged. "I've seen worse."

Mapleshade rolled her eyes. *Trust ShadowClan cats to get competitive about deaths they have watched.* She dodged around a rock and emerged among a cluster of RiverClan cats. Instantly pelts bristled and she felt eyes burn into her.

"There may be a truce," snarled the black warrior Rainfall. "But don't push your luck, ThunderClan mouse dung."

Mapleshade ducked her head. "I mean no harm," she mewed. "I'm not staying."

"Good," growled a cat she couldn't see.

Mapleshade forced her hair to lie flat as she wove among the hostile warriors. She couldn't blame RiverClan for being angry. ThunderClan had triumphed in the last clash over Sunningrocks; defeat was the bitterest wound of all.

"Remember what happened to Birchface and Flowerpaw," Rainfall murmured in her ear, so close that Mapleshade could feel the heat of his fish-breath. "Those rocks belong to us, and we'll kill as many of your Clanmates as we need to until you give them up."

Mapleshade stumbled as a memory seared through her brain: Appledusk, a light brown RiverClan warrior with piercing green eyes, striking Birchface so hard that the ThunderClan cat lost his footing and slipped from the very top of Sunningrocks. He landed with a splash in the swollen river. His apprentice Flowerpaw leaped in after him and struggled to keep Birchface's head out of the water but the current was too strong and they were swept downstream into the half-submerged crossing rocks. For one terrible moment, dark tabby and dappled gray heads rose above the surface, screeching in fear, then both vanished into the tumbling foam. Their bodies were found just beyond the stones, washed up on the ThunderClan shore as if they were making a last desperate effort to go home.

Mapleshade swallowed a burst of rage at the warriors around her. Why did RiverClan insist on fighting over a bunch of rocks that were clearly on ThunderClan's territory? She lowered her head and pushed her way through the knot of hostile cats. She made it to the edge of the hollow where the shadows clustered more densely, dark enough to hide among. Suddenly a pale brown shape loomed in front of her, and Mapleshade's nostrils flared at the scent of fish. She looked up, her heart pounding.

"What are you doing here?" hissed Appledusk. His long front claws caught the moonlight as he sank them into the grass.

Mapleshade's words seemed to be stuck in her throat. She stared into the RiverClan warrior's holly-colored eyes and tried to breathe normally. She wondered if any of her Clanmates were watching.

Appledusk took a step closer and lowered his head until his muzzle brushed the tip of Mapleshade's ear. "You must know how dangerous it is for you to be here. What would happen if your Clanmates saw you talking to me?"

Mapleshade leaned forward until her cheek pressed against Appledusk's feather-soft chest fur. "I had to speak with you," she murmured. "It's been too long. I waited for you at the syc-amore tree every night, but you never came."

The tom's breath warmed the back of her neck. "I know," he purred. "But since the battle, we've doubled our border patrols, even after dark. I can't cross the river without being spotted." He took a step back, and Mapleshade felt a rush of cold air on her pelt. "I'll try to get across at new moon. Things might have calmed down by then."

"If only you hadn't killed Birchface," Mapleshade whispered. "Of all the cats to lose in the battle, it had to be Oakstar's son!"

She felt Appledusk stiffen beneath his pelt. "It was an accident," he growled. "I never meant for him to fall into the river."

Mapleshade closed her eyes. "That's not the way my Clanmates see it. They blame you for both of our losses."

"Then they are fools." Appledusk shuddered, then relaxed. "But Sunningrocks has always made our Clans a little mousebrained." He licked the top of Mapleshade's head. "Thank StarClan you didn't get hurt in the battle."

Mapleshade gazed up at him. *Oh my precious warrior. I love you with all my heart.* "There's something you need to know," she mewed.

Appledusk was looking over her head, toward the pool of moonlight where his Clanmates stood. "Can't it wait?"

"I don't think so." Mapleshade took a deep breath. "I'm expecting your kits."

There was a flash of green as Appledusk opened his eyes wide. "Are you sure?"

Mapleshade nodded. The RiverClan warrior curled his tail over his back. "I'm going to be a father," he purred. "Incredible." He tipped his head to one side. "But these kits will be half-Clan. Half *RiverClan*. How will your Clanmates feel about that?"

"They won't know," Mapleshade answered. She noticed Appledusk flinch. "At least, not at first," she went on. "I will raise them as ThunderClan until they have been fully accepted. Then every cat will be able to cope with the truth. Why should it matter that their father lives in a different Clan?"

The fur on Appledusk's shoulders twitched. "You have great faith in your Clanmates," he murmured.

"No, I have faith in StarClan, and in the warrior code."

"You think StarClan approves of what we are doing?" Appledusk narrowed his eyes.

"I think our warrior ancestors know that our Clans need kits and we are providing them. How can our innocent kits not have their blessing? They will grow up to be fine warriors, loyal to ThunderClan and RiverClan equally." Mapleshade turned away before Appledusk could say anything else. "I must return to my Clanmates before they come looking for me. Perhaps it's best if we don't see each other again until after the kits have come." She looked back over her shoulder. "But I will be thinking of you every day, my love."

As she padded into the shadows that ringed the hollow, Mapleshade heard rapid paw steps. "Appledusk! There you are! I've been looking for you!" Mapleshade stopped, hoping her white patches weren't glowing in the moonlight. A dark orange she-cat was pressing herself against Appledusk's shoulder. "One of the ShadowClan elders is telling a story about a cat that swallowed a live frog," she mewed. "Come and listen, it's really funny."

With a worried glance at the shadows where Mapleshade crouched, Appledusk followed the she-cat back to the cluster of cats. The orange warrior curled her tail until it was resting on Appledusk's back.

Mapleshade curled her lip. *Stay away from him, Reedshine. He's mine! These kits will make sure of that!*

"Mapleshade, wake up!" A small ginger face poked through the branches that sheltered the warriors' den. "Beetail wants you to go on the dawn patrol. You're late!"

"All right, Nettlepaw, I'm coming." Mapleshade heaved herself to her paws. Last night she had felt the kits stirring inside her for the first time. *Is it because your father knows about you now?* She craned her head around to lick the rumpled fur on her flank, then pushed her way out of the den. She felt strangely heavy, unbalanced by her swollen belly.

The air in the clearing was still and cold, tasting of old leaves and damp earth. The little orange apprentice bounced around Mapleshade. "Hurry up! When did you get so slow?"

Mapleshade flicked him lightly with her tail. "What would Deerdapple do if you spoke like that to her, hmmm?"

Nettlepaw looked down at the ground at the mention of his mentor. "She'd probably make me pick ticks off Rabbitfur for a moon," he admitted.

Mapleshade purred, too full of joy about her kits to be short-tempered. "You're lucky that I won't punish you, then. Now, off you go and let me speak to Beetail."

The apprentice scampered off with a squeak. Mapleshade

headed over to the ThunderClan deputy, who was standing beside the entrance to Oakstar's den. The dark brown tabby nodded as Mapleshade approached.

"I'd like you to join the dawn patrol, please," he meowed. "Frecklewish is leading it."

"Actually, there's something I need to tell you," Mapleshade began. Her paws tingled. "I won't be able to carry out my usual duties for a while. I'm expecting kits."

Beetail blinked. "Oh. Right. I . . . er . . . wasn't expecting that. Well, you must only do what you feel up to. Does Oakstar know?"

"Not yet. Why don't I help out in the camp today?" Mapleshade suggested. She couldn't resist glancing at the curve of her belly. "I could fetch some soaked moss for the elders, if you like."

"That would be great," mewed Beetail. He shifted his paws. "And, er, congratulations."

"Thank you," purred Mapleshade. "It's wonderful news, isn't it?"

"Indeed," Beetail meowed. "And these kits . . . their father . . . ?"

"I will be raising them alone," Mapleshade answered firmly.

The deputy looked startled for a moment, then dipped his head. "May StarClan light your path, and the path of your kits."

Still rumbling with delight, Mapleshade turned and headed back across the clearing. Since she wasn't needed on the dawn patrol, she could go back to her nest until the rest of the Clan stirred. She knew she had to save her strength for when the kits arrived.

She was dozing in dappled sunlight when she was roused by paws thrumming outside the den. Frecklewish burst in, her speckled golden fur fluffed up and her eyes sparkling. "Beetail told me your news!" she purred. "I'm so happy for you!"

Mapleshade sat up and curled her thick white tail over her paws. "Thank you." *You see, Appledusk? My Clanmates will only be delighted to have new kits in the camp!*

Frecklewish stood beside Mapleshade's nest looking uncharacteristically shy. "Beetail also said that you would be raising these kits alone," she mewed.

Mapleshade tensed. She had not anticipated questions about her kits' father so soon.

Frecklewish looked down at the floor of the den. "Is . . . is that because their father is dead?" She lifted her gaze, and Mapleshade almost winced at the blaze of hope in her eyes. "Are these Birchface's kits?" Frecklewish whispered. "Is my brother going to live on through you?"

The air in the warriors' den was suddenly so thick that Mapleshade couldn't catch her breath. *Is StarClan offering me a way for my kits to be accepted by their Clanmates? I can't lie, not if I want them to know the truth later.* She stared at Frecklewish, unable to speak.

The golden she-cat didn't seem to need a response from Mapleshade. She nodded slowly, and the light in her eyes burned even more brightly. "I'm right, aren't I? Oh, thank StarClan! And thank *you*, Mapleshade. You will never know how much this means to me. I . . . I thought I would never be happy again after Birchface was killed in that terrible battle. But now I can help you to raise his kits, teach them that their father was a true ThunderClan hero, watch them take his place in the Clan . . ." She broke off and stepped gently into the nest until she was crouched beside Mapleshade. She stretched out her front paw until it rested on Mapleshade's orange-and-white flank. "I hope Birchface can see us," she murmured.

Mapleshade took a deep breath. *I have not lied out loud. This was all Frecklewish's doing. But I cannot turn down this chance to have my kits welcomed with the love they deserve. Appledusk will understand that I have to put ThunderClan first, for now at least.* She unfurled her tail until it was resting on Frecklewish's shoulder.

"You have answered my prayers, Frecklewish," she mewed softly. "My kits and I are no longer alone."

Frecklewish's dark amber gaze shone back at her. "Never," she vowed. "These kits will be the best thing ever to happen in our Clan."

CHAPTER 2

Oh StarClan, make it stop! Mapleshade writhed in agony and sank her claws into the dried moss.

"Relax," Ravenwing instructed, placing one paw on her rippling flank.

You try to relax with this happening to you, Mapleshade wanted to screech at the medicine cat, but she barely had enough breath to survive the spasm that wracked her body. She clenched her jaw and resisted the urge to sink her teeth into Ravenwing's thick-furred black leg.

"It's a tom!" gasped Frecklewish. "Oh, he's magnificent!"

Ravenwing turned to look. Mapleshade sprawled in the nest with her eyes closed, trying not to think about the pain yet to come. Something wet and squirming was shoved against her muzzle. She opened her mouth to protest—and smelled the sweetest scent she had ever known. She lifted her head and blinked down at the dark brown bundle of slick fur beside her. *Oh Appledusk, you have a son. And he's beautiful!*

"Lick him, Mapleshade," Ravenwing mewed. "It will help him to breathe."

For a moment Mapleshade wanted to tell the other cats

to get out, to leave her alone with this tiny precious creature. Nothing would ever be as special as this heartbeat, when she met her first kit. Then her body buckled under another wave of pain and she cried out. Ravenwing hastily pulled the kit away. "You take him, Frecklewish," he ordered.

"Gladly," came the she-cat's mew. "Come here, little one. Let's get you clean and dry."

Mapleshade tried to say that she could take care of her own kits but the spasm grew stronger and suddenly there was another kit lying beside her, his mouth wide open in a soundless mew, his fur patched with ginger and white like his mother's.

"Another tom," Ravenwing announced. "You're doing great, Mapleshade." He ran his paws along her body. "One more, and that's it. Come on now, stay focused."

An irresistible longing to be alone with her kits gave Mapleshade a fresh surge of strength and the final kit slithered out almost at once.

"A she-cat!" purred Ravenwing. "Smaller than her brothers, but in excellent shape. Your turn to take over, Mapleshade." He nudged all three kits into the curve of Mapleshade's belly. She propped herself up and twisted around to gaze at them in astonishment. *I did it, Appledusk! Two sons and a daughter!*

"They are gorgeous," Frecklewish whispered, her voice husky with emotion.

Ravenwing nodded. "You did a great job, Mapleshade. We'll leave you alone to rest, but I'll come back with some herbs for you after sunhigh. Do you feel okay?" There was a flash of concern in his dark blue eyes, and Mapleshade felt a surge of sympathy toward the young medicine cat. He had been in sole charge of ThunderClan for just two moons since the death of Oatspeckle, and this was one of the first deliveries he'd had to supervise.

"I couldn't be better," she told him. Her throat felt dry and sore. "Could I just have some water, please?"

"I'll fetch it," Frecklewish offered, hopping out of the nest and vanishing through the brambles.

Ravenwing watched her leave. "You have made her feel as if life is worth living again," he commented. "She took the loss of her brother hard."

Mapleshade buried her muzzle in the soft, damp fur of her kits. "These kits are my gift to the whole of ThunderClan," she murmured. "I will thank StarClan for them every day for the rest of my life."

The medicine cat touched her lightly with the tip of his tail. "And ThunderClan thanks you," he meowed.

As will RiverClan, Mapleshade added silently. *The feud over Sunningrocks will be forgotten when the Clans realize that they share these perfect warriors!*

"Are you receiving visitors?" rumbled a voice at the entrance to the nursery.

"Of course! Come in," Mapleshade mewed somewhat breathlessly while trying to coax the she-kit off the top of her head. At three sunrises old, they astonished Mapleshade with their ability to be all over the nursery at once, while at the same time constantly nuzzling at her belly.

Oakstar's broad dark brown face appeared through the branches. "Hello, little ones," he purred.

The she-kit jumped at the sound of his voice. Releasing her tiny claws from Mapleshade's ear, she slithered onto the moss with a thump.

"This is Oakstar, the leader of ThunderClan," Mapleshade told her kits. She tried to nudge them into a line. But their eyes were still closed and the smell of a different cat was just too much to resist, so all three tottered toward Oakstar with their stubby tails held straight up, mouths open in high-pitched mews.

Oakstar gently herded them back to Mapleshade with his paw. "I'm not just their leader," he reminded her. "Birchface was my son. These cats are my kin." His eyes clouded with emotion as he stared down at the kits. "If only Birchface could see them."

Mapleshade's fur felt hot and prickly. "I'm sure he's watching from StarClan," she murmured. Beside her, the kits started nuzzling at her belly and fell silent as they began to suck.

"My son was a great warrior," Oakstar went on. "The Clan is honored if his spirit lives on through his kits."

There was a rustle of bramble fronds and Frecklewish appeared with a vole in her jaws. She set it down beside the nest. "I took first pick of the fresh-kill pile for you," she told Mapleshade with pride.

"Thank you," Mapleshade meowed hoarsely. She wondered if it would be rude to ask Oakstar to leave. His scrutiny was making her more and more nervous.

Frecklewish turned to Oakstar. "Aren't the kits perfect?" she purred. "I can see Birchface so clearly in each of them!"

Mapleshade glanced at the tiny bodies in the curve of her belly. Apart from the tom who was patch-furred like her, they were the exact soft brown shade of Appledusk's fur. Birchface had been a dark brown tabby, almost black. Her heart pounding, she waited for Oakstar to comment but instead he asked if she had chosen names for them.

Mapleshade used her tail to indicate each kit without disturbing them. "I thought Larchkit for the brown tom, Patchkit for his brother, and Petalkit for their sister." She paused as her tail-tip rested on the tiny she-kit. She was the fluffiest of all and her ears were so small they barely peeked out of the fur on her head. Mapleshade felt as if her heart would burst with love. *If only you could see them like this, Appledusk!*

"Excellent names," Oakstar meowed.

"Didn't you want to name one of them after Birchface?" Frecklewish asked. She sounded disappointed.

Mapleshade didn't lift her gaze from her kits. "I want them each to be their own warrior," she explained quietly. "Not an echo of a cat that has gone before."

To her relief Oakstar purred. "ThunderClan is blessed to have you as a queen, Mapleshade. I look forward to watching these kits grow up."

"I can't wait to see RiverClan's faces when they hear about them at the next Gathering," Frecklewish hissed.

Mapleshade's heart began to beat faster. "I wish I could be

there to see that, too. Make sure you tell them that I've had three perfect, strong kits who are going to be great warriors!" she told Frecklewish. "Especially Appledusk. Tell him first."

The pale ginger she-cat blinked. "Why would I speak to that mange-fur?" she growled. "He killed Birchface!"

"Exactly!" mewed Mapleshade hurriedly. "He needs to know that ThunderClan is stronger than ever, thanks to these kits."

Frecklewish nodded. "Of course." She unsheathed her front claws and sank them into the mossy litter on the floor of the nursery. "Our enemies have even more reason to fear us now!"

Oakstar curled his lip, showing a glint of yellow teeth. "It will do no harm for RiverClan to know that they may have robbed us of two fine cats, but thanks to Birchface, there will be three more warriors ready to defend what is rightfully ours."

Mapleshade felt a stir of alarm. "The warrior code says we must show mercy to the warriors we have defeated," she pointed out.

"Appledusk didn't show any mercy to Birchface and Flowerpaw!" Frecklewish hissed, lashing her tail.

It was an accident! Mapleshade wanted to shriek. *Birchface fell! Flowerpaw should never have followed him into the river!* But she controlled herself. She couldn't let Frecklewish suspect she had any sympathy for Appledusk. Not yet.

Oakstar was starting to back out of the nursery. "Right now, the most important thing is that Mapleshade's kits are safe and well," he meowed. There was a grim note to his voice that made Mapleshade's fur stand up. "We will raise them to be great warriors like their father," Oakstar vowed, "and let them avenge his death when they are ready." He turned and vanished into the clearing, leaving the bramble wall trembling.

Frecklewish bent over the furry little bodies and touched her muzzle lightly to each squirming rump. "They are my brother's gift to the Clan," she murmured. "And the most precious creatures in the whole forest!"

Mapleshade fought down the urge to bat Frecklewish away. *These are my kits, not yours!* She knew that the ginger she-cat's friendship would go a long way toward her kits being loved by all of ThunderClan. By the time the kits were ready to be apprenticed, the truth about who their father really was would be unable to shake the loyalty of their woodland Clanmates. Even Oakstar would understand, once he valued the kits for themselves rather than any legacy they might carry. *And once RiverClan gets to know them, those cats will feel the same!*

CHAPTER 3

"Watch this, Larchkit!" Wrinkling her muzzle in concentration, Petalkit gripped the bundle of dry moss in her jaws and shook it violently.

Her brother grabbed the moss from her and tossed it across the clearing. Both kits scrambled after it, Petalkit winning by a nose. She flopped down on top of the moss. "Mine!" she declared.

"Don't you want to join in?" Mapleshade asked Patchkit, who was lying in the curve of her belly. His fur matched hers so perfectly that it was impossible to tell where one stopped and the other began. "It looks like they're having fun."

Her son shook his head. "I'm fine here," he mewed. He snuggled in a little closer. "You need me to keep you warm, don't you?" His green eyes blinked anxiously at her.

Mapleshade stifled a purr of laughter. She could barely feel his tiny body against hers. It was a rare cloud-free day in the rainwashed leaf-fall, and the sunbeams were just strong enough to bring cats out of their dens to bask, though there was a chill in the ground that warned of leaf-bare just around the corner.

"You're doing a great job," she told Patchkit. "I might have to share you with the elders to stop them getting cold."

Patchkit's green eyes opened wide in alarm. "No! I want to stay with you forever and ever! Even when I'm an apprentice!"

Mapleshade nuzzled the top of his head. "That won't be for another four moons, little one. By then you'll be so big and strong, you'll be glad to leave the nursery and start your warrior training!"

"No I won't," muttered Patchkit, burying his face in her chest fur. "I never want to leave you."

Petalkit and Larchkit were standing side by side, looking at the moss.

"You've ripped it to pieces!" Larchkit protested. "It doesn't roll away now, look." He prodded the pile of dusty brown shreds with his paw.

Petalkit shrugged. "It was trying to escape and I caught it!"

One of the elders, a gray tabby named Rabbitfur, padded stiffly over to the kits. "Looks like she's killed it," he observed. "Want to play a different game?"

"Yes please!" mewed Larchkit.

Rabbitfur used his front paw to roll a small stone into the middle of the clearing. Then he nudged a twig with his nose until it lay a bit less than a fox-length from the stone. Mapleshade propped herself up to watch.

"I want you to stand by this stick," Rabbitfur meowed, pointing with his tail, "and pounce on that stone without touching the ground in between."

Petalkit blinked. "But that's almost at the other side of the clearing!"

"I'd have to grow wings to jump that far!" mewed Larchkit.

"Don't be mouse-brained," snorted Rabbitfur. "Your father could leap twice that distance, and land on the smallest leaf without disturbing a fly."

Mapleshade felt a stir of alarm in her belly. Beside her, Patchkit sat up and tipped his head to one side. "Rabbitfur's really bossy!" he squeaked.

Petalkit was crouching down beside the twig, wiggling her rump as she braced herself for the jump. With a grunt, she heaved herself forward, but her hind paw caught on the stick. She lurched sideways, snapping the twig, and sprawled on the ground at Rabbitfur's paws.

"Humph!" he muttered. "Try again."

This time Petalkit managed to clear the stick but she barely made half of the distance to the stone. Rabbitfur shook his head. "Your turn, Larchkit," he rumbled.

The little brown tom looked very determined as he hunkered down. He sprang into the air, almost as high as Rabbitfur's ears, but came down almost vertically, like an acorn falling from a tree.

Rabbitfur had to dodge out of the way to avoid being squashed. "Watch out!" He gave his chest fur a couple of licks. "Birchface managed to pounce without flattening any cats," he grunted.

Mapleshade couldn't listen to any more. She jumped out, dislodging Patchkit, who rolled over with a squawk, and trotted into the clearing. "Perhaps they take after me, Rabbitfur," she meowed. "I can't pounce, either."

The old tom narrowed his eyes. "You're not that bad," he rasped. "I can't believe any kit of Birchface would be heavy-footed as a badger." He glanced at Petalkit, who was licking the paw that had caught on the stick.

The blood was roaring in Mapleshade's ears now. "I will not have my kits judged before they have even begun their warrior training!" she hissed. "Patchkit, come here! We're going for a walk in the forest!"

Patchkit scampered over, but Petalkit was pouting. "I want to stay here and practice jumping," she mewed. "I want to be as good as Birchface."

Rabbitfur looked pleased. "You should be very proud of who your father was," he purred. "I remember the time we were stalking a pheasant over by Twolegplace. I'd never seen a bird that big, but Birchface was fearless—and so quiet, I couldn't hear him over the breeze in the leaves!"

"I think the kits need to stretch their legs outside the camp," Mapleshade meowed, interrupting Rabbitfur's memories. "Come on, you three! No arguments, Petalkit."

Patchkit's green eyes—so like Appledusk's, they made Mapleshade's heart flip over—were huge. "Are we allowed outside? I thought we had to stay in the camp until we are old enough to be apprentices."

"I'll be with you so you'll be perfectly safe," Mapleshade told him. Oakstar and Beetail were out on patrol and Frecklewish had gone to check the barrier of stones at Snakerocks.

Rabbitfur had wandered back to his sunny spot outside the elders' den. Apart from some dozing cats, the clearing was empty. No one would take much notice if she took the kits out.

Suddenly Mapleshade couldn't bear to be in the ravine another moment. With a whisk of her tail, she trotted toward the tunnel through the gorse. The kits bundled after her, chirping with excitement.

"I'm going to catch a badger!" Larchkit boasted.

"I'm going to watch that badger eat you first!" retorted Petalkit.

Patchkit was running at Mapleshade's heels. "Don't let a badger eat me!" he whimpered.

Mapleshade paused beside the tunnel entrance and turned to lick Patchkit's ears. "I'll never let anything bad happen to you," she promised. With one more glance to check that they weren't being scrutinized, she ushered her kits into the branches.

"Ow, it's prickly!" squeaked Petalkit.

"Don't stop," Mapleshade urged. With a rapid beat of paws on hard earth, the kits burst out of the tunnel and stopped dead, staring around.

"Wow, outside of the camp is really big!" breathed Larchkit.

"It's even bigger at the top of the ravine," Mapleshade meowed. She nudged her kits toward the path that led up to the trees. Her fur prickled at the thought of being seen by a returning patrol.

The kits scrambled up the slope, Petalkit in the lead. They

looked even tinier among the tree trunks, the towering oaks and beeches that overhung the ravine. Mapleshade hurried them along a little-used path beneath dense ferns; the kits wanted to stop and sniff every leaf, every mark on the ground, but Mapleshade kept them moving, ducking beneath the sweet-smelling fronds and hoping the fern scent would cover their tracks.

The undergrowth began to thin out, and the sound of splashing water drifted through the trees. Larchkit pricked his ears. "What's that?" he mewed. As he tried to peer through the stalks, he stumbled over a fallen twig and landed on his nose. Mapleshade whisked him back to his paws before he could let out a wail. *I'm glad Rabbitfur didn't see that*, she thought. She couldn't deny that these kits were clumsier than their ThunderClan kin.

Patchkit had kept going while Mapleshade picked up his brother, and Mapleshade heard his sudden squeak of surprise. "Water! Water everywhere, look!"

His littermates bundled forward to stand beside him at the edge of the bracken. Mapleshade joined them, and looked out at the dazzling brightness of the river as it flowed past, swift and sparkling.

"It's the most beautiful thing I've ever seen," Petalkit whispered.

"Where did it come from?" mewed Larchkit.

Mapleshade thought for a moment. "I don't really know," she admitted. "Farther upstream is a deep gorge beside Wind-Clan's territory —"

"Can we go there?" Petalkit demanded.

Mapleshade shook her head. "No, little one. It's too far for you to walk today. But one day you'll see it, I promise."

Patchkit, usually so timid and happy to let his littermates try everything first, tottered over the stones to the edge of the water.

"Be careful!" Mapleshade warned.

Her son turned to look at her, his eyes shining and droplets of water glinting on his whiskers. "It's okay," he mewed. "Watch!"

Before Mapleshade could stop him, he launched himself forward and slipped into the water. For one heartstopping moment, he vanished, then his ginger-and-white face bobbed up on the surface. "Look at me!" he squealed.

Larchkit and Petalkit raced down the shore and plunged in. For a few strides their little paws dug into the pebbles while the water lapped their fluffy bellies, then they were swimming through the rolling water.

Mapleshade felt a burst of love like the sun coming out. *Oh Appledusk! Our kits are half RiverClan, for sure!*

Patchkit reached a branch sticking out of the water and hauled himself onto it. Water streamed from his pelt, leaving it as glossy as a crow's feathers. He looked no bigger than a mouse with his fur flattened to his sides, and his flanks heaved as he caught his breath. Mapleshade felt a jolt of concern.

"Are you okay?" she called.

Patchkit nodded, still panting too hard to speak. Mapleshade paced up and down on the shore. She hated the idea of getting her paws wet, but she wasn't sure if Patchkit had enough strength to swim back on his own. The other kits were playing hide-and-seek in a clump of reeds close by the shore. "Larchkit, Petalkit, go help your brother!" she meowed.

Suddenly the rushes on the far shore rustled and a dark gray head appeared. Mapleshade froze. It was Spiketail, the River-Clan deputy. In the middle of the river, Patchkit slumped on the branch, his cheek resting on the slick bark.

"What is that kit doing?" growled Spiketail. He stepped onto the shore, the fur along his spine bristling.

Mapleshade opened her mouth to speak but two more warriors were emerging from the rushes beside Spiketail.

"Is ThunderClan sending their youngest cats to invade us?" asked Milkfur, her white pelt glowing against the stones.

The third cat met Mapleshade's gaze across the river. From this distance, his green eyes were unreadable. "I think one kit is hardly a threat to our territory," he meowed. "I'll return him to where he belongs." He waded into the water, his pale brown fur turning black as he slid beneath the surface.

"Larchkit, Petalkit, come here!" Mapleshade hissed. The kits waded toward her, looking scared.

"Is that RiverClan warrior going to catch us?" Petalkit squeaked.

Mapleshade watched Appledusk's head bob steadily closer to the branch. "No," she mewed. "You're safe, don't worry."

Appledusk mewed something to Patchkit, too quietly for Mapleshade to hear. Patchkit slithered down the branch and into the water. The RiverClan warrior steadied him with one paw, then began to propel him toward the ThunderClan shore. Mapleshade realized that the other kits were trembling from cold and she bent her head to lick their fur.

"Are we in trouble?" Larchkit mewed.

"Hush, everything's fine," Mapleshade murmured between licks.

Appledusk waded out of the river with Patchkit dangling from his jaws. He set the kit down on the stones and nudged him to his feet. "I think this one's worn out from all that swimming," he commented. His eyes burned into Mapleshade's. "You took a risk, bringing them this close to our boundary."

"I wanted to show them the river," Mapleshade meowed. She angled her body so that the kits were bundled behind her, out of earshot. She could hear Larchkit asking Patchkit what it had been like to swim so far out.

Appledusk leaned forward until his muzzle was almost touching Mapleshade's cheek. "They are wonderful," he breathed. "Strong and brave, and as confident as any River-Clan cat in the water. I am so proud of you." He straightened up and raised his voice. "I don't want to see you or these kits anywhere near the river again," he meowed. The longing in his eyes told a different story.

Mapleshade bowed her head. "Of course, Appledusk. Thank you for bringing Patchkit back."

Appledusk glanced once more at the kits, then headed back into the water.

"Those kits are not old enough to be out of the nursery!" Milkfur called across the river. "What were you thinking of, bringing them here? They could have drowned!"

"You may have won Sunningrocks, but the river still belongs to us," yowled Spiketail. "Appledusk has been merciful this time, but from now on, stay away from our territory."

Mapleshade herded the kits into the bracken. They were bouncing on their paws—even Patchkit, whose fur was fluffing up like thistledown as it dried.

"That was the best thing ever!" squeaked Larchkit.

"When can we come here again?" Petalkit asked. "Swimming is way more fun than jumping!"

"I swam the farthest, didn't I?" mewed Patchkit proudly.

Suddenly a dark shape blocked the path. Mapleshade looked up and met Ravenwing's searching blue gaze. The medicine cat glanced down at the kits. "What were they doing in the river?" he asked.

Mapleshade's paws started to tingle. "Did . . . did you see them?" she whispered.

Ravenwing nodded. "I saw *everything*. What's going on, Mapleshade?"

Before Mapleshade could reply, the kits tumbled over themselves to tell him about their adventure.

"A RiverClan warrior had to save Patchkit—" mewed Larchkit.

"He did not! I was just resting!" Patchkit interrupted crossly.

"It's fine, no one was in any danger," Mapleshade meowed as Ravenwing narrowed his eyes.

"The RiverClan cat was really nice!" squeaked Patchkit.

"He said I was very brave, and a really good swimmer!"

"Did he?" mewed Ravenwing. "What else did he say?" He took a step closer.

Mapleshade curled her tail around the kits. "Come on, little ones, time to go home."

Ravenwing didn't move out of the way. "I've seen an omen, Mapleshade," he murmured. "I wonder if you know anything about it?"

There was something in his voice that made Mapleshade's fur prick. "Why would I know anything about an omen? I'm not a medicine cat."

Ravenwing stared at her without blinking. "A tiny stream appeared in my den, in a place where no stream has run before. It carried with it three pieces of water reed." He swept his paw over the ground as if he was tracing the path of the rivulet. "Water reed doesn't grow in ThunderClan territory," he went on. "It doesn't belong inside our boundaries. Do you understand?"

Mapleshade shrugged. "There's been so much rain this leaf-fall, bits and pieces must be washing all over the place." She tried to keep her voice light but there was a cold, heavy feeling in her belly, as if she had swallowed a stone from the river.

Ravenwing watched the kits play with an acorn, shuffling it from one to the other with their paws. "I think this omen means that the river has washed three strange cats into ThunderClan—three cats who don't belong there."

Mapleshade's heart was pounding so hard, she could hardly

breathe. "What are you trying to say?" she whispered.

Ravenwing gazed at her, and suddenly he didn't seem like a young, inexperienced cat anymore. Knowledge glittered in his eyes like frosty stars. "Birchface is not the father of these kits, is he? Rabbitfur told me what happened today, how they showed no signs of being able to stalk or pounce like him. And don't tell me that they take after you instead," he added, cutting Mapleshade off as she opened her mouth. "You tread as lightly as any ThunderClan warrior." He looked past her, at the river splashing beyond the shade of the trees. "I watched your kits swim in that river as if they were fish. I think these kits were fathered by a RiverClan cat. Appledusk, I'd guess, judging by the color of their fur and by the way he spoke to you when he brought Patchkit back."

Mapleshade felt the ground sway beneath her paws. "ThunderClan is blessed to have three beautiful, strong kits," she hissed. "The truth will be revealed at the right time. It's not my fault that everyone assumed Birchface was their father."

"I cannot let you lie to our Clanmates!" Ravenwing spat. "And now that I know the truth, I cannot lie, either."

"I have told you nothing," Mapleshade mewed through clenched jaws.

"You have told me plenty," Ravenwing responded, and there was sadness in his sky-colored eyes. "The truth must come out."

"Please don't say anything!" Mapleshade begged. "These are ThunderClan's kits!"

"They are half RiverClan," Ravenwing corrected, his voice

as hard as ice. "Our Clanmates deserve to know. I'm sorry, Mapleshade. Sorry for you, but even sorrier for these kits. They will end up suffering for the lies that you have told." He whirled around and vanished into the bracken.

Mapleshade stared after him. *StarClan, help me!* For a moment she considered taking her kits and running deeper into the forest, hiding her kits away from any cat who might harm them. But then she looked at Petalkit balancing the acorn on her head while her brothers tried to knock her off her paws and dislodge it. *ThunderClan loves these kits and won't do anything to hurt them. I always planned to tell them the truth. It's just happening sooner than I thought.*

CHAPTER 4
♣

By the time they reached the path leading down to the ravine, the kits were dragging their paws with weariness. "Nearly there, little ones!" Mapleshade mewed encouragingly. She hoped she would be able to settle them in the nursery and give them a feed before Ravenwing came looking for her.

Patchkit stumbled on the pebbly slope so Mapleshade let him lean against her shoulder and took almost all of his weight as they descended to the gorse tunnel. Petalkit let out a huge yawn. "I'm so sleepy!" she murmured.

"I'm hungry," Larchkit squeaked. "My belly is rumbling louder than a badger!"

They pushed through the gorse tunnel, ducking their heads to keep the sharp twigs out of their eyes. Mapleshade followed, nudging Patchkit in front of her. When she emerged, Larchkit and Petalkit had stopped dead at the entrance. "Come on," Mapleshade urged, her attention on Patchkit as he swayed on his feet.

"I think something's happening," Petalkit whispered.

Mapleshade looked up. The clearing was ringed with cats, all staring at them. Oakstar stood on Highrock, silhouetted against the trees. Ravenwing was crouched below him, his gaze fierce. The deputy Beetail was next to the medicine cat, his striped coat ruffled as if he had been interrupted mid-groom. Mapleshade started to tremble.

Patchkit pressed himself against her. "What's wrong?" he whimpered.

"Nothing for you to worry about," Mapleshade told him. "Go stand over there." She pointed with her tail to a clump of bracken at the edge of the clearing. The three kits trotted over in silence and huddled together.

"Come here, Mapleshade," Oakstar commanded.

On legs that seemed to be made of stone, Mapleshade walked forward until she was standing in the center of the clearing. "What is it, Oakstar?"

The dark brown tom twitched the tip of his tail. "Who is the father of your kits?" he asked. "Tell the truth!"

Before Mapleshade could speak, there was a flurry of ginger fur beside her. Frecklewish pushed past a cluster of warriors and joined Mapleshade below Highrock. "We know it's Birchface!" she called up to Oakstar. "Why are you asking this?"

"I want Mapleshade to tell us herself," Oakstar mewed, his voice soft with menace. "She let me believe that my son Birchface was their father. I cannot imagine that one of my warriors would dare to tell such a lie."

Mapleshade shifted her weight onto her hind paws so she could hold the leader's gaze. "Any Clan would be proud to have these kits grow up to serve them," she declared.

"Even if they knew the kits were half-Clan?" Ravenwing meowed. "We deserve to know the truth, Mapleshade. Appledusk is their father, isn't he?"

For a moment, the whole forest seemed to hold its breath. Then there was a screech of pure horror and Frecklewish launched herself at Mapleshade. "Is this true?" she yowled, clawing at Mapleshade's face. "What have you done?"

Mapleshade stumbled backward. "Stop!" she gasped. She tried to raise her front paws to shield herself but Frecklewish had pinned her down.

Suddenly the weight was lifted from Mapleshade's belly and she opened her eyes to see the she-cat being hauled away by Bloomheart and Seedpelt. Mapleshade staggered to her paws. Blood pooled in her eye from a torn eyelid, and her cheek stung from a well-aimed blow. All around her, the cats hissed and muttered.

Frecklewish shook off the warriors and glared at Mapleshade. "You have betrayed my brother's name!" she spat. "You have betrayed us all with your lies and your disloyalty. You don't deserve to be called a warrior and nor do those . . . those half-Clan creatures." She curled her lip toward the three kits, who cowered beneath the ferns. "Their father killed Birchface and Flowerpaw! Get them out of here!"

Mapleshade shook scarlet droplets onto the grass. "Why does it matter who their father is?" she demanded furiously. "I have given ThunderClan three fine kits. I am a queen and I should be treated with respect. StarClan knows we need more warriors, and here they are!" *Have my Clanmates gone mad, that they would turn against me like this?*

Oakstar bounded down from Highrock and stood in front of her. His yellow eyes gleamed with hatred and he thrust his head forward until his breath blew hotly on Mapleshade's muzzle. "Have you forgotten that Appledusk murdered my son and Flowerpaw? Of all the cats, why did you have to choose *him*? You cannot possibly expect my forgiveness." He stepped back and raised his head. "You have betrayed the warrior code and lied to your Clanmates. We will not raise these kits within the walls of our camp, nor the boundaries of our territory. Take them and leave. You are no longer a warrior of ThunderClan."

Mapleshade stumbled backward. "You can't mean that! These kits belong to ThunderClan! You have to let us stay!"

Oakstar shook his head. "No, I do not." He gazed around at the Clan. "Ravenwing told me about an omen he received, a mysterious stream of water that washed three pieces of reed into his den. Reeds don't belong in our territory, and certainly not in the heart of our camp. These kits will bring nothing but danger!"

"Get rid of them!" screeched Frecklewish. "Drive them out!"

"Oakstar's right, they don't belong here," growled Bloomheart.

Mapleshade stared at the gray tabby in horror. "You were my mentor, Bloomheart! You know I would never betray my Clan!"

"You already have," he replied gruffly. "I am ashamed of

you." He turned away, and Mapleshade felt her heart break into pieces.

"I will never forget this," she hissed, slowly turning to glare at each one of her Clanmates. "You have betrayed me and my kits. You will live to regret this day forever, ThunderClan, and that is a promise." She stalked over to her kits and swept her tail around them. "This is no longer our home," she told them. "Come."

She prodded them back through the gorse tunnel and up the path. Petalkit fell over and grazed her nose on a stone, but was too tired to protest. She simply picked herself up and stumbled on as if she knew there was no point in complaining. Mapleshade felt her heart break a little more.

"Why don't they like us anymore?" whimpered Patchkit as they headed into the trees. It had started to rain, and fat drops thudded onto the ferns around them.

"Because they're mouse-brained, bat-blind, and fox-hearted," Mapleshade hissed.

"Those are bad words!" Larchkit mewed. "You're not supposed to say them!"

"It's the truth," Mapleshade answered grimly.

"What were they saying about our father?" Petalkit asked. "Don't they like Birchface either?"

Mapleshade felt an overwhelming urge to lie down and slip into the darkness of sleep. "I'll tell you everything later," she promised. "First we must get across the river."

"We're going swimming again?" chirped Patchkit. "But that RiverClan cat said we had to stay away from the water."

"Everything is different now," Mapleshade murmured.

When they emerged from the shelter of the trees, the rain was pelting so hard that Mapleshade could hardly keep her eyes open.

"I don't want to go swimming anymore," Larchkit moaned. "I want to go home."

"I wish we were in the nursery." Petalkit sniffed. "It's too wet to be outside."

"We have no home!" Mapleshade snapped. She had to raise her voice over the pounding of raindrops on the shore. "Forget about ThunderClan and the nursery." She stared at the river. The tops of the stepping-stones were just visible among the wind-stirred waves. "We don't have to swim all the way," she told the kits. "Do you see those rocks? We just have to swim from one to the next until we get to the other side."

"But then we'll be in RiverClan!" Patchkit squeaked. "We're not supposed to go there!"

"It's all right," Mapleshade mewed, trying to sound calm. "Your father will be pleased to see us."

Larchkit tipped his head on one side. "I thought our father was dead!"

Mapleshade took a deep breath. "Remember that nice RiverClan cat who helped Patchkit today? He is your father. Not Birchface."

Larchkit wrinkled his nose. "But that doesn't make sense. Our father can't be from RiverClan. We're ThunderClan cats!"

"You're half RiverClan," Mapleshade told him. "That's

why you liked the water so much today."

The three kits' eyes stretched wider until they were like moons. "Is that why our Clanmates are mad at us?" asked Petalkit.

"Yes," mewed Mapleshade. She felt the hackles rise along her spine. "But they are wrong," she growled. "They'll change their minds soon and until then, we'll live in RiverClan. Everything will be okay." She nudged Petalkit closer to the river. "Come on, we need to cross before it gets dark."

The little brown kit hung back. "I don't want to!" she wailed. "There's too much water!"

"You'll be fine," Mapleshade insisted. She herded Larchkit and Patchkit alongside their sister. "I'll be right behind you."

Patchkit looked over his shoulder. "Promise we'll be okay?"

"I promise."

The ginger-and-white tom stepped bravely into the waves. Almost at once the water washed over his head but he fought his way up, spluttering. His littermates followed him. Mapleshade watched the three small heads bob to the first stepping-stone. They scrambled out and stood belly-deep in water, shivering.

"Wait for me!" Mapleshade called. "I'm coming!" Gritting her teeth, she waded into the river. The water sucked at her fur, chilling her to the bone. She forced herself to strike off from the shore and churn her paws, propelling herself toward the stepping-stones. *I have to do this for my kits*, she told herself, hating every moment.

Suddenly there was a roar from somewhere upstream.

"Swim faster!" screeched Petalkit. "Something's coming!"

Mapleshade glanced sideways to see a wall of water bearing down on her, sweeping branches and debris ahead of it. She paddled furiously but the current was dragging her away from the stones, not toward them. "Hold on!" she screeched to the kits as the wave crashed over her head.

Mapleshade was thrust to the bottom of the river by the force of the flood. Branches thudded against her and when she opened her eyes, she saw nothing but bubbles and churned-up pebbles. With her chest screaming for air, she clawed her way to the surface and burst out, gasping. Her flailing front paws struck something hard; unsheathing her claws, she managed to haul herself onto the rock. Somehow she had made it to the first stepping-stone. She looked around.

The kits had gone. Mapleshade stared into the water in horror. *My kits! Where are you?* Any hopes that they had struck out for the second stone vanished when she saw three tiny shapes being swept downstream.

"Help!" wailed Petalkit before a wave pushed her under.

Mapleshade launched herself off the stone and paddled furiously toward her kits. A pale shape bobbed in front of her. She reached out and managed to hook one claw into sodden fur. It was Patchkit. His eyes were closed.

"Wake up!" Mapleshade screeched. "You have to swim!"

A faint mew came from somewhere beside her. Mapleshade lifted her head and peered through the waves. Larchkit was clinging to a branch that hung into the river. Gripping Patchkit in her jaws, Mapleshade battled her way over to the tree. She tried to boost Patchkit out of the water but he was too heavy and he slipped out of her grasp.

"No!" Mapleshade yowled as he vanished into the black river.

Larchkit lost his grip on the branch and splashed into the water beside her. Mapleshade sank her teeth into his scruff but the pull of the current was too strong. Larchkit was ripped away from her and swept away with just one tiny cry.

"Mapleshade! Mapleshade! Grab hold of the branch!" There was a frantic shout from the shore. Mapleshade saw Appledusk wading into the river, his fur fluffed up in alarm. He gestured with his tail to the overhanging tree. "Hold on and I'll drag you out!"

Mapleshade was only dimly aware of hooking her claws into the branch beside her. She felt herself being dragged through the water, and then strong jaws were in her pelt, hauling her onto the stones. Appledusk loomed over her. "What in the name of StarClan are you doing? Where are the kits?"

Two more shapes appeared beside him. "What is a ThunderClan cat doing in the river?" asked one. Mapleshade recognized the voice of Splashfoot, a young tom.

"Is it Mapleshade?" asked his companion.

"I think so, Eeltail," mewed Splashfoot. He peered closer, his pale gray fur glowing in the failing light.

"My kits," Mapleshade rasped. "Save . . . my kits . . ."

Appledusk's face appeared above her, his eyes huge with horror. "Are you telling me the kits are in the river?"

Mapleshade nodded, too weak to speak.

Eeltail was already bounding along the shore. "If kits are in there, they are going to be in big trouble!" she called over her shoulder. Splashfoot raced after her.

Appledusk crouched beside Mapleshade. "I will find them, I promise," he whispered. Then he raced away from her.

Mapleshade closed her eyes. *StarClan, help my kits*, she prayed. *None of this is their fault. Take me if you must, but please, spare them.*

She lay still, feeling the water run off her fur, until she heard paw steps crunching over the stones. She lifted her head and saw Appledusk approaching. In the darkness, she couldn't see his expression. "Did you find them?"

"Yes," he meowed. "We found them."

Mapleshade hauled herself to her paws. "Where are they?"

Wordlessly, Appledusk turned and led her downstream. He pushed his way into a dense clump of reeds and beckoned Mapleshade forward with his tail. Eeltail and Splashfoot were standing over three small dark shapes. Eeltail looked up, her eyes brimming with pity. "I'm so sorry," she mewed. "We couldn't save them."

A ghastly shriek split the air. Mapleshade wondered where the noise was coming from until she realized that her mouth was wide open. She shut her jaws with a snap and took a step toward her kits. Her legs buckled and suddenly she was lying beside them, desperately licking each one in turn.

"Wake up, little ones," she urged. "We made it across the river. You are safe now!"

But the bodies rolled limply under the strokes of her tongue, and three pairs of eyes stayed closed.

Mapleshade pressed her muzzle against Patchkit's cold cheek. "You promised you would never leave me," she whispered. *You promised you would keep me safe.* His voice echoed inside her head. "I'm sorry!" Mapleshade wailed. "I was trying to find us a new home. I didn't know where else to go."

"What are you talking about?" Appledusk sounded stunned. "Do you mean that you deliberately tried to cross the river? In the middle of a flood?"

Mapleshade twisted around to look at him. "ThunderClan threw us out," she explained. "We had nowhere else to go."

"I don't know what's going on here, but we need to take these kits to Darkstar," meowed Eeltail. "He needs to know about this."

For a moment Appledusk looked as if he was going to disagree, then he nodded. "You're right. Come on, we'll take one kit each. Mapleshade, follow us."

The RiverClan warriors gently picked up the drenched little shapes and carried them slowly back along the shore. Mapleshade stumbled behind them, too numb to think clearly. Beside them, the river had calmed and lapped at the shore like a cat's tongue, making soft, comforting noises in the still air. Mapleshade waited for Appledusk to send the other warriors on ahead, to find some excuse to be alone with her so they could mourn their kits together before facing the rest of his Clan. But he didn't turn back to look at her. *He hasn't even asked what I named them.*

The warriors threaded between tall reeds on a narrow path of dense brown soil. It opened into a clearing which was raised up from the water by heaps of more soil on top of tightly woven branches, like a huge nest. Mapleshade caught the glint of many pairs of eyes watching from among the reeds and her wet fur bristled.

An orange she-cat ran up to Appledusk. Mapleshade recognized her at once; it was Reedshine, the warrior who had been fussing over Appledusk at the Gathering.

"Did someone fall in the river?" Reedshine gasped. "Are you okay?"

The RiverClan warrior set down Petalkit's body as gently as if she were sleeping, and touched his tail to Reedshine's flank. "I'm fine. I need to speak with Darkstar."

Reedshine stayed where she was, her gaze flicking to Mapleshade and back again. "Why is she here? What's going on, Appledusk?"

There was a stir of movement at the far end of the clearing, and Darkstar stepped out of the reeds. All the cats fell silent.

Appledusk stepped forward. "Three kits have drowned in the river," he announced.

Ask me their names! Mapleshade screeched silently.

Appledusk looked at his paws. "I . . . I am their father."

Mapleshade held her breath. This was Appledusk's chance to plead for mercy on her behalf, to explain that Mapleshade deserved to be given a place in RiverClan because she had borne his kits.

Darkstar's eyes narrowed to tiny slits. "What do you mean, Appledusk? What are you talking about?"

"I'm so sorry, Reedshine," Appledusk whispered. "Please forgive me."

Reedshine twitched the tip of her tail. "Forgive you for what?"

Mapleshade looked at the concern in Reedshine's eyes and felt something inside her turn to ice. This was not just a Clanmate to Appledusk.

Appledusk bowed his head and went on. "Many moons ago, I met with Mapleshade in secret."

There was a gasp from his Clanmates, and one of them, a rumpled old tabby, hissed, "Traitor!"

Mapleshade kept her gaze fixed on Darkstar. *She has to take pity on me. I have lost my home and my kits. I have nothing left except Appledusk.*

"You knew about these kits?" Darkstar asked. The tip of her tail was twitching.

Appledusk nodded, and Reedshine let out a soft wail. "Mapleshade told me she would raise them in ThunderClan," Appledusk meowed. "I . . . I knew I had made a mistake so I said nothing to my Clanmates."

A mistake? Mapleshade almost winced at the pain in Appledusk's pale green eyes. Almost, but not quite. The ice was spreading through her faster than a leaf-bare frost. *Soon I won't be able to feel anything*, she thought.

"I should never have betrayed my Clan by meeting with Mapleshade," Appledusk went on. "I will regret it for the rest of my life, and I can only beg for your forgiveness."

"What brought these kits here tonight?" Darkstar queried,

looking down at the three pitiful shapes.

Mapleshade opened her mouth to explain but Appledusk spoke first. "Mapleshade's Clanmates learned the truth and she had to leave. The river is flooded and the kits were too young to swim across." His voice faltered. Mapleshade stared at him. *You're making it sound as if this was my fault!*

Darkstar mewed, "The loss of any kits is a loss to all of us. But you broke the warrior code, Appledusk. How can I ever trust you again?"

Reedshine padded forward until she was standing alongside Appledusk with her fur brushing his. "There is no cat more loyal to RiverClan than Appledusk," she declared. "If I am willing to forgive him for his past mistakes, then so should you, Darkstar."

There were murmurs from the cats at the edge of the clearing. They sounded impressed by Reedshine's confidence.

Darkstar waited until the clearing was silent again, then nodded. "This is not the season for losing warriors. Appledusk, I believe that you are sorry for what you did, and that you have been punished enough by the death of your kits. I will allow you to remain in RiverClan—but know that I and the rest of the Clanmates will be watching you. You will have to earn back our trust."

Appledusk dipped his head so low that his muzzle almost touched the reeds beneath his paws. "I will never forget your mercy, Darkstar," he murmured. "Thank you. I promise my loyalty lies only with RiverClan, and my Clanmates." He glanced sideways at Reedshine, who blinked at him.

Darkstar gestured with her tail. "Rainfall, help Splashfoot and Eeltail to bury these kits. The accident of their birth is not their fault. They may lie in peace in our territory now."

Mapleshade struggled to find her voice. "What . . . what about me?" she croaked. "May I stay here with my kits?"

The RiverClan leader stared at her. "No, you may not. You will leave this territory at once and never set foot across the border again. Like Appledusk, I believe that the loss of your kits is punishment enough. Otherwise, rest assured my warriors would have clawed your fur off for what you have done."

"But night is falling!" Mapleshade protested. "Where will I go? Appledusk, help me!"

The pale brown warrior shook his head. "Why should I? It's your fault that these kits are dead. I never want to see you again."

Reedshine pressed herself even closer to Appledusk's flank. "Go away, Mapleshade," she hissed. "You have caused enough trouble tonight."

Mapleshade looked down at her drowned kits. "I cannot leave them," she whispered. "They are everything to me."

"And now they are dead," Appledusk growled. "Be thankful we have shown you some mercy, Mapleshade. Get out, before we make you leave."

Mapleshade stared at the cat whose face had occupied her mind for so many moons. She thought she had known every swirl of his fur, the angle of every whisker, but now she didn't recognize him at all. The coldness swelled inside her until she felt it burst out of her eyes, and there was a jolt of satisfaction as Appledusk flinched away from her gaze. "You told me you loved me!" Mapleshade hissed. "I went through the agony of bearing your kits! And now you treat me worse than prey. You will regret this, Appledusk. That is my last promise to you."

She turned and stumbled out of the clearing, blindly following paths through the reeds until she reached scent markers that suggested she was at the RiverClan boundary. She was dimly aware of crossing hard gray stone, then a massive shape loomed out of the shadows, a sharp-edged Twoleg den of some sort. She found a hole in the wall and slipped through into a musty, hay-scented space. Mapleshade slumped down on a clump of dusty dried stalks and shut her eyes. Sleep dragged her away, and her dreams were filled with the sight of her kits spiraling away from her in churning black water, screeching for help that never came.

CHAPTER 5

Mapleshade fought her way out of sleep, coughing and scorched with fever. *Where am I?* She struggled out of her prickly nest and looked around. A fresh-killed mouse lay beside her, and Mapleshade's belly rumbled. She couldn't remember the last time she had eaten. She bent down to take a bite, then the memory of where she was and what had happened flooded over her and she retched violently. *My kits! Appledusk!*

"Hello? Are you all right?" An anxious mew made Mapleshade look up. A small black-and-white tom was standing at the foot of the huge stack of hay that filled the den. Daylight filtered through cracks in the wooden walls, highlighting tiny specks of dust that floated in the air.

"Where am I? Who are you?" Mapleshade rasped.

The little cat picked up a bundle of dripping moss that lay at his paws and carried it over to her. "You need to drink," he urged. "My name is Myler, and this is my barn. You went to sleep so quickly last night that I didn't have time to introduce myself. How are you feeling?" He peered at her and Mapleshade shied away. "You still look exhausted," Myler observed. "Eat the mouse, then I'll let you get some more rest.

"I'm not staying," Mapleshade hissed. "I don't want your fresh-kill."

"But there's plenty to share," Myler insisted. "I can catch more for myself, don't worry."

Mapleshade staggered forward, almost knocking the tom off his paws. "Leave me alone," she growled. "I don't need your help."

She searched for the gap in the wall where she had come in. Behind her, Myler was meowing something about giving shelter to strangers and having plenty of room in the barn. Mapleshade didn't bother to listen. What could some kittypet possibly give to her? *My life is ruined! I did nothing wrong, and yet I have lost everything!* The image of her three dead kits hovered at the edge of her vision, as if she would be able to see them clearly if only she could turn her head fast enough. *Mama, help me!* they wailed.

"I can't," Mapleshade whispered. "Oh my precious loves, I am so sorry."

Trembling with hunger, Mapleshade plunged into the wispy undergrowth that edged RiverClan's territory. She stayed well clear of the border as she headed uphill, toward the gorge. She knew there was a wooden Twoleg bridge just below the sheer walls of rock where she would be able to cross back to ThunderClan territory. She felt an irresistible pull inside her, back to the place where she had spent her whole life. There was no solace in the spindly willows of RiverClan, and the vast open moor that stretched up above the gorge made her shudder with fear. Instead she yearned for the denseness of sturdy trees and thick green undergrowth rooting her to the ground, filling her senses with familiar sounds and scents.

Mapleshade reached the wooden bridge and raced across, ears flattened and fur spiked. The noise of the river tumbling below dragged her mind back to the moment she had let go of Patchkit. *The water was too strong! It was not my fault that my kits died*, she reminded herself. She jumped off the bridge onto dry, sandy ground that sloped up toward Four Trees directly in front of her. If she turned and followed the river downstream, she would be in ThunderClan territory. Trying to ignore the sound of the water, she took a few steps toward the boundary, already tasting the scent markers on the still air.

Then she froze. She could not cross the border. She had been driven out—exiled by her own Clanmates. If she took one step into her former home, she would be treated worse than a rogue. An image swam into Mapleshade's mind of a small black cat, eyes narrowed with suspicion, spouting words that rang with righteous indignation. *Ravenwing!* This was all his fault. He had jumped to conclusions, shattered the Clan's trust in her, forced her Clanmates to judge her for something beyond her control. Because of his actions, Patchkit, Larchkit, and Petalkit had died. Every breath that Ravenwing took was a breath he had denied Mapleshade's kits.

Rage swelled inside Mapleshade's head until the sounds of the forest faded away and her vision blurred. She stumbled along the edge of the border, not caring when her claws scraped on stones or brambles dragged at her pelt. Her skin throbbed with heat and she was dimly aware of being thirstier than she had ever been in her life, but even when her paws splashed through a tiny stream, she couldn't muster the energy to stop and drink. Eventually she could walk no farther, and she flopped down where she was, in a narrow ditch beside a holly bush that smelled of home.

Mapleshade closed her eyes and listened to the thudding of her heart. It seemed to grow louder and louder, until the leaf mulch she was lying on started to quiver. With a jolt she opened her eyes and saw a ginger face staring down at her in dismay.

"Mapleshade!" squeaked Nettlepaw. "You're not supposed to be here!"

"Then pretend that I'm dead," Mapleshade growled. "I may as well be."

Nettlepaw's gaze darted around the ditch. "Where are the kits?" he whispered. "Are they in RiverClan?"

Mapleshade felt the numbness creeping over her once more. "They drowned in the river."

"Oh no!" Nettlepaw's eyes grew huge.

Mapleshade let her cheek rest on the cold dirt. "Leave me alone."

With a muffled meow, Nettlepaw turned and fled. Mapleshade wondered if she would ever climb out of the ditch. There was another patter of paw steps above her. Mapleshade opened one eye. Nettlepaw was pushing a bundle of herbs down toward her.

"I was collecting these for Ravenwing," he mewed. "But

I think you need them more. You don't smell good, Maple-shade." He peered earnestly at her. "Please eat them. I . . . I'm sorry about your kits. Frecklewish saw what happened in the river, but I hoped you made it to the other side."

Mapleshade sat up with a hiss. "Frecklewish was *watching*?"

The apprentice looked scared. "Y-yes. She followed you to make sure that you left. She . . . she said you fell off the stepping-stones."

"And yet she did nothing?" Mapleshade rasped. "Those kits were helpless! How could she watch them drown?"

Nettlepaw started to back away. "I don't know. She must have thought they were okay. She said there were RiverClan cats on the far shore."

"They were not okay!" Mapleshade snarled, arching her back and sinking her claws into the mulch.

"Nettlepaw! Where are you?" a cat called from the other side of the holly bush. Nettlepaw let out a whimper and raced away.

Mapleshade sank back down into the ditch. She chewed the leaves without tasting them, feeling a stab of satisfaction that she had taken them from Ravenwing. How could he carry on gathering herbs, treating his Clanmates, as if nothing had happened? Mapleshade burned with the need to see him, to make him regret spilling the secret that was hers, and hers alone. She looked up at the moon, which had appeared in the twilight sky. In one sunrise it would be at its half, when the medicine cats traveled to the Moonstone. Mapleshade might be forbidden from entering ThunderClan's territory, but no cat could keep her away from the path that led to Mothermouth. Ravenwing would be alone on his journey, unprotected by warriors who were stupid enough to listen to his accusations and doom-mongering.

She felt the herbs working inside her, restoring strength to her legs. With a grunt, she jumped out of the ditch and started trotting away from the border, into the bramble thickets that encircled the hollow at Fourtrees. It wasn't safe to stay so close to ThunderClan, not when patrols might be looking out for her. She didn't know if Nettlepaw would keep quiet about finding her, though presumably he wouldn't admit to giving her the herbs.

Mapleshade dropped down the steep slope into the hollow, paused briefly to look up at the four gigantic oaks, then carried on, scrambling up the other side and plunging into the trees that bordered WindClan's territory. There was a strong smell of fox, which made her fur prickle, but it was stale rather than fresh, and would hide her own scent from curious border patrols.

She felt rather than heard the thrumming of terrified paws over the ground; peeping out of the bracken, she saw a rabbit hurtling across the moor toward her, pursued by a patrol of WindClan cats. Mapleshade hardly had time to think before the rabbit ran straight into her in a tumble of paws and fur. She bit down hard on its neck and it went limp. The warriors were still racing toward her so Mapleshade grasped the rabbit in her jaws and hauled it up the nearest tree. Her claws tore on the smooth bark and the rabbit dragged at her teeth but at last she reached the lowest branch and crawled onto it with her fresh-kill. She heard the WindClan cats scramble to a halt below.

"Where did that rabbit go?" asked one of them.

Another was circling the trunk, sniffing the ground. "The trail ends here, but that's impossible. Rabbits don't climb trees."

"I don't know how you can smell anything," grumbled an old tom with patchy brown fur. Mapleshade thought his name was Midgepelt. "It stinks of fox around here."

Mapleshade held her breath, waiting for one of the cats to look up and see her. There was little leaf cover this far down the trunk, and she couldn't climb higher without making a noise. But the patrol sniffed around for a moment more, then headed back to the open moor, grumbling about vanishing prey. *Fools!* Mapleshade thought as she bit into the rabbit.

She spent the night under a clump of ferns a little deeper into the forest. She woke shivering beneath a light coat of frost, missing the warmth of her kits. *Wherever you are, I hope you are warm,* she thought through chattering teeth. Her belly was still full from the rabbit so she headed straight into the open, hoping it was too early for the WindClan dawn patrol. She had traveled to the Moonstone once before, as an apprentice. Mapleshade remembered her excitement at being inside WindClan's territory with impunity; how she had longed to be seen by a patrol and challenged! But now she darted from rock to clump of gorse, cursing the lack of cover on the empty moor.

At last she reached the foot of the slope and crouched beside the Thunderpath. The stench of monsters caught in her throat and made her eyes water, but there were few of the noisy beasts around this early. She only had to wait a few moments before silence fell heavily in the valley and she was able to dart across the hard black stone. On the other side, she plunged through the long soft grass and into a hedge. She recalled passing a Twoleg den with cows and a dark, hay-scented barn where she and the other apprentices had paused to hunt. She decided to stay well clear this time, in case she ran into any of the other medicine cats traveling early to the Moonstone.

After crossing a broad expanse of grass and pushing through another hedge, Mapleshade saw the dark brown tops of some Twoleg dens that looked like the barn. She swerved to the far side of the next stretch of grass and trotted through a row of trees to where the ground started to slope steeply up. Tilting back her head, she stared at the jagged rocks that marked the top of the ridge. The sun was striking them, turning them rosy and warm-looking, but their outlines still looked like teeth against the pale sky.

Mapleshade's belly rumbled and she realized that if she didn't eat now, she would be hungry for the rest of the day up on the hillside. She ducked back under the trees and quickly picked up the scent of a mole snuffling in the sunshine. Not her favorite fresh-kill but too easy to miss. She struck the flat-tened black body with her front paw and tucked in for a meal. Afterward she felt stronger, clearer-headed. She bounded up the side of the ridge, scattering loose pebbles under her paws. As the weak sun set the jagged stones ablaze, Mapleshade leaped onto a boulder and opened her jaws to screech at the valley below.

I am ready for you, Ravenwing! You will pay for what you have done!

The life that she had known was over; if she couldn't be a warrior, then she would dedicate every beat of her heart to avenging the deaths of her kits.

CHAPTER 6

The sun dragged slowly across the sky. Mapleshade's belly was still
full from the mole; besides, she was too tense to eat. Her claws
were blunt after her long day of walking, so she sharpened
them on a stone. A hawk swooped overhead and Mapleshade
imagined it feasting on Ravenwing's body after she had finished with him. He would bleed a river of blood, every drop
spilled for her helpless kits. . . .

At last the sky faded and the shadows between the rocks
grew thicker. Mapleshade fluffed up her fur against the chill
and crouched on top of a boulder, watching for any sign of
movement at the foot of the hill. Suddenly a darker shadow
flitted across the grass. Ravenwing was here! Alone and early,
as he usually was. Mapleshade unsheathed her claws and let
them scratch against the stone. She stayed very still, hardly
breathing, as Ravenwing climbed the slope toward her.
Mapleshade tensed her hindquarters, ready to leap down onto
the medicine cat, but then she paused. If she attacked him out
here, she might be seen by the other medicine cats. And where
was the satisfaction in a simple ambush? She should follow
Ravenwing down to the Moonstone and tackle him there, at

the source of his precious omens.

Mapleshade pictured the long, stifling tunnel from her visit as an apprentice. Her pelt pricked at the thought of entering that darkness again, but then the wails of her kits echoed in her ears and she slid soundlessly off the boulder just a heartbeat before Ravenwing padded past. Mapleshade could hear him breathing heavily after the climb. She waited until he vanished into the gaping maw of Mothermouth before slipping out and trotting after him.

The hole swallowed her up at once, thick black shadows pressing around her until there was no glimpse of moonlight when she looked back at the entrance. Mapleshade padded over the stone floor, trying to keep her steps as light as possible. But Ravenwing must have heard something because he stopped, invisible in the dark ahead of her, and called out. "Who's there?"

Mapleshade froze, convinced that her heart was thudding loud enough for the medicine cat to hear. But after a moment Ravenwing carried on, his paw steps the softest whisper in the silence. Faint gray light appeared ahead, silhouetting the medicine cat's ears. *The Moonstone!* Mapleshade realized she had dropped into the hunting crouch and was stalking forward one step at a time, her tail flattened behind her. She reached the opening to the cave and almost gasped out loud at the sight of the Moonstone glittering in the silver light. Ravenwing knelt in front of it, his head bowed.

With a hiss, Mapleshade sprang forward, claws extended. She landed on his back, sending him rolling onto the smooth cold stone. She caught a glimpse of his eyes, bright in the reflected moonlight.

"Mapleshade!" Ravenwing choked. "What are you doing here?"

Mapleshade let her claws sink into the fur around his throat. "Avenging the death of my kits," she snarled. "If I could kill you three times over, I would!" She knew she had nothing to say to the medicine cat. Nothing would bring back her kits. He simply did not deserve to live when they were dead. She bit down on Ravenwing's neck and the black cat went limp beneath her.

There was the sound of paw steps approaching down the tunnel. Mapleshade let Ravenwing fall to the floor and slipped behind the crystal.

"Great StarClan!" she heard Larkwing, the WindClan medicine cat, hiss. "Ravenwing! What happened?"

There was a grunt from his companion—peeking around the edge of the Moonstone, Mapleshade saw Sloefur, the ShadowClan medicine cat, sniff at Ravenwing's unmoving body. "He's dead," Sloefur announced in horror. He looked around and Mapleshade ducked behind the crystal.

"We can't leave him here," meowed Larkwing. "Come on, help me get him back to the surface."

Mapleshade listened to the sound of them dragging Ravenwing up the tunnel. She waited until the rays of the moon had slid past the hole in the roof and the cave was plunged into darkness. Mapleshade's heart pounded, but she reminded herself that she had nothing to be afraid of. The only dangerous thing in the shadows was her. She wondered if the medicine cats would continue with their gathering, but they did not come back to the cave. Mapleshade figured they had returned to their Clans to deliver the terrible news.

When the tiny patch of sky above the hole turned white with dawn, Mapleshade stretched her cold, stiff legs and padded back up the tunnel. Outside Mothermouth stood a heap of small stones that had not been there before. A tuft of black fur poked through a gap in the pile. Mapleshade sniffed and recognized Ravenwing's scent. Rather than carry him all the way back to the forest, his fellow medicine cats had decided to bury him here, marking his final nest with a careful mountain of rocks.

Mapleshade curled her lip. What memorial was there to her kits? Nothing but the cold wet dirt inside RiverClan's territory. She struck out at the pile of stones, knocking them to the ground. Her claws caught on the rocks and her pads stung but she kept flailing until the heap was destroyed and Ravenwing's body was exposed to the gray dawn. Mapleshade looked up and caught sight of a hawk circling overhead. *Here's your next piece of fresh-kill*, she thought with satisfaction.

The hawk swept down closer, and Mapleshade bounded away from the scattered stones. She bounded down the hillside without looking back. She had avenged her kits! *Were you watching, my precious kits? I killed him for you! I hope you never see Ravenwing in StarClan. He should be in the Place of No Stars for all eternity.*

She reached a hedge at the edge of a stretch of thick soft grass and crawled under the branches. Suddenly she was too tired to walk another step. Ignoring the rumbling in her belly, she closed her eyes.

"Mama!"

"Help me!"

Two drenched faces appeared in front of Mapleshade, eyes huge and pleading, mouths open in tiny wails. The sound of the flooded river roared in Mapleshade's ears.

"Patchkit! Petalkit!" she screeched. She thrashed with her front legs, trying to reach them as the water sucked them away, but her paws thudded against cold hard earth.

Mapleshade opened her eyes. She was lying under the hedge beneath Highstones. Why had she dreamed of her kits? Where was Larchkit?

"Mama! Save us!" Two voices echoed again.

Mapleshade shook herself and sat up. Ravenwing had died—did that mean only one kit had been avenged?

StarClan, why are you doing this to me? I fell in love, that's all! And now I am made to suffer more than any cat has before.

An image drifted into her mind of a pale brown cat sitting among ferns, looking out at a churning black river as it swept three little shapes away. *Frecklewish!* According to Nettlepaw, she had seen the kits struggling, but had done nothing to save them. They may not have been Frecklewish's kin, but the warrior code said that no kit should be left in danger, regardless of Clan.

Frecklewish needed to pay for the lost kits, just as Ravenwing had done.

Mapleshade stood up, shaking on exhausted paws. This

would be harder to achieve because Frecklewish only left ThunderClan to go to Gatherings, when she would be surrounded by her Clanmates. And even inside the border she was rarely alone. Mapleshade needed to find a way to attack her within the territory, the safest place for a warrior to be. Thinking hard, she started to pad along the bottom of the hedge. A tendril of ivy caught at her foot and almost tripped her. Hissing, Mapleshade snatched her paw away. The ivy lay on the ground, quivering like a glossy green snake.

Snakerocks! Mapleshade pictured the nest of adders that had been blocked in with stones. Perhaps there was something deadly inside ThunderClan's borders after all!

CHAPTER 7

❧

Mapleshade trekked back to the forest, skirting the edge of Wind-
Clan under cover of darkness and heading for ThunderClan's
border with Twolegplace. She knew she would have to wait
for Frecklewish to pass by on patrol; even then, Mapleshade
would need the luck of StarClan to get the she-cat alone. She
plunged into the lush green grass at the foot of the Twoleg
fences, then scrambled up and over the wooden barrier, dropping down into the small, strongly scented enclosure on the
other side.

Almost at once, a fat gray-and-white tom heaved himself
through a tiny flap in the side of the Twoleg den and lum-
bered toward her, mewling.

"Get out of here! You're one of those stinking forest cats,
aren't you? My housefolk don't want you in their backyard!
Shoo!"

Mapleshade waited until the kittypet was a mouse-length
away, then shot out one paw and raked his face. The kittypet
leaped backward, screeching. Blood dripped from his blunt
muzzle. "Ow!" he wailed.

Mapleshade stayed where she was. The kittypet glared

at her through screwed-up eyes before turning and shuffling back to the den. When the flap banged shut behind his plump haunches, Mapleshade studied the enclosure. A tree grew beside the fence with broad enough branches to support her, and dense leaves to hide her from view. She would wait there for Frecklewish. She scrambled up the tree and settled on a bough that looked out over the forest. She had caught a squirrel at Fourtrees and drunk from a stream so her belly was comfortably full. Resting her chin on her paws, she let herself doze, one ear pricked for any sounds from below.

At dusk four ThunderClan warriors came past, creeping along the bottom of the fence as if they feared the kittypets were about to attack. Mapleshade curled her lip in scorn. She had thought her Clanmates were braver than that. Frecklewish was not among them, though. As night fell, Mapleshade dropped down from her branch into the long grass, hoping to hunt. ThunderClan scent surrounded her and for a moment she felt a pang of longing; then she pictured her Clanmates driving her and her kits away, and she thought of Frecklewish watching her kits drown, and her fury returned. She quickly caught a blackbird that was wrestling with a worm and carried it back to the tree. Behind her, the gray-and-white tom was bundled out of the den by a cross-sounding Twoleg. Mapleshade watched the kittypet squat on the grass, its eyes huge with fear, then race back inside. *Ha! He knows this territory is mine now!*

Mapleshade slept fitfully, the bark digging into her belly fur and sending a damp chill through her bones. She woke with the first glimmer of dawn, feeling pangs of hunger. The blackbird had been old and scrawny. Mapleshade scanned the forest for signs of movement. All was still beneath the trees. She jumped down and padded into the ferns, scanning for prey. A tiny rustle alerted her to a mouse scrabbling at the foot of a sycamore tree. Mapleshade stalked forward, hoping her flashes of white fur wouldn't startle her prey. The mouse was intent on nibbling a seed so Mapleshade was able to pounce unseen, killing the creature with a single blow to its neck.

Then she froze. She heard voices! Bloomheart was among them, directing his patrol to split up and hunt before meeting again at the lightning-struck elm. There wasn't time to get back to the Twoleg fence, so Mapleshade crouched beneath a clump of bracken with her fresh-kill. Paw steps came closer, then a glimpse of pale brown fur through the green stems. *Frecklewish!* StarClan had brought her right to Mapleshade. But she couldn't attack her here, not when the others were so close by.

Mapleshade backed carefully out of the bracken, dragging the mouse. Its body was still warm so the scent it left would seem fresh. Sure enough, she heard Frecklewish sniffing the air and uttering a low growl that suggested she had picked up the trail. Mapleshade let the mouse scrape along the ground a little more before daring to pick it up and move forward with it dangling from her jaws. She couldn't risk being seen by Frecklewish before she had reached Snakerocks.

Mapleshade deliberately pushed her way through the thickest undergrowth so that the mouse left a generous trail of scent. She hoped that her own scent would be lost among general ThunderClan odors; she didn't think she had been out of the Clan long enough to smell unfamiliar. She could only just hear Frecklewish stalking her; the she-cat was one of the best hunters in the Clan and moved as lightly as a butterfly's wing over the leaf-strewn ground.

Suddenly dark gray stones loomed over the stems of bracken. Mapleshade swerved, still carrying the mouse, which felt heavier and heavier in her jaws. She padded around the base of the rocks and emerged into the clearing on the other side. There was hardly any trace of cat scent; clearly the warriors were concerned that the adders might escape from their prison. Mapleshade hoped the snakes were still there, but had no time to check. She left the mouse on the ground and raced to the heap of smaller stones that had been piled in front of the adders' nest. She pushed aside as many as she could, leaving a gaping black hole, then ducked behind a boulder.

Frecklewish emerged cautiously from the bushes, her jaws parted to scent the air and her fur bristling. She looked puzzled when she saw the dead mouse. Mapleshade sprang out from behind the rock and snarled at her.

"You let my kits die!"

Frecklewish stumbled backward in shock. "Mapleshade! You shouldn't be here!" She arched her back. "Leave or I'll call the rest of the patrol."

Mapleshade lashed her tail. Out of the corner of her eye she saw a tiny flicker of movement from the pile of stones. Was that a snake slithering into the light? Mapleshade took a step closer to the rocks. "Too scared to fight me yourself, Frecklewish?" she hissed. "You prefer watching helpless kits drown, don't you?"

The brown she-cat stiffened. "I thought your kits would be saved," she rasped. "I never meant for them to die."

Mapleshade sniffed. "I don't believe you! You're a fox-hearted coward. I bet you're glad they are dead!"

Frecklewish bounded toward Mapleshade, her eyes flashing with anger. "I wish *you* were dead!" she spat. "You betrayed my brother's name!"

Mapleshade dodged sideways just as Frecklewish lunged at her. With a yelp, the she-cat stumbled into the pile of stones. Before she could find her footing, there was a hiss and a sleek dark green head darted forward, tongue flicking.

"Adder!" gasped Frecklewish. There was a blur of movement, then Frecklewish staggered backward, screeching. "It bit me! Help!"

"Like you helped my kits?" Mapleshade growled. "Never! I hope you die in agony!"

Frecklewish yowled again, a wordless shriek of pain. Almost at once paw steps thrummed toward them through the trees.

"Frecklewish, is that you?" called Bloomheart.

Mapleshade slipped into a clump of bracken at the far side of the clearing. She knew she should flee before the patrol arrived but she wanted to watch Frecklewish die. With a crackling of undergrowth, Bloomheart and two other ThunderClan warriors, Seedpelt and Thrushtalon, burst into the clearing.

"Keep watch for snakes!" Bloomheart ordered. His Clanmates spun around and scanned the rocks. Bloomheart bent over Frecklewish, who was curled on the ground with her paws over her eyes. "It's all right, Frecklewish, we're here now."

"My eyes!" wailed Frecklewish. "I can't see!"

Bloomheart lifted his head. "Oh StarClan, if ever we needed Ravenwing, it is now! Why did you take him from us?" Then he shook himself and faced his Clanmates. "Seedwhisker, we need soaked moss, as fast as you can. We have to wash the venom out of her eyes. Thrushtalon, fetch every scrap of fennel you can find in the medicine stores. We have to try to save Frecklewish's eyesight."

The two warriors darted away. Bloomheart placed his paw on Frecklewish's flank. "Lie still," he meowed. "We're doing everything we can."

"But ThunderClan doesn't have a medicine cat!" Frecklewish whimpered. "Am I going to die?"

"Not on my watch," Bloomheart vowed.

Mapleshade felt bile rise in her throat as her former mentor soothed the cat who had watched her kits drown. Frecklewish's eyes were a seeping, clouded mess. Even if she survived, she would never watch anything again. Mapleshade knew she had to leave before the rest of ThunderClan rushed to help Frecklewish. She crept through the undergrowth to the thickest part of the forest, then raced back to the Twoleg fence. Cries of alarm filtered through the trees as more warriors arrived at Snakerocks. The sounds faded as Mapleshade scrambled over the fence and crouched on the bare brown earth, panting.

Only one voice echoed in her ears now: Patchkit, her tiniest, most defenseless kit. "Help me, Mama!"

Her daughter, Petalkit, had found peace with the attack on Frecklewish. Like Larchkit, her desperate cries had been silenced. For a moment Mapleshade's breath was crushed beneath a wave of grief for the son and daughter she might never see again. Then she clenched her jaw and pictured the final cat who had to suffer for the death of her kits.

"Not long now, Patchkit," she vowed. "Soon you will be free!"

CHAPTER 8
❧

As dusk fell, bringing with it a cold, damp wind, Mapleshade jumped down from the fence into the forest and followed the boundary along the edge of Twolegplace. Raindrops pattered around her as she reached the pine trees, whose spindly trunks and whispering needles gave little shelter. Mapleshade padded softly over the forest floor, staying well outside the Thunder-Clan border as she skirted the Treecutplace—silent and dark now—and plunged back into dense undergrowth. Brambles scraped her pelt and blocked her way, but Mapleshade kept pushing through, ears pricked for the first sounds of the river.

By now the rain was falling more heavily, rattling the leaves and stalks around Mapleshade's ears. She gasped when she suddenly emerged from a clump of stiff grasses to find herself at the top of a steep bank with the river sliding past, thick and black and deadly, just a tail-length below. She scrambled backward with a hiss. For a moment she thought she saw three small shapes twisting and tumbling in the water, but it was only a reflection of starlight.

Mapleshade stared at the reeds growing on the far shore. Somewhere in there was the RiverClan camp, perched like a bird's nest above the sodden ground. If she strained her ears past the sound of the rain, she could almost hear the murmurings of cats as they settled down for the night. Mapleshade pictured Appledusk lying in his den with Reedshine curled beside him, her orange pelt merging with his soft brown fur. The hair rose on Mapleshade's neck and she bared her teeth. *Appledusk will regret the day he met me! All those times he said he loved me, all the promises he made—they were nothing but lies! He never wanted my kits, so he let them drown. He could have saved them, I know he could have!*

Behind her, the sky was lightening above the trees. Dawn was a while off, but Mapleshade felt more comfortable traveling in darkness, so instead of giving in to the urge to sleep, she picked her way downstream along the bank. There was a ridge of little stones stretching across the river down here—she had used them to cross to meet Appledusk on the other side once. There was no way Mapleshade was going to swim across the river, but she could wade if she had to.

She reached the stones, invisible in the dark but recognizable by the way the noise of the river changed as it flowed over them. Shuddering, Mapleshade jumped down the bank and waded in. Her belly fur was instantly soaked and she gasped at the cold. She forced her legs through the current, feeling the water tug against her and splash her flanks. The river was much slower and shallower than when she had tried to cross with her kits, but she still hated every paw step, and she hissed with relief when she hauled herself onto the far bank. She lay there for a while, panting, as the water trickled from her fur. It had stopped raining but the sky was thick with clouds and the wind was growing stronger, scented with more rain to come.

Mapleshade forced herself to stand and keep going. Plunging into the reeds, stiff and springy so that they flicked her face and tripped her tired paws, she pushed forward until she detected RiverClan border marks, then retraced her steps so that she was following the edge of the territory safely out of scent-range. Dense reeds gave way to softer undergrowth dotted with low, slender-branched willow trees. Her belly rumbled but she didn't dare hunt in case it alerted the River-Clan cats. Sounds carried too easily on this side of the river.

Gradually the ground became firmer and drier beneath her paws, and the air filled with green, leafy scents rather than the taint of fish. Mapleshade reached a dense stand of trees, leafier and sturdier than the other willows. The territory border was just close enough that she could look down from the branches and watch for passing cats. With a sigh as she recalled just how much time she had spent up a tree recently, Mapleshade clawed her way up the nearest trunk and eased her way onto one of the lower boughs. Without knowing the habits of RiverClan warriors, she hadn't been able to think of a plan to trap Appledusk alone. She would just have to learn what she could from watching.

Mapleshade fluffed up her fur against the cold and waited. She was rewarded quite soon by a cluster of paw steps crackling nearer: an early hunting patrol, chattering and crashing through the undergrowth as if they wanted to alert all the prey to their approach. Mapleshade curled her lip, thinking of ThunderClan's stealth. The patrol passed right under her branch without noticing her.

Before their noise had faded, more cats approached. The breeze carried a scent that made Mapleshade's nostrils flare. A heartbeat later, the bracken parted to reveal a pale brown cat, broad-shouldered beneath his thick, glossy fur. *Appledusk!* Once again, StarClan had brought Mapleshade's prey right to her paws.

But then the stalks rustled and a plump gray apprentice bundled out. He crouched down and leaped forward, stubby front legs outstretched. Appledusk shook his head. "You need more height than that, Perchpaw," he chided. "You must be prepared to fight full-grown warriors when you go into battle."

The young cat's blue eyes stretched wide. "I will get taller, won't I?"

Appledusk purred. "Of course you will, but you still need to learn how to jump."

"Why don't I spring at you to show him how it's done?" asked a voice. An orange she-cat slipped into the clearing. Mapleshade's hackles bristled. *Can't Reedshine let Appledusk do anything on his own?*

Appledusk went to meet his Clanmate and rubbed his cheek against hers. "I'm not letting you do anything," he mewed. "Think of our kits!"

Reedshine glanced at her belly, barely swollen beneath her pelt. "I'm not sick!" she protested.

"I know you're not," meowed Appledusk. "But our kits are too precious to risk Perchpaw injuring you by mistake!"

Mapleshade gripped the branch so tightly that two of her claws snapped off. She barely noticed the jolt of pain. How could Reedshine be expecting kits already? How many lies had Appledusk told? She bunched her quarters beneath her, ready to leap down the moment Reedshine and Perchpaw left Appledusk alone, but the three cats moved off together with Perchpaw earnestly discussing battle tactics.

Mapleshade crouched in the tree and seethed with rage. A cold wet figure pressed against her flank, screeching for help. Mapleshade tried to curl her tail around her last remaining kit, but there was nothing but empty air beside her. She was dimly aware of being hungry and thirsty, and exhausted after her trek through the night, but nothing mattered now except taking revenge on the cat who had destroyed her world. She would wait here for as long as she had to—for the rest of her life, if it meant she could finally silence Patchkit's wails.

She must have dozed, because she woke with a start much later when the air was filled with misty rain and the ferns were filling up with shadows. Something was approaching through the undergrowth. Mapleshade stiffened, wondering if StarClan would bring Appledusk to her twice in one day. Then a bundle of fur blundered into the clearing and skidded to a halt at the foot of the tree.

"Take that, ThunderClan mouse-dung!" Perchpaw squealed, slapping his paw down onto a twig. As the twig snapped, he spun around, ears flattened. "Creep up on me, would you? You're as fox-hearted as your Clanmate!" He lurched forward and crushed a large clump of moss. Then he straightened up and looked down at his enemy. "Oops. I could have taken that back to the elders' den. I'll look for some more."

He trotted toward Mapleshade's tree, peering at the roots. Mapleshade let go of the branch and plummeted straight down onto the apprentice's back, knocking him to the ground with an *oof*. Before Perchpaw could figure out what was happening, Mapleshade grabbed his scruff in her teeth and hauled him past the tree, across the border. Her eyes bulged with the effort; the fat apprentice weighed more than a badger!

Perchpaw yowled and thrashed but Mapleshade sank her teeth farther into his pelt until he stopped struggling. "Who are you? What do you want?" he growled.

Mapleshade placed one paw heavily on his shoulders and snarled, "Keep still or I'll rip your throat out."

Perchpaw blinked. "I'm a RiverClan warrior! Let me go!"

"No you're not," Mapleshade hissed. "You're a stupid apprentice. It's all right, I'm not interested in killing you. I only want you as bait."

When Perchpaw tried to speak, she forced his face into the ground, muffling his protests. Then she squatted down, resting most of her bulk on his haunches, and waited.

"Perchpaw! Perchpaw, where are you?"

Mapleshade almost purred. A moment later, Appledusk trotted into the clearing, his eyes troubled. "Why can't you do what you're told for once?" he complained, looking around. "If I find out you've been practicing battle moves instead of collecting moss, you're going to be in big trouble, Perchpaw!"

Mapleshade gripped Perchpaw's neck fur in her teeth and dragged him out from behind the tree. She let the apprentice fall to the ground. "Is this what you're looking for, Appledusk?"

The warrior stared at her in horror. "You were told to leave our territory!"

Mapleshade twitched the tip of her tail. "And you thought I would? You're more mouse-brained than I thought. You killed our kits, and now you must pay."

Appledusk bared his teeth. "What are you talking about? *You* killed our kits, making them cross the river. Let Perchpaw go and get out of here before I call for a patrol."

Mapleshade jumped over Perchpaw and stood in front of the brown warrior, pelt bristling, paws planted firmly. "You can have that useless lump of fur back," she snarled. "But you'll have to fight me first."

CHAPTER 9

❧

Appledusk took a step back. His eyes clouded and he suddenly looked weary. "Mapleshade, I don't want to fight you," he meowed.

"I'm not giving you a choice!" Mapleshade hissed. She bunched her hindquarters beneath her and lunged at him.

Appledusk dodged away. "Just leave!" he gasped.

There was a crackle of stalks behind him and Reedshine appeared. "What's going on?" Her gaze fell on Mapleshade. "What's she doing here?"

Half-blind with fury, Mapleshade hurled herself at the orange she-cat. "You and your kits must die!" she screeched. "Appledusk is mine!" She unsheathed her claws, aiming for Reedshine's face.

There was a thud of paws, then silence, and a solid brown shape flashed in front of Mapleshade. Her claws struck home, piercing fur and flesh, and a spurt of blood leaped out at her. With a grunt, Appledusk dropped at her feet, blood pouring from his throat.

In the same moment, a heavy weight struck Mapleshade from behind. Perchpaw gripped her with his paws and bit down hard on her neck. Mapleshade staggered forward and almost fell. Perchpaw slid off her back. Mapleshade could feel him trembling against her flank; then she realized that she was the one shaking. *Why? I'm not frightened.*

"He's dead!" Reedshine shrieked, crouching beside Appledusk. She stared up at Mapleshade, her horrified eyes ringed with white. "You killed him!"

Mapleshade tried to take a step forward but her legs felt strangely heavy and her vision was blurred. *Is it raining?* she wondered. Something hot and wet spilled down her front legs, and there was a dull ache behind her ears. She shook her head and bright red droplets spattered the ground like tiny fallen leaves.

Something small and ginger and white stirred beside Appledusk's unmoving body. "You killed him, Mama!" shrilled Patchkit. His little tail was held high with triumph. "We are all free now!" He started to fade against his father's light brown fur.

Mapleshade stumbled toward her son. "Wait!" she gasped. "Don't leave me!"

Reedshine rose up from behind Appledusk and hissed at Mapleshade. "Don't come any closer! What you have done here is more terrible than anything a Clan cat has done before. But you have not won, Mapleshade. Appledusk will live on in his kits, and in their kits, and their kits in turn. His spirit will not die. He will be part of RiverClan *forever*!"

Mapleshade swayed, feeling the soil sticky beneath her paws. "Then I will watch over all your kin and punish each one for what you did to me," she rasped. "My vengeance is not finished yet. It will never be finished!"

She lurched toward the bushes behind the willow tree. She dimly heard Perchpaw start to follow her, but Reedshine called him back. "She has done enough harm," Mapleshade heard her mew. "Let her crawl away to die alone."

Mapleshade forced her way through the undergrowth. She felt no pain, just a strange numbness that seemed to be spreading through her body. She reached the edge of the bushes, and the walls of the Twoleg den where she had slept on the first night of her exile loomed up in front of her, but Mapleshade was too weak to go any farther. She slumped to the ground, feeling dirt and tiny stones grind into her blood-soaked fur. She closed her eyes, waiting for the faces of her kits to appear and thank her for everything she had done.

But there was nothing behind her eyes except swirling darkness, battered by an icy wind and unbroken by even a glimmer of stars. Mapleshade felt the first stirrings of fear. "StarClan, where are you?" she wailed into the endless night. "Where are my kits?"

A small furry face appeared blurrily in front of her eyes. "Patchkit?" Mapleshade gasped. She tried to reach out with one paw.

"It's you!" exclaimed the cat. "Do you remember me? I'm Myler. We met once before." Mapleshade felt his nose press along her flank. "You're badly hurt," mewed the little cat. "You poor thing. Come on, let's get you inside."

With surprising strength, he boosted Mapleshade to her feet with his shoulder and guided her into the Twoleg den.

Mapleshade collapsed onto a pile of hay. *I have lost everything*, she thought. *What do I have left to live for?*

There was a bustle of movement beside her and the black-and-white cat started dabbing at her fur with a piece of wet moss. Mapleshade was too weary to push him away. She half opened one eye and saw blood flowing freely down her shoulder, pooling beneath her.

"There's too much, too much," fretted Myler. He dabbed more frantically. "Did a Clan cat do this to you?"

Mapleshade closed her eye again and nodded.

The little cat sighed. "Ah, there is no end to their wildness and thirst for blood," he muttered. "You should have left while you had the chance."

Leave? How could I ever leave? I swore to avenge the deaths of my kits, and that's what I have done. And yet that vengeance is not over, because Appledusk will live on in Reedshine's kits. I will never be finished.

Myler curled up beside her, hardly flinching as his fur pressed against her bloody body. "I'll stay with you," he promised. "You're safe now."

Mapleshade unsheathed her scarlet, broken claws. "Leave me alone," she rasped, forcing herself to lift her head and glare at her companion. "I don't need anyone."

The black-and-white cat stood up and looked down at her with sadness in his eyes. "I think you are wrong," he whispered. But he turned and padded into the hay-scented darkness.

For a moment Mapleshade longed to call him back, but sleep was dragging at her, heavier than stones, stronger than the river. She closed her eyes and watched her mind fill with churning shadows, pierced by shrieks of terror that made her jump. She realized that she could feel ground beneath her paws, cold and sodden and stinking like the river. Somehow she could walk again, strength flowing back into her limbs and her vision clearing.

She emerged into a half-lit clearing surrounded by gray tree trunks. Although she felt no fear, she was aware of being watched by unseen eyes. "Am I dead?" she meowed out loud, listening to her voice echo between the trees. "Is this StarClan?"

She looked up, but there were no stars in the thick black sky above her, not even a glimmer of silver beyond the rustling leaves. Instead, what light there was seemed to come from fleshy fungus growing on the roots of the trees, and from the slimy trunks themselves.

"Not StarClan," whispered a voice from somewhere behind her. "This is the Dark Forest, the Place of No Stars. We welcome you, Mapleshade."

Mapleshade spun around. "Who are you? Show yourself!"

"Never," hissed the voice. "You have come here to walk alone in your blood-soaked memories."

Instead of dread, Mapleshade felt a surge of triumph. If she was here because of what she had endured, then there would be other cats like her, cats who would understand what she had gone through, who knew what it was to stand up to their enemies and dole out immeasurable pain.

She would find these cats, whatever that voice had told her, train them to be as strong and fearless as she was, and use them to cause more trouble for the Clans than the warriors could imagine in their worst dreams.

Mapleshade had found a place where she truly belonged. From here, she could cause more suffering than when she had been alive, and fighting her battles alone. For all eternity, Appledusk's kin would mourn the day he had destroyed the life of a ThunderClan warrior. Just as she had promised to Reedshine, Mapleshade's desire for vengeance would never sleep.

WARRIORS

GOOSEFEATHER'S
CURSE

ALLEGIANCES

THUNDERCLAN

LEADER   DOESTAR—pale fawn-and-white she-cat with amber eyes

DEPUTY   PINEHEART—red-brown tom with green eyes

MEDICINE CAT   CLOUDBERRY—very old long-furred white she-cat with yellow eyes

WARRIORS   (toms and she-cats without kits)

MUMBLEFOOT—brown tom with amber eyes

LARKSONG—tortoiseshell she-cat with pale green eyes

ROOKTAIL—black tom with blue eyes

APPRENTICE, STORMPAW

WINDFLIGHT—gray tabby tom with pale green eyes

APPRENTICE, SWIFTPAW

HAREPOUNCE—light brown she-cat with yellow eyes

APPRENTICE, ADDERPAW

SQUIRRELWHISKER—brown tabby she-cat with amber eyes

APPRENTICE, ROCKPAW

HOLLYPELT—black she-cat with green eyes

APPRENTICE, SMALLPAW

RAINFUR—speckled ginger-and-white she-cat with amber eyes

STAGLEAP—gray tabby tom with amber eyes

LITTLESTEP—black-and-white tom with blue eyes

FLASHNOSE—dark ginger cat with white muzzle

QUEENS (she-cats expecting or nursing kits)

DAISYTOE—gray-and-white she-cat with yellow eyes (mother to Moonkit, a silver-gray she-cat with pale yellow eyes, and Goosekit, a speckled gray tom with blue eyes)

FALLOWSONG—light brown she-cat (mother to Poppykit, a dark red she-cat with a bushy tail and round amber eyes, Heronkit, a dark brown tabby tom with yellow eyes, and Rabbitkit, a thick-furred light brown tom)

APPRENTICES (more than six moons old, in training to become warriors)

STORMPAW—blue-gray tom with blue eyes

ADDERPAW—mottled brown tabby tom with yellow eyes

SWIFTPAW—tabby-and-white she-cat with yellow eyes

SMALLPAW—gray tom with very small ears and amber eyes

ROCKPAW—silver tom with blue eyes

ELDERS (former warriors and queens, now retired)

MISTPELT—thick-furred gray she-cat with green eyes

NETTLEBREEZE—ancient ginger tom

SHADOWCLAN

LEADER   **HOUNDSTAR**—brown-and-white tom

DEPUTY   **CEDARPELT**—very dark gray tom with a white belly

MEDICINE CAT   **REDTHISTLE**—dark ginger she-cat
     APPRENTICE, SAGEPAW (white she-cat with long whiskers)

WINDCLAN

LEADER   **HEATHERSTAR**—pinkish-gray she-cat with blue eyes

DEPUTY   **GORSEFOOT**—gray tabby tom

MEDICINE CAT   **CHIVECLAW**—dark brown tom with yellow eyes
     APPRENTICE, HAWKPAW (mottled dark brown tom with yellow eyes)

WARRIORS   **DAWNSTRIPE**—pale gold tabby with creamy stripes

RIVERCLAN

LEADER   **VOLESTAR**—brown tabby tom

DEPUTY   **HAILSTEP**—thick-pelted gray tom

MEDICINE CAT   **ECHOSNOUT**—old black-and-white she-cat

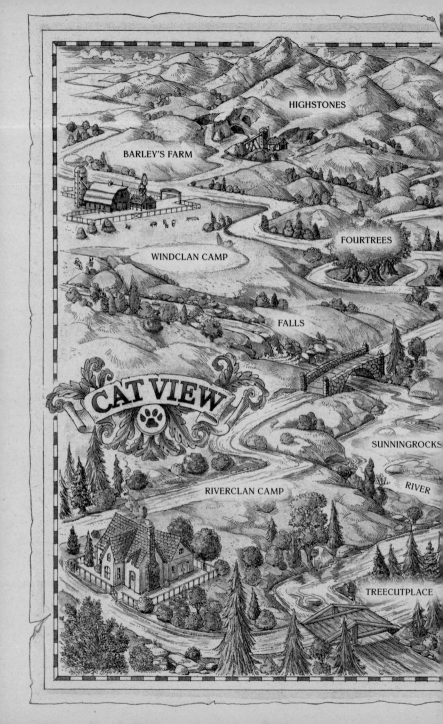

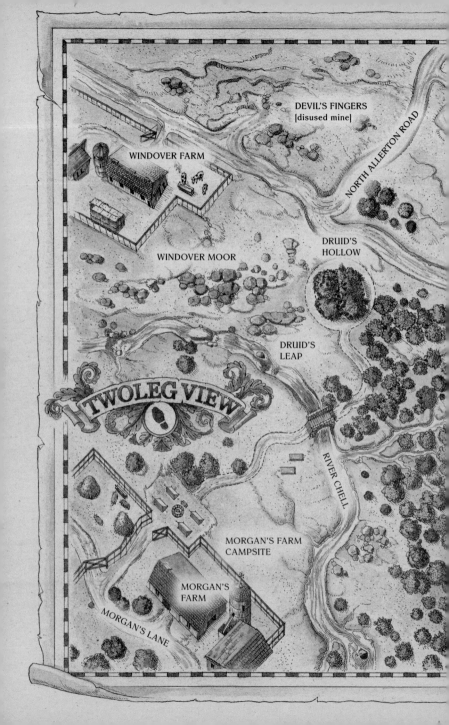

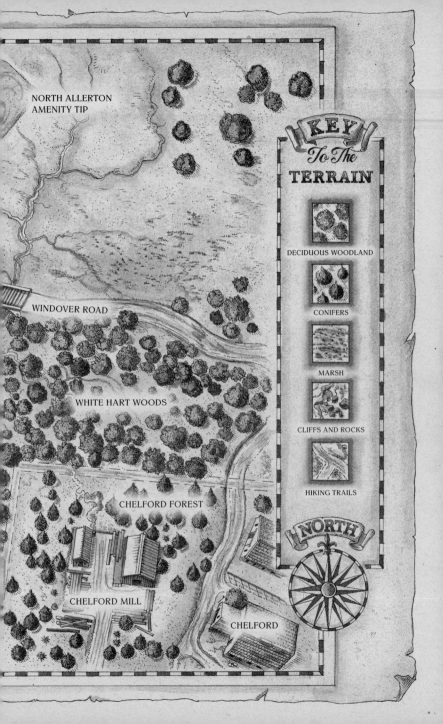

CHAPTER 1

"The leader of TigerClan unsheathed his claws until they pierced the smooth spotted throat of the cat who sprawled beneath him. He lifted his magnificent black-striped head and glared at the warriors standing at the edge of the trees. 'This is *my* forest!' he roared. 'One step closer and I'll rip the fur from your leader's bones!'"

Goosekit whimpered and buried his nose under his thick gray tail. The elderly she-cat nudged him with her muzzle. "Don't be scared, little one," she purred. "It's only a story."

"But TigerClan is so mean!" Goosekit mewed, his voice muffled by fur.

"Goosekit! Where are you? Come outside!"

Goosekit lifted his head and scowled. "That's my mother," he muttered.

"It's a lovely day! You should be out here, not moldering in the den!"

The old she-cat nuzzled the top of his head. "Go on, scamp," she meowed. "We can finish the story later."

"But I want to hear it now!" Goosekit wailed. "What if I

meet the leader of TigerClan when I'm a warrior? I need to know how to fight him!"

"There'll be time later, I promise. Now go find your mother. She's right; it is a beautiful day." The she-cat prodded him with her fat brown paw, and Goosekit stumbled reluctantly out of the nest.

He pushed his way through the thorns and emerged blinking into the sunlit clearing. The brambles that circled the clearing sparkled from the recent fall of rain, and the air was heavy with the scent of unfurling leaves and warm fresh-kill. Goosekit's belly rumbled, and he turned toward the pile of prey, but before he could take a step, a damp and prickly ball of moss knocked his legs from under him.

"Oof!" he grunted, tumbling onto his side.

A gray-and-white she-cat bounded over and stared down at him. "Oh, Goosekit!" she meowed. "Are you all right?"

"Of course he's all right!" huffed a silver-gray she-kit. She trotted up on sturdy, fluff-covered legs. "Aren't you?"

Goosekit lifted his head. "Yes, I'm fine, Moonkit," he panted. "I didn't see the moss ball coming, that's all."

Moonkit prodded him with her forepaw. "Get up! I want to play!"

A dark red kit with round amber eyes bounced up and flicked the moss ball away. "Come on, Moonkit! Bet you can't catch this!"

Goosekit's littermate spun around and raced after the ball as it rolled across the clearing. Poppykit followed, her longer legs keeping up easily. There was a flash of dark brown fur as her brother Heronkit charged to meet them. All three kits crashed together in a flurry of paws and tails, while the ball of moss kept rolling until it reached the fresh-kill pile.

Watching them, Goosekit winced. His mother licked the top of his head. "You should join in more," she urged him. "You won't get hurt."

Goosekit looked up at her. "Really? Then why is Rabbitkit in Cloudberry's den again? Did he fall off the half-tree? Get stuck in a bramble?"

Daisytoe shook her head. "He got a thorn stuck in his nose. He's clumsy because he hasn't grown into his paws yet."

Goosekit looked down at his small furry feet. "I don't want to stay this size forever," he muttered. "What if I never grow big enough to be a warrior?"

"That's not what I meant," Daisytoe began. She broke off as the gorse bushes at the entrance to the clearing quivered and several cats burst through.

A tortoiseshell she-cat with leaf-green eyes was at the head of the patrol. She dropped her catch—a plump young pigeon—on the fresh-kill pile and trotted over to Daisytoe. "You'd have loved it out there today," she mewed. "The prey was practically falling into our paws!"

For a moment Daisytoe looked wistful. "Maybe next moon, Larksong," she replied. "I need to get the little ones weaned first."

The black tom who had followed Larksong through the tunnel came to join them. A red squirrel dangled from his jaws. He placed the squirrel on the ground and brushed the tip of his tail along Daisytoe's flank. "I caught this for you," he purred.

"Thanks, Rooktail," Daisytoe meowed, her eyes lighting up.

There was a gasp from the other side of the fresh-kill pile. Goosekit saw a broad-shouldered gray apprentice staring at him. "Wow, Goosekit, is that really you? Or just a lump of moss shaped like you?"

Goosekit sighed as the cat trotted over and sniffed him. "I haven't seen you outside for days!" the tom went on. "Look, Rooktail! Your son doesn't melt in sunlight!"

The black warrior twitched his ears. "That's enough, Stormpaw. Go see if the elders want anything to eat."

Moonkit ran over, her stubby tail straight up in the air. "Stormpaw! Watch this! I've been practicing that move you showed me!" She crouched down, waggling her haunches, then sprang forward with her front paws raised. Her ears were flat back, and she curled her lip to reveal tiny sharp teeth. "Pretty fierce, huh?" she panted, dropping back onto all four paws.

Stormpaw nodded. "You scared me for sure! Do you want to help me take fresh-kill to the elders? Then I'll teach you another battle move."

"Yes, please!" Moonkit bounced on the spot, her yellow eyes shining.

Rooktail narrowed his eyes at Stormpaw. "You're the apprentice," he reminded him. "Don't let the kits do your duties for you!"

"But I want to help!" Moonkit protested. "I hope Stormpaw

can be my mentor when I'm an apprentice."

"Of course he won't be," Goosekit mewed. "He'll only just be a warrior!"

"Maybe, but he'll be the best warrior in ThunderClan!" Moonkit declared loyally. "Even better than Doestar!"

Stormpaw shuffled his paws. "Come on, Moonkit," he muttered. "Let's feed these elders."

Goosekit watched them pick up a blackbird from the fresh-kill pile and start hauling it toward the elders' den, where two ancient cats sat outside with the sun warming their pelts. Moonkit's eyes bulged with the effort of dragging the heavy bird. Goosekit winced as they almost collided with a slender white-furred tom, but somehow they missed him and the tom walked on and vanished into the gorse tunnel.

The other two cats on the hunting patrol, Harepounce and her apprentice, Adderpaw, were depositing their prey on the pile. Adderpaw twitched his tail toward Goosekit. "Come and try this mouse! I caught it myself," he added proudly.

Goosekit trotted over and sniffed at the brown-furred, still-warm body. It was huge, almost as big as him. Its nose was wrinkled slightly, exposing long front teeth, and its paws were clenched in tight little curls. Goosekit winced. He had shared some fresh-kill with his mother and Moonkit, but he preferred milk. Eating fresh-kill made his jaws ache.

"Don't you want it?" Adderpaw asked, sounding disappointed.

Goosekit gripped one of the mouse's front legs and started to heave it off the pile. As his hind paws scrabbled on the sandy earth, he was shoved roughly aside. A ragged ginger shape loomed over him.

"Watch out, Nettlebreeze!" Adderpaw called. "There's plenty of prey."

Nettlebreeze turned his cloudy gaze on the apprentice. "What? Did you say something?" He twitched his ears, and a lump of something yucky dropped onto Goosekit's head.

"Hey!" Goosekit protested. "Get off me! This is my mouse!" He shook his head, and a tick covered in mouse bile fell onto the floor.

The ancient cat bent his head and sniffed him. "Don't you know the warrior code? Elders and kits eat first!"

"I am a kit!" Goosekit mewed.

"Then you should learn to respect your elders," Nettlebreeze growled. He placed one paw on the mouse. "Leave me to eat in peace."

Goosekit backed away, his fur fluffed up with indignation. But he knew better than to pick a quarrel with the oldest cat in ThunderClan—maybe the oldest cat in all four Clans. Goosekit suspected Nettlebreeze had been alive when the four great oak trees had been nothing more than acorns. His tail spiked as he pictured the hollow that his mother had described to him, flanked by steep slopes and watched over by the mighty oaks. As soon as he was six moons old, Goosekit would be an apprentice, able to go to the Gathering every full moon and meet cats from the other Clans. Goosekit wasn't sure how much fun that sounded. He already felt a bit alarmed by how many cats there were in ThunderClan.

Goosekit headed back toward the nursery, swerving to avoid Heronkit and Poppykit, who were wrestling over a stick. Their littermate, Rabbitkit, watched, a large leaf stuck on his pricked nose. "Go on, Poppykit!" he cheered, sounding as if he had his head stuck in a patch of ferns.

Goosekit was about to push his way into the den when Daisytoe stopped him. "Stay outside with me," she urged. "It's too nice to be inside. Don't you want to play with your denmates?" She nodded toward Moonkit, who was stalking across the clearing beside Stormpaw. The tip of her tongue poked out as she concentrated hard on copying his low, stealthy movement. Two full-grown warriors watched them, half hidden in the shadows under the brambles.

Goosekit curled into his mother's warm belly fur. "I'd rather stay with you," he mewed. "There are too many cats here."

Daisytoe purred. "No more than usual! These are your Clanmates, Goosekit. The cats who will feed and protect and train you until you are ready to patrol alongside them. They will always look after you."

"Stormpaw won't," Goosekit growled. "He's going to try to kill me."

Beside him, Daisytoe stiffened. "Don't say that! Stormpaw will look out for you, like all your Clanmates."

Goosekit shook his head stubbornly. There were pictures crowding into his head, as clearly as if they were right in front of him. "There will be a badger," he insisted, "and Stormpaw will leave me to fight it on my own."

"You're letting your imagination run away with you!" Daisytoe scolded him. "Stop it! You haven't even seen a badger yet."

"I know what they look like," Goosekit argued. "Big, with a long pointy face. They are black and white like magpies, but striped like TigerClan. They are angry and fierce and they eat kits!"

Daisytoe wrapped her tail around him. "You'll have to train hard and become a big strong warrior, won't you? Then you can fight off all the badgers on your own. Meanwhile, I think you should stop listening to the elders' stories. They're putting mouse-brained ideas into your head!"

Goosekit nestled closer to his mother's belly. In his head he saw the huge black-and-white creature looming over him, yellow teeth bared, drool hanging from its jaws. "I'm going to be really scared," he muttered. "I don't like badgers. Stormpaw is the meanest cat in ThunderClan!"

CHAPTER 2

Goosekit crouched in the ferns, not daring to breathe. He could hear paw steps coming closer on the hard-packed earth, and the soft noise of his stalker tasting the air.

"I know you're in there!" a voice growled. Goosekit tensed, ready to push himself deeper into the ferns, but there was a rattle of fronds, and a dark red shape appeared in front of him with a yowl of triumph.

"Found you!" Poppykit declared. Her amber eyes shone. "Great hiding place, Goosekit! The smell of Cloudberry's herbs really hid your scent!"

Goosekit followed her out of the ferns, shaking shreds of greenery from his fur. Behind them, a voice rasped, "Are you kits playing hide-and-seek near my den again? I've told you not to flatten those ferns! They keep out the drafts!"

Poppykit rolled her eyes. "Cloudberry is such a grump! I bet she never played when she was a kit."

Goosekit nodded. "Playing probably wasn't allowed back then!"

"Hey, you found him!" Heronkit called from the half-tree outside the apprentices' den. All the apprentices were out on patrol, and it was too cloudy for the elders to bask outside, so the kits had the clearing to themselves.

Moonkit jumped down from the tree stump. "Your turn to look for us, Goosekit!" she called. "No peeking!"

Goosekit stood at the base of the half-tree, faced the rough brown bark, and closed his eyes. He flexed each toe in turn, letting the tip of his claws press briefly into the earth. When he had tested each claw, he opened his eyes and turned around. The clearing was empty apart from Fallowsong, Daisytoe's denmate, rolling a ball of soiled bedding out of the nursery.

"They seemed determined to find the best hiding places!" she purred to Goosekit. "Good luck!"

Goosekit ran to the nursery first. His legs felt strong, and he could feel new muscles flexing underneath the pelt on his shoulders. In two moons he would become an apprentice. He couldn't wait to start learning how to hunt and fight so he could be a great warrior like his father, Rooktail. But he didn't want to learn from Stormpaw like his sister, Moonkit. She had stars in her eyes whenever she looked at that big-headed apprentice. No, Goosekit wanted to learn from ThunderClan's best warriors, like Rooktail or even Doestar herself.

He slipped quietly into the nursery and looked around. It was dark and musty inside, full of warm scents of milk and fur. Daisytoe was out on patrol, and without the queens inside, the den looked much larger. Goosekit poked his muzzle into a heap of bedding. No sign of his denmates here. He whirled around and headed back into the clearing. His ears caught a faint sound from behind Highrock, just past the entrance to Doestar's den. Goosekit stared at the spot and opened his jaws to taste the air. The breeze carried a faint, familiar scent to him. He marched forward and pushed aside a prickly tendril that curled around the base of the rock.

Rabbitkit and Poppykit blinked at him. "That was quick!" Rabbitkit mewed. "We thought you'd never find us here!"

"I heard you moving around," Goosekit replied.

Poppykit scowled. "That was Rabbitkit," she complained. "I sat on a nettle!"

Goosekit twitched his tail. "Go wait by the half-tree while I find the others."

He stood outside Doestar's den and gazed around the clearing, looking for branches that were moving too fast for the breeze, or flashes of pale fur between the leaves. Poppykit and Rabbitkit had stomped over to the half-tree and were lying beside it.

"Hey!" A low voice caught Goosekit's attention. A young black-and-white tom was beckoning to him from the shadows beside the warriors' den. "Are you looking for two kits?"

Goosekit nodded.

"The dark brown tom went behind the elders' den," mewed the tom. "And I think I saw the other one go into those ferns."

Goosekit's fur spiked. If Cloudberry caught Moonkit beside her den, they'd be in big trouble! "Thanks!" he called to the black-and-white cat. He bounded to the elders' den and squeezed behind it, screwing up his eyes so they didn't get poked by thorns. He almost fell over Heronkit, who was trying to make himself invisible by crouching behind a clump of thistles.

"Watch out!" Heronkit protested, wriggling out of the way.

"Sorry," Goosekit puffed. "At least I found you! Go join the others by the half-tree. I need to find Moonkit."

He turned around, not easy in the tiny, prickly space, and struggled back to the clearing. He could see the tips of some ferns waving beside the rock that sheltered the medicine cat's den. Goosekit hoped that he would find Moonkit before Cloudberry did. He ran over to the tunnel that led into the dense ferns and stuck his head between the pale green stalks.

"Moonkit! Are you in there?"

There was no reply. Goosekit sighed and pushed his way in. The scent of fresh and dried herbs was overwhelming this close to the medicine den, and it was impossible to pick up any other smells. But he spotted a tiny paw print in a damp patch of earth, and a dent at the stalks of some ferns, as if something had brushed past not long ago. He followed the trail and spotted pale gray fur glowing among the greenery.

"I see you, Moonkit!" he called softly.

There was a hiss of annoyance and his sister started heading toward him.

"Come on, before Cloudberry sees us," Goosekit urged. He turned and began pushing through the ferns just as a stir of movement close by suggested that Cloudberry had poked her head out of her den.

"Swiftpaw, is that you?" the old cat called.

Ducking his head, Goosekit nudged Moonkit past the last

clump of stalks and into the clearing.

"I can't believe you found me so quickly!" Moonkit wailed.

"He found all of us too quickly," meowed Heronkit, narrowing his eyes. "I bet he cheated!"

"I did not!" Goosekit protested. His fur grew hot. He hadn't asked the black-and-white cat to help him! Any of the others could have been told where he was hiding when it was their turn to look.

"You must have," Poppykit insisted. "You didn't look anywhere else except where we were hiding!"

"I told you that I heard Rabbitkit move!"

"I don't believe you," Poppykit hissed. "I don't want to play with you anymore."

"Me neither," huffed Heronkit. He deliberately turned his back on Goosekit. "Come on, let's play something else. Without him."

Moonkit shot Goosekit an apologetic look. "It does seem like you cheated," she whispered.

Goosekit flattened his ears. "Whatever. I don't want to play with you anyway." He stomped toward the nursery. Maybe he'd find an elder to tell him more stories about LeopardClan and TigerClan. Those were real adventures, not like stupid games of hide-and-seek.

There was a rattle of branches as a patrol returned through the gorse tunnel. Goosekit sat down in the shadows beside his den and watched the long-legged, powerful-looking warriors spill into the clearing. Cloudberry puffed her way out of the ferns to meet them.

"Is all well on the borders, Windflight?" she asked the gray tabby who was sniffing at the fresh-kill pile.

Windflight nodded. "Twolegplace was as quiet as Fourtrees at new moon," he commented. "Those cats we chased off two sunrises ago haven't dared showed their noses again!" He lifted his head and looked around the clearing. "Is Swiftpaw back? I want to take her out for some battle training with Harepounce and Adderpaw."

Cloudberry narrowed her eyes. "I assumed she'd met up with you and joined the patrol. I haven't seen her since she left."

"No, she didn't join us. I thought you told her to fetch comfrey leaves and come straight back," Windflight meowed.

A dark ginger cat with a white muzzle trotted over to them. "Are you talking about Swiftpaw? Is something the matter?"

"Nothing to worry about, Flashnose," Windflight mewed. "Swiftpaw is taking longer than we expected to fetch herbs, that's all."

Flashnose turned in a tight circle. "She went out before we did. Something must have happened to her!"

Windflight touched her rump with the tip of his tail. "She'll be fine. She's almost a warrior now, and she's smart enough to take care of herself. Just like her mother," he added.

But the ginger she-cat refused to be comforted. "We must find her! What if she came across a fox?" She looked at the den below Highrock. "Is Doestar back yet?"

Cloudberry shook her head. "You're the first patrol to return. No one here but the kits and elders."

Another patrol returned, this time carrying the rewards

of good hunting. As they started to drop their catch on the fresh-kill pile, Flashnose called to them, "Did any of you see Swiftpaw in the forest?"

Daisytoe tucked the tail of her fat gray squirrel onto the pile. "Not a whisker," she meowed. "I thought she went to fetch herbs."

"She did, but she's not back yet," Windflight explained. "I'm sure she's fine—"

"You can't be sure!" Flashnose hissed. "Swiftpaw is too young to be out on her own."

"We'll go back out to look for her," Rooktail meowed, coming to stand beside Flashnose. The other warriors in his patrol nodded.

Daisytoe trotted over to the kits, who were watching, huge-eyed. "Come on, into the nursery," she prompted. "I want you to stay there until I come back." As she ushered them past Goosekit, she included him with a sweep of her tail. "You too, little one."

"But we could help look for Swiftpaw!" Moonkit protested as Daisytoe pushed them into the den.

"Definitely not!" Daisytoe mewed. "It's bad enough that an apprentice has gone missing. We'll be back soon." She whisked around and Goosekit listened to the warriors thundering through the gorse. Their paw steps faded as they climbed the ravine and disappeared into the trees.

Rabbitkit scrabbled crossly at the dried moss. "We totally could have helped!" he grumbled. "I'm nearly as big as the apprentices!"

Heronkit nodded. "It would be just like playing hide-and-seek!"

"Except we wouldn't cheat," mewed Rabbitkit, glaring at Goosekit.

Goosekit wasn't in the mood for defending himself again. When the others started to play a game of spot the ant at the far end of the den, he slipped through the brambles. The clearing was deserted except for Cloudberry dozing near the entrance and, tucked below Highrock, the black-and-white tom who had helped Goosekit find his denmates.

Goosekit trotted over to him. "You're an apprentice, aren't you?" he asked.

The tom stopped licking his chest fur and looked up. "That's right."

"Why aren't you looking for Swiftpaw? Can you go find her, please?"

The black-and-white cat looked unsure. "I don't think I can go by myself," he mewed.

A long-tailed warrior with brown striped fur padded past. "Hey!" the black-and-white cat called. "An apprentice has gone missing!"

The warrior stopped and fixed clear amber eyes on Goosekit. "Which one?"

"Swiftpaw," Goosekit replied. "She's got tabby-and-white fur and yellow eyes. Have you seen her?"

"Quite small, carrying herbs?" meowed the brown tom.

Goosekit nodded. "That's her!"

The warrior turned to walk away. "Oh yes, I saw her," he

purred. "She was just below Sunningrocks, in the reeds."

Goosekit started to call after him, but the sun was in his eyes and he couldn't see where the warrior had gone. The clearing was starting to fill up with another returning patrol, and the ravine echoed with cries of alarm as Cloudberry woke from her snooze and told them what had happened.

Goosekit ran over to the warriors. Taking a deep breath, he stopped and stretched himself as tall as he could. "I know where Swiftpaw is!" he blurted out.

CHAPTER 3

Several heads turned toward him.

"She's in the reeds by Sunningrocks," Goosekit went on.

Larksong pricked her ears. Beside her, Hollypelt looked skeptical. "You've never even left the camp," she meowed. "How do you know about the reeds beside Sunningrocks?"

Goosekit pressed his paws into the solid earth. "A warrior told me he saw Swiftpaw there."

"Which warrior?" asked Larksong, looking around.

"I . . . I don't know," Goosekit admitted. "He's not here now."

Harepounce rolled her eyes. "Fancy that."

"I'm not lying!" Goosekit insisted, digging his claws into the earth in frustration.

Larksong looked closely at him. Then she lifted her head. "We'll need to check the whole territory," she pointed out. "So we may as well start with Sunningrocks. Mumblefoot, Hollypelt, will you come with me?"

"Because a kit said so?" Hollypelt mewed. "I don't think so. Doestar and Pineheart will be back soon. I'll wait for them to organize search patrols."

"I'll come with you," Mumblefoot meowed, padding over to Larksong. He glanced at Goosekit. "It would be a funny thing for a kit to make up, don't you think?"

Larksong nodded. She whisked around and plunged back into the gorse with the sturdy brown tom at her heels. More cats emerged into the clearing before the thorns stopped quivering. This patrol was led by Doestar and Pineheart. The ThunderClan leader's face darkened as she heard about Swiftpaw. Hollypelt told her about the cats who had already gone out to search.

Doestar turned to her deputy. "It sounds as if Snakerocks and the Thunderpath boundary have been covered. I want you to take a patrol to the treecutplace and along the border with Twolegplace."

Pineheart dipped his head. "We'll go at once." He summoned the three warriors standing closest to him with a flick of his tail, then led them into the tunnel at a run.

Almost at once, Flashnose, Rooktail, and their patrol returned to the clearing. Their tails drooped, and Flashnose's eyes were brimming. "We searched all the way to Snakerocks and back," she murmured. "But there was no sign of her."

Doestar rested her cream-colored tail on Flashnose's shoulder. "There are warriors spread through the whole forest," she meowed. "We'll find Swiftpaw, I promise."

Suddenly there was a crackle of branches, and a small, sodden figure draped in green slime stumbled out of the gorse.

"Swiftpaw!" Flashnose screeched, flinging herself on her daughter.

Larksong appeared behind Swiftpaw, her tortoiseshell coat dripping with bright green riverweed. "She was well and truly stuck!" the warrior reported. "Mumblefoot and I thought we'd never get her out of the reeds!"

Mumblefoot joined them. His brown fur stood on end, and there was a piece of reed stuck behind one ear.

"I hurt my leg," Swiftpaw whimpered. "I was following a frog and I got all tangled up. I thought the river was going to swallow me!"

"You're safe now, my precious," Flashnose purred. She lifted her head and gazed at Larksong and Mumblefoot. "Thank you for finding her! You saved her life!"

Larksong curled her tail over her back. "It's Goosekit you should thank. He told us where Swiftpaw had gone."

Flashnose tipped her head on one side. "How did you know? And why didn't you tell us at once?"

"A warrior told me," Goosekit mewed. "A dark brown tom."

"Are you sure it wasn't Squirrelwhisker?" mewed Rooktail.

Goosekit shook his head. "No! I know the difference between a tom and a she-cat!"

Pineheart stood over him, looking stern. "There are no other dark brown warriors in ThunderClan, Goosekit. Who told you where Swiftpaw was?"

Goosekit looked around, wishing the amber-eyed warrior would appear from the shadows. "I told you! I don't know his name!"

Daisytoe left her sister licking the slime from Swiftpaw's fur and came over to stand beside Pineheart. "You have to tell the truth," she meowed. "Have you been outside the camp on your own? Is that how you knew where Swiftpaw had gone?"

"No!" Goosekit yowled. "I *am* telling the truth!"

There was a faint scent of herbs as Cloudberry padded over. "I don't think we need to make a fuss about it," she rasped. "Swiftpaw is back, and that's what matters. Daisytoe, go help Flashnose clean her up before I take a look at her leg. Goosekit, you come with me."

Feeling very small beside the ancient white medicine cat, Goosekit followed her to where Doestar was standing. The leader looked at them questioningly. "Is something wrong, Cloudberry?"

"I'm not sure," she admitted. "Goosekit, I want you to describe the cat who told you where Swiftpaw was. Everything you can remember, from his nose to his claws."

"And you're not going to be angry with me?" Goosekit checked.

Cloudberry shook her head.

Goosekit closed his eyes and pictured the brown-furred warrior. "He had long legs, but he wasn't as tall as you, Doestar. His fur wasn't as thick as Cloudberry's, and his tabby stripes were really dark, almost black. Darker than Squirrelwhisker's." He opened his eyes and looked at the senior cats.

Doestar was staring at Cloudberry. "He must be mistaken," she murmured.

Cloudberry shrugged. "You would think so."

"Do you think it's a sign?" Doestar queried.

"I can't see how it could be," Cloudberry meowed. She twitched her tail. "I'll talk to him."

Doestar nodded. "I think you should." She walked away to join the others.

Cloudberry looked down at Goosekit. "That cat you saw. Has anyone ever described him to you before?"

Goosekit shook his head.

"And he didn't tell you his name?"

"No!" Goosekit was starting to feel frustrated. Why did it matter who had told him where Swiftpaw was, as long as the apprentice had been found?

Cloudberry gazed around the clearing. "Are there any cats here now whose names you don't know?"

Goosekit shrugged. Was he going to get into trouble for not knowing the names of every one of his Clanmates? There were so many of them!

"It's okay if you don't know," Cloudberry urged him gently, as if she could tell what he was thinking.

Goosekit narrowed his eyes against the bright sun. "Well . . . the black-and-white cat washing himself by the Highrock. I think he's an apprentice. There's an elder who tells great stories; I don't know her name, but she often comes to see me in the nursery. She has brown fur and green eyes. And there's a cat beside Nettlebreeze who I haven't seen before."

Beside him, Cloudberry tensed. "Tell me about that cat," she whispered.

Goosekit wondered if Cloudberry was losing her sight. "She's got pale orange fur, a white belly, and four white paws.

She's watching him as if he's just a kit!" He purred with amusement at the thought of cranky, ancient Nettlebreeze ever being in the nursery.

Cloudberry nudged Goosekit's shoulder. "Let's go ask Nettlebreeze her name." She started to walk across the clearing. Goosekit trotted beside her, thinking it would be more polite to speak to the ginger cat directly.

As they reached the elders' den, Cloudberry hissed, "Let me do the talking." She raised her voice. "Hello, Nettlebreeze. You look comfortable out here. Tell me, do you know a pale orange she-cat with a white belly and white paws?"

The fur rose along Nettlebreeze's spine. "That's my mother, Dawnfeather," he growled. "Why are you asking about her? Has she spoken to you from StarClan?"

"StarClan?" Goosekit yelped. "But she's right—"

Cloudberry clamped her tail over Goosekit's mouth. "She asked me to tell you that she is watching over you, Nettlebreeze. All is well."

The old ginger tom grunted and put his chin on his paws. "It's a nice thought, I'm sure," he muttered, closing his rheumy eyes.

Goosekit bounced on his toes as Cloudberry steered him across the clearing to her den. They plunged through the soft green ferns and entered the den beneath the broad expanse of rock.

Cloudberry sat down and curled her tail over her paws. "You can talk now," she puffed.

"What's going on?" Goosekit squeaked. "That orange

she-cat was beside Nettlebreeze all the time! Why couldn't he see her?"

"Because she's dead," Cloudberry replied, fixing her yellow gaze on Goosekit. "She died many seasons ago, before I came to ThunderClan." She shifted her bony haunches on the dusty ground. "The striped brown tom who told you where Swift-paw was? I think that was Beetail. He was Oakstar's deputy when I arrived. He was a great warrior, wise and kind."

"He . . . was?" Goosekit echoed. "You mean he's dead too?"

Cloudberry nodded. "As are the other cats you described, the black-and-white apprentice and the brown elder. I don't know who they are. They must have lived in ThunderClan a long time ago. Only you can see them, no one else."

"That's not fair!" Goosekit whimpered. "Why can I see all the dead cats?"

"I don't know," Cloudberry admitted. "StarClan didn't tell me." She rolled a piece of moss under her paw until it crumbled. "You have a great gift, Goosekit," she mewed softly, "but it is not one that all the cats will appreciate. You must keep it to yourself. Do you understand?"

Goosekit put his head on one side. "But they might like to know that their ancestors are here in the camp!"

There was a flash of temper in Cloudberry's eyes. "It doesn't work like that!" she spat. "Warriors are raised to be suspicious of anything that doesn't come from the warrior code—and preferably from inside their own boundaries!"

Goosekit suddenly remembered what his mother had told him about Cloudberry, how she came from RiverClan after the ThunderClan medicine cat Ravenwing was murdered. Had the ThunderClan cats been unwelcoming at first? Even though they needed a new medicine cat?

Cloudberry had stood up and was pacing anxiously around her cave. "You will have to become my apprentice," she mewed, jerking his thoughts back to the present.

Goosekit gulped. That wasn't what he had planned. He was going to be a great warrior like Rooktail!

"Hopefully StarClan will guide me in how to train you to use your gift," Cloudberry went on. She stopped and stared at him. "What do you think, Goosekit? Would you like to be a medicine cat?"

CHAPTER 4

Doestar stood on top of the Highrock, her pale cream-and-fawn fur looking like clouds against the clear blue sky. "By the powers of StarClan, I give you your warrior name," she declared. "Swiftpaw, from this moment you will be known as Swiftbreeze. StarClan honors your courage and your willingness to learn, and we welcome you as a full warrior of ThunderClan."

The tabby-and-white she-cat dipped her head self-consciously as around her the Clan exploded with cheers for the new warriors. "Stormtail! Adderfang! Swiftbreeze!"

Moonkit cheered too, but Goosekit, crouching beside her outside the nursery, felt too anxious to speak. The warriors started to swirl around the clearing, and the noise of chatter grew until it sounded like a flock of birds had filled the ravine.

"Wait!" Doestar silenced them from her place on the rock. "I have one more ceremony to perform. We have a new apprentice among us."

The warriors circled back to sit below Highrock, muttering in confusion. "None of the kits are six moons old, are they?" Goosekit heard Littlestep ask Flashnose.

"No, I thought Fallowsong's kits would be made apprentices

next moon," the ginger she-cat replied.

Among the cats closest to the nursery, Goosekit saw Fallowsong glance questioningly at his mother. Daisytoe looked away without speaking. Goosekit suddenly wondered if his mother was unhappy that he was going to be made an apprentice so soon. Was she afraid of breaking the warrior code? *It's okay; I have a gift!* Goosekit sank his tiny claws into the earth, frustrated that he had to keep it a secret even from his own mother.

Beside him, Moonkit craned her neck to spot Heronkit and his littermates. "No way!" she squeaked. "Who's going to be made apprentice? Heronkit didn't say anything to me!"

"Goosekit, come forward!" Doestar's voice rang out across the clearing.

There was a stunned silence. Goosekit stumbled toward the Clan leader and stood beneath the Highrock. Doestar sprang elegantly down from the rock and touched the top of Goosekit's head with her chin before addressing the Clan. "Cloudberry is taking Goosekit to train as a medicine cat," she announced. "Goosekit, from this day on, until you receive your full medicine cat name, you will be known as Goosepaw. Your mentor will be Cloudberry, and I hope she will pass down all she knows to you."

Goosepaw felt the leader's breath hot against his ear fur as she licked his head. "Good luck, little one," she whispered, and Goosepaw felt the knot in his belly grow tighter. He kept his head lowered and screwed his eyes shut as there was an outburst of meowing behind him.

"What's going on? He's only four moons old!"

"He's far too young to be a medicine cat!"

"I don't want him to look after me if I get injured!"

Then a new voice, quieter and more rasping than the rest, but with a strength that made the other cats fall silent: "As your medicine cat, I ask you to trust me in this as you do in all other things," Cloudberry meowed calmly. "This is the right thing to do, I promise."

"Did StarClan tell you to do this?" challenged a voice that Goosepaw recognized as Rainfur's.

There was a pause; then Cloudberry mewed, "Yes. Our ancestors have chosen Goosepaw for a special path. I must do everything I can to help him follow that path."

Goosepaw took a deep breath and turned around. To his relief, a few cats called his name: "Goosepaw! Goosepaw!" He nodded gratefully to Larksong, Mumblefoot, and his sister, Moonkit. But the other kits were glaring at him, and the new warrior Stormtail curled his lip to show his long yellow teeth.

An image of an ugly badger, its black-and-white snout drawn back in a fierce snarl, flashed across Goosepaw's mind.

As Doestar vanished into her den and Pineheart began organizing patrols, the crackling tension in the air faded, and Goosepaw began to breathe more steadily. Several other cats nodded to him, not always recognizable among the blur of bodies and faces. Goosepaw wondered if they were dead cats; he tried to tell the difference, but it wasn't easy. He was fairly sure he saw Nettlebreeze's mother beside the entrance to the elders' den, and the striped brown tom who'd told him about Swiftpaw.

Nettlebreeze lurched past him, smelling of mouse bile and chewed grass. "Don't go getting any fancy ideas," he growled. "Kits becoming apprentices at four moons? It would never have happened in my day."

Goosepaw scowled, but Moonkit appeared on his other side, murmuring, "Don't listen to him. He's just cross because he's covered in ticks."

Goosepaw turned to face his sister. His fur felt hot with embarrassment. "I'm sorry," he blurted out. "I know it's not fair for me to become an apprentice before you."

Moonkit stopped him with a sweep of her tail. "I'm proud of you," she mewed. "Why wouldn't I be? You're going to be a medicine cat!"

"But . . . won't you miss me?" Goosepaw pressed. "I'll have to sleep in Cloudberry's den now."

Moonkit was looking past him at the warriors milling around. "I'll be fine," she mewed distractedly. "Do you think I could talk to Stormtail? Or will he think I'm a dumb kit now that he's a full warrior?"

Goosepaw followed her gaze. Stormtail was talking to Windflight and Squirrelwhisker, boasting about the size of the pigeon he had caught during his assessment. Goosepaw shrugged. "If you're willing to listen to how great he is, I'm sure he'd love to talk to you," he muttered.

Moonkit was already trotting across the clearing toward the warriors. Goosepaw felt the air stir behind him. Cloudberry was watching him from the entrance to her den. Goosepaw realized she was waiting for him. He dragged his paws toward the gap in the ferns, feeling as if he were falling into a deep hole from which there was no way out.

Goosepaw stared at the dizzying blackness waiting to swallow him. Every hair on his pelt stood on end, rippling in the soft wind that swept over the rocks. A huge white shape loomed toward him, carrying the scent of ancient stone.

"Come on, Goosepaw," Cloudberry grunted. "The moon will rise soon." She turned and headed back down the tunnel.

Goosepaw took one last glance over his shoulder. The hill rolled away behind him, down to the faint gray line that was the Thunderpath, before rising again to WindClan's bare moorland. Beyond that was the dense, dark mass of trees where ThunderClan slept, oblivious to the medicine cats' long journey for the half-moon Gathering. Goosepaw's feet hurt from the trek, and his mind still whirled with everything he had seen: not just the Thunderpath, the farm with noisy dogs, and the huge grassy fields, but also the faces of unknown cats, cats who his companions couldn't see.

A scrawny gray tom had died at his paws on the border of WindClan, and the hedge beside the Thunderpath had echoed to the wails of a lost kit calling for her mother. Goosepaw had tried to speak to them both, but they had looked straight through him as if they couldn't see him. Did that mean these things hadn't happened yet? he wondered. Was he seeing visions of things that would happen in the future? He shivered and ran to catch up to Cloudberry.

Here at Mothermouth there were three cats watching Goosepaw, their pelts so faint he could see the rocks behind them. They nodded encouragingly as he braced himself to enter the tunnel; Goosepaw decided they must be StarClan cats whose lives were already behind them. Far below, in the darkness, he could hear the medicine cats settling on the hard stone floor: Redthistle and Sagepaw from ShadowClan, Chiveclaw and Hawkpaw from WindClan, and Echosnout from RiverClan.

Goosepaw took a deep breath as if he were about to plunge into an icy river and stepped into the tunnel. The cold of the stone after the warm, heavy night took his breath away. "That's right, follow me," rumbled Cloudberry from up ahead. Goosepaw tucked in close to her furry haunches, inhaling her familiar herby scent, as they padded down and down.

After what seemed like forever, Goosepaw began to see his mentor's shape outlined against a fuzzy paleness. The tunnel opened up into a cave almost entirely filled by a huge glittering rock, bigger than Highrock, almost as big as the Great Rock, which Goosepaw had seen at Fourtrees on the journey here.

"I still think he's too young to be here," muttered Echosnout, lowering herself onto the stone floor at the far side of the cave. "Four moons old? He should be suckling at his mother's belly." Goosefeather knew she had been Cloudberry's mentor in RiverClan, and the old medicine cat seemed to think she could still boss the ThunderClan medicine cat around.

"If Cloudberry believes that he needs to begin his training

now, then who are we to argue?" meowed a deep voice. That was Chiveclaw from WindClan. He had been kind to Goosepaw on the journey, helping him squeeze under a prickly hedge and reassuring him that the hollering dogs couldn't get close.

"Why did I have to wait until I was six moons until you made me your apprentice?" whispered Hawkpaw. "Didn't StarClan send you a sign about me?"

Chiveclaw sighed in the darkness. "You became my apprentice when it was right for you," he replied. "Now be quiet and close your eyes. Make sure you're touching the Moonstone with your muzzle, remember."

Cloudberry nudged Goosepaw, and he shuffled forward on his belly until his nose scraped the sharp rock. He closed his eyes, then opened them again.

"Cloudberry?" he breathed.

"What is it?"

"We're going to see StarClan now, right?"

"Yes. You have to be very still and quiet for them to come to you."

"But I see them all the time, don't I? In the camp, on the way here. I bet if I looked around I could see some of them now!"

Cloudberry let out a sigh. "You haven't seen the most important StarClan cats yet. You need to be at the Moonstone for that."

Goosepaw wriggled around to look at his mentor. "How do you know? I can't tell you the names of all the cats I've seen. What if I don't need to do this at all? I could be a medicine cat already!"

"You've been my apprentice for precisely one quarter moon. Do you know any herbs? How to treat sickness? What to do if a queen is struggling to kit? No. You are most definitely *not* a medicine cat," Cloudberry mewed. She prodded his cheek with her front paw. "Put your nose against the Moonstone and go to sleep."

"Will you two be quiet?" hissed Echosnout.

"Sorry," whispered Cloudberry. She leaned forward and pressed her broad, flattened muzzle against the stone.

Goosepaw lay with his nose getting colder and colder as the cats beside him drifted off to sleep. He listened to their breathing slow down and felt the air grow still. He sighed. This stone was far too uncomfortable to go to sleep on, and his paws tingled from walking so far. He opened his eyes a chink. Above him, the crystal glowed from the light of the half-moon pouring down through the tiny gap in the roof. Goosepaw could see the shapes of the sleeping cats clearly on either side of them. Redthistle's apprentice, Sagepaw, stirred in her sleep, her white fur glowing like the rock. Goosepaw sighed. This was totally boring. He was getting cold, and he wasn't sleepy at all. He wondered how much trouble he would get into if he went back up the tunnel.

"Goosepaw! Goosepaw!"

Goosepaw stiffened. Someone was whispering. Had one of the apprentices woken up?

"Goosepaw!"

A pair of eyes gleamed like green stars in the shadows beside the Moonstone. Two more orbs appeared, blinking, then more and more, until Goosepaw was surrounded by cats staring at him. They started to move toward him, a mass of shifting pelts turned to shades of gray and silver by the moonlight.

"We have been waiting for you, Goosepaw!" breathed one of them.

"A long time," hissed another.

"We watched you being born!"

"And now you must listen to us. We have so much to tell you."

Goosepaw took a step back, flattening his ears. "Wait. There are so many of you. . . . Can you speak one at a time, please?"

A black cat loomed into his face. "ThunderClan is doomed!"

"There will be a cat who burns like fire!"

"Trust no one, not even your Clanmates. Too many hearts are fickle."

"Beware the striped face and snapping teeth!"

Goosepaw tried to edge toward the tunnel. "Stop!" he begged. "You're scaring me!" He looked at the medicine cats, but they were still sleeping, still lost in their dreams of StarClan. But which cats were these around him now? Why hadn't they waited for him in his dreams?

"So much water, more than any cat has seen before . . ."

"You will find friends in unexpected places. Listen to what midnight tells you."

"The lake will run red with the blood of brothers!"

Goosepaw stubbed his toe on the entrance to the tunnel.

With a yelp he turned and fled up the steep stone.

"ShadowClan will soar above you all!"

"Leopard and Tiger will feast on your bones!"

"Rivers of blood, washing away everything the Clans have known . . ."

Goosepaw ignored the pain in his feet as he raced up the tunnel. He could feel soft air on his whiskers, and a few moments later he burst into the open, flanks heaving and gasping for breath. He stumbled to a halt beside a pile of rocks and let the silence of the night wash over him. The StarClan cats had stayed in the tunnel. He was alone.

"Goosepaw! What are you doing?"

Goosepaw spun around. Cloudberry was standing at the mouth of the tunnel, glaring at him. "You can't leave the Moonstone before the ceremony is over! I still have to name you as my apprentice before StarClan. Come on, the others are waiting."

"StarClan knows who I am already," Goosepaw panted. "They came to me, all of them, with so many prophecies. I couldn't listen to them all; I was so frightened. They told me that terrible things are going to happen!" He broke off in a wail.

Cloudberry walked over and pressed her shoulder against him. "It's all right, young one. Calm down. We'll have to figure out a way for you to control those visions."

Goosepaw stared wildly at the she-cat. "They're not visions! These cats are actually here, all around us!"

"Then you'll have to find a way to ignore them," Cloudberry

meowed. "There's more to being a medicine cat than talking with StarClan. There are herbs and ways of healing to learn, and omens to find. The other cats must see you preparing to be a medicine cat in the ways that they expect. Remember, no one must know about your . . . your gift." She said the last word reluctantly.

This isn't a gift, Goosepaw thought. *I don't want to have all these cats around me! I don't want to be a medicine cat! I just want to be a warrior.* He lifted his head and gazed at the star-flecked sky.

Find some other cat to talk to, StarClan!

CHAPTER 5

"Comfrey, marigold, borage, chickweed . . ."

"No, no, this one's chickweed, and that's mallow." The she-cat reached out with one plump brown paw and patted the scraps of leaf. "Try again."

"I don't want to!" Goosepaw flopped back on the sun-warmed stone and looked up at the cloudless sky. The only sound was the river running beside Sunningrocks, punctuated by the occasional plop of a vole entering the water. "It's too hot to remember anything. Tell me a story about Leopard-Clan, Pearnose. Please!"

"You're not a kit anymore, Goosepaw! And you don't deserve to be a medicine cat apprentice if you don't start learning your herbs. Now, can you tell me what this is and what you'd use it for?"

Goosepaw stared at the limp green leaf hanging from Pearnose's paw. It looked like comfrey, except that comfrey was furrier. Could it be chervil? No, that was thinner and darker. "Tansy, for treating coughs?" he guessed.

Pearnose shook her head. "No, it's yarrow for vomiting. But you're right that tansy is good for coughs."

"See? I think my brain has melted. I can't remember any-thing!" Goosepaw insisted.

"Who are you talking to?" Soft paw steps on the stone behind him made Goosepaw spin around. Moonpaw was watching him, her eyes narrowed.

"Uh—no one," Goosepaw stammered, standing up so quickly that he mixed up his piles of leaves.

Moonpaw came over and studied the herbs. "Wow. They all look the same."

"Tell me about it." Goosepaw sighed.

"Are you sure there's no one here?" Moonpaw pressed, looking around.

"Well, can you see anyone?" Goosepaw challenged.

"No, but . . ." *Your gift must be a secret!* Cloudberry's words echoed in his mind. Goosepaw sighed. "Sometimes I talk to myself, that's all. It's easier to remember all the herbs if I say them out loud."

"That's kind of freaky." Moonpaw's blue eyes burned into him. "Cloudberry doesn't talk to herself."

"I'm not Cloudberry," Goosepaw retorted.

"Moonpaw! Where are you?"

Goosepaw spotted a dark gray shape moving through the reeds on the far side of Sunningrocks. An image of a long pointed face, striped black and white and taut with fury, filled his mind. He pushed it away with an effort. "Stormtail's look-ing for you," he told his sister. "You'd better go."

Moonpaw was already bounding across the rocks. "Com-ing!" she yowled.

"Any cat would think he was your mentor!" Goosepaw called. "Don't make it too obvious how you feel about him, Moonpaw. It'll just make his head even bigger."

The silver-gray she-cat paused and looked back at him. "At least Stormtail is normal," she retorted. "Why do you have to be so . . . so *different*?" She whisked around and disappeared among the ferns.

Goosepaw grumpily swept the herbs into a pile.

"Hey! Don't mix them up!" Pearnose protested. "It may be greenleaf, but every leaf is worth saving."

"I'll pick some more," Goosepaw snapped.

"Not if you can't remember what they look like," Pearnose teased. Her tone softened. "Look, I know what it's like to be apprenticed to a medicine cat when your denmates are preparing to be warriors. It feels as if they'll never understand what you do. But nothing—no herb name, no healing trick—is more important than being loyal to your Clan. And that includes *all* your Clanmates, especially when you are a medicine cat."

"It would be easier to be loyal if they didn't treat me like a rogue," Goosepaw complained. "Perhaps I should just accept that I'll never have any friends because I walk a different path than they do."

Pearnose snorted. "Sometimes, Goosepaw, I think you make your path more different than it needs to be. When you're as old as me, you'll realize that all cats—kits, apprentices, leaders, elders—are all the same underneath their fur. Your Clanmates need to be able to trust you, to see you as one of them, if you are going to treat them when they are sick

or injured. Now take these herbs back to the camp and check
Nettlebreeze for ticks again. I don't think you used enough
mouse bile on him yesterday."

Goosepaw stood up. *At least Moonpaw only has one mentor to boss
her around!* Sometimes he felt as if Cloudberry and Pearnose
would wear his ears off with their constant nagging!

He plunged into the ferns, reveling in the feeling of the
fronds brushing against his pelt. He imagined this was what it
would be like to plunge into a cool green river, cut off from the
sky and trees and all the forest scents. . . . Goosepaw stopped.
He could smell something beneath the ferns: newly cut wood
overlaid with a sharp, sour tang that made his nose wrinkle.
He had smelled it before, but where? *Twolegplace!* It was the
scent of the wooden boundary at the very edge of Thunder-
Clan territory. But he was nowhere near. Why could he smell
it here?

Goosepaw's ears filled with a loud buzzing noise. He
dropped the herbs as the ground rocked beneath his feet, making him lurch sideways. Now he could smell other cats—musty,
unwelcome scents as well as the stifling odors of Twolegs and
too-bright flowers. *Kittypets?* What were they doing so far into
ThunderClan territory?

Goosepaw blinked. The ferns had vanished—or at least
faded until they seemed to be very far away. Instead he was
at the edge of dense pine trees, standing in lush green grass
beside the wooden Twolegplace border. Abruptly the buzzing
in his ears was pierced by the shrieks and yowls of fighting
cats, a writhing knot of fur that lurched toward him, then

jerked away. Goosepaw stared in horror as more kittypets streamed over the wooden border and plunged into the fight. He strained to make out individual pelts—from the scent he knew that it was a ThunderClan patrol being attacked, but were these his Clanmates, or cats from long ago?

Goosepaw peered closer, trying to recognize each cat, but they were moving too fast, and too tangled up with their attackers. He winced as a thick-set ginger-and-white kittypet sank its teeth into a brown tabby neck.

"Those kittypets are stronger than you'd think," purred a voice in Goosepaw's ear.

He whirled around to see a tortoiseshell-and-white she-cat standing beside him. Her amber eyes gleamed with delight as she watched the battling cats.

"Who are you?" Goosepaw whispered.

The cat twitched her ears without taking her gaze from the fight. "Have I been forgotten so soon?" she murmured.

Goosepaw jumped as a cat thudded to the ground near his paws, flung by a kittypet with long black fur. He tried to make out the wounded cat's face, but the buzzing had returned in his ears, and suddenly he was surrounded by ferns again. Goosepaw blinked. He was back on the path from Sunning-rocks. The battling cats, the strange she-cat watching them, the pine trees, and the Twolegplace border had disappeared.

But Goosepaw couldn't forget the shrieks of terror, and the bitter taste of fear clung to his tongue. He had never been sub-merged so completely in a vision before. Everything had been louder, brighter, more vivid than his previous visions. Pelt bristling, he raced through the bushes and plunged down into the ravine. He burst into the clearing, startling the apprentices who were standing at the fresh-kill pile.

"Are you being chased by a fox?" Heronpaw called.

"Goosepaw always smells of leaves. He's more likely to be chased by a rabbit!" Poppypaw teased.

Moonpaw and Rabbitpaw huffed with laughter. Stormtail looked up from the other side of the fresh-kill pile. "You want to watch out, Goosepaw," he purred. "Even rabbits can be dangerous when you don't know how to look after yourself."

Rabbitpaw reared up onto his hind legs and boxed the air. "This rabbit's always dangerous!" he meowed, bringing his front paws down on Heronpaw.

The dark brown tom shrugged him off. "Stop messing around!"

Goosepaw noticed his sister watching him with a frown, as if she was worried about how he would react. He forced his fur to lie flat and lowered his tail. "No foxes or rabbits after me today," he mewed. "Something spooked me, that's all." The shrieks of battling cats rang in his ears for a moment, and he shook his head to clear it. "Have you left any fresh-kill for me?" he asked.

"Goosepaw? Is that you?" Cloudberry pushed her way out of the ferns, sniffing. "Did you bring back the herbs that I gave you?"

Goosepaw's belly lurched. He had dropped all the leaves when he had the vision of the kittypet attack. "Er, not quite . . . ," he began.

He was interrupted by Pineheart appearing from Doestar's den. "Is Squirrelwhisker's patrol back yet?" he meowed, looking around the clearing.

Larksong looked up from the pigeon she was sharing with Mumblefoot. "No, they're still out."

Pineheart narrowed his eyes. "But they went out before your patrol. What's taking them so long?"

Goosepaw froze. He pictured the warrior who had fallen at his feet in the thick of the battle. The image wasn't as clear as it had been before, but he remembered brown tabby fur, terrified amber eyes, long pale whiskers . . . Was it *Squirrelwhisker's* patrol being attacked by kittypets? Goosepaw was about to say something when he caught Moonpaw's eye. *She wants me to be normal, right?* He couldn't be certain it was his Clanmates in the fight. Goosepaw shut his mouth and turned back to the fresh-kill pile.

His first mouthful of vole felt as if it was choking him. The yowls of frightened cats kept echoing in his ears, and all he could smell was fear and blood and the sickly scent of Twolegplace.

"Are you okay?" Moonpaw asked him quietly.

Goosepaw shook his head. Abandoning the vole, he padded to the leader's den beneath the Highrock. Cloudberry was inside, talking to Pineheart and Doestar. Goosepaw stopped at the entrance and coughed.

"Goosepaw?" Doestar called. "Come in."

It was dark inside the den, and Goosepaw could hardly make out the shapes of the three cats. He stood in the doorway, blinking. "Cloudberry, I need to speak to you," he mewed.

One of the shapes moved toward him. "What is it?" She sounded cross, and Goosepaw's heart sank. Was his mentor in the mood for hearing about this?

"I saw something on the way back from Sunningrocks," he whispered, hoping Doestar and Pineheart weren't listening. "I . . . I was by Twolegplace, watching a battle between ThunderClan cats and kittypets. I think Squirrelwhisker was one of the cats."

Cloudberry leaned closer to him, her breath hot on his muzzle. "Do you think it was a vision of the future?"

Goosepaw swallowed. "I don't know," he confessed. "My other visions have felt different, more . . . distant. This one felt as if I was right in the middle of it."

The old she-cat narrowed her eyes. "You mean it could be happening right now?"

Goosepaw shrugged. "Like I said, I don't know. But I thought I should tell you."

Cloudberry straightened up. "You did the right thing." She turned to the other cats inside the den. "We should send a patrol to find Squirrelwhisker and the others. They could be in danger."

Doestar stood up, her pale fur glowing in the shadows. "What do you mean? Has StarClan sent you a sign?"

Cloudberry glanced at Goosepaw. "Not to me," she meowed. "But I think we should treat it seriously."

Goosepaw ducked his head as he felt Doestar's eyes rest on him. There was a pause; then the leader mewed, "Pineheart, take a patrol of warriors and follow Squirrelwhisker's tracks. Cloudberry, do we know where we might find them?"

The medicine cat touched Goosepaw's flank with her tail. Without looking up, he muttered, "By Twolegplace."

"Right," meowed Doestar. "Go quickly, Pineheart."

The deputy hesitated, shifting from paw to paw. "Really? Because an apprentice says so?"

Goosepaw stared at a crack in the ground, wishing he could disappear into it.

Beside him, Cloudberry lifted her head. "And because I say so. Goosepaw and I are your medicine cats, remember."

Goosepaw risked a glance at Pineheart. The fox-colored tom was glaring at Cloudberry. Suddenly the scent of kitty-pets grew stronger, filling Goosepaw's nose and mouth until he thought he was going to choke. He whirled around, frightened that the kittypets had stormed the camp and were about to invade Doestar's den. But everything was quiet, and none of the cats beside him had moved.

"Just go, Pineheart," Doestar ordered. "Say nothing to the others about the possibility of trouble, but there's nothing to be lost by making sure Squirrelwhisker's patrol is safe."

The deputy dipped his head and slipped past Goosepaw out of the den. Doestar looked at Goosepaw for a few moments, then turned to Cloudberry. "I hope I was right to trust you," she murmured.

I'm not making this up! Goosepaw thought fiercely.

Cloudberry brushed her tail against him. "Come on," she mewed. "We need to sort out our stocks if there are going to be wounds to treat." Nodding to Doestar, she led him out of the den.

The apprentices were watching the gorse tunnel, which still quivered from the rapid exit of Pineheart's patrol. "What's happening?" asked Rabbitpaw.

"Pineheart has gone to check that Squirrelwhisker's patrol is okay," Cloudberry replied lightly. "Nothing to worry about." She padded into the ferns, then looked back at Goosepaw, who had stopped. "What's wrong?"

Goosepaw stared at the gorse, picturing Pineheart and the warriors racing through the forest to the border with Twoleg-place. Would they be in time to help Squirrelwhisker? "I wish I could have gone with them," he mewed.

"You're not trained to fight," Cloudberry reminded him. "That's not what a medicine cat does. Now, are you going to help me with these herbs? Seeing as you left a good portion of them somewhere in the forest today. . . ."

Goosepaw was trying to brush a wad of cobweb off his paws when he heard the thunder of cats entering the camp. He rushed out of the den with sticky white web trailing behind him. "Wait for me!" Cloudberry called behind him, but Goosepaw ignored her and plunged through the ferns.

The clearing was thronging with cats, swirling like fish in a tiny pool. Goosepaw stood on tiptoe and spotted Pineheart, Stormtail, Larksong . . . all cats who had gone to look for the missing patrol. The crowd shifted, and suddenly Goosepaw saw a dark brown shape huddled on the ground, oozing scarlet trails. Squirrelwhisker! He started forward, but Cloudberry was already running past him.

"Let me through!" she yowled, and the cats stepped aside to let her crouch beside the injured warrior. Goosepaw saw the rest of Squirrelwhisker's patrol now: Stagleap, Rockfall, Flashnose, all battered and bleeding and looking shocked but on their feet.

"They were being attacked by kittypets," Pineheart reported to Doestar. "They were outnumbered, and the kittypets took them by surprise. We sent them packing with a few scratched ears, I promise."

"Thank StarClan you found them!" gasped Fallowsong. She had been on a hunting patrol, which had just returned.

"They were lucky that Pineheart went looking for them," Rainfur agreed.

"It was nothing to do with luck," Doestar meowed.

Goosepaw felt his fur grow hot. Cloudberry glanced over her shoulder at him and gave a faint shake of her head, as if warning him that his secret would be safe with her. But Doestar was already bounding onto the top of Highrock and calling the Clan together.

"Let all those cats old enough to catch their own prey gather below!" she yowled. "We need to thank StarClan for the victory over the battle with kittypets today—and not only StarClan." She looked down at Goosepaw, who felt the cats around him take a step away, leaving him in a bare patch of sand. "Squirrelwhisker and her patrol owe their rescue to one of their Clanmates. An apprentice, no less! It was Goosepaw's vision that led Pineheart straight to the attack. Cats of ThunderClan, we have a powerful medicine cat among us! And Cloudberry, if you agree, I would like Goosepaw to receive his full name as a sign of our gratitude and pride."

Goosepaw blinked. Behind him, he heard the apprentices muttering in disgust.

"He's only been training for three moons!" Poppypaw complained.

"I've only been an apprentice for a moon!" wailed Moon-paw. "That's not fair!"

"What makes you so special?" growled a voice in Goosepaw's ear. It was Stormtail.

Goosepaw spun around and glared at the warrior. "You have no idea what I can do!" The image of a badger loomed over him. *If all my visions come true, then so will this one! Stormtail is going to try to kill me with a badger!* Goosepaw sank his claws into the earth to keep himself steady. "I know what you're going to do," he hissed. "And I'll be ready, just you wait and see!"

Stormtail looked baffled. "You're weird."

Cloudberry stepped out of the crowd and dipped her head. "You are very generous, Doestar. I will gladly give Goosepaw his full name at the next half-moon. But I am sure he knows that he still has much to learn, and his training will continue until I am called to StarClan." She fixed her clear yellow gaze on Goosepaw and he nodded.

Goosepaw ignored the glares of fury coming from Rab-bitpaw and Stormtail. They were only jealous. He glimpsed

Squirrelwhisker through the crowd, raising her head just enough to nod gratefully to him. Goosepaw felt a stirring of pride in his belly.

No other cat sees as much as I do! I will keep my Clan safe forever!

CHAPTER 6

♣

"Goosepaw, do you promise to uphold the ways of a medicine cat, to stand apart from rivalry between Clan and Clan, and to protect all cats equally, even at the cost of your life?"

Goosepaw bowed his head in the glittering light of the Moonstone and tried to ignore the murmurs that came from the shadows. As always, the little cavern was full of watching eyes, voices whispering to him on the cusp of his hearing, dire threats and prophecies echoing around the stone walls. It seemed as if every cat in StarClan came here to pour their warnings into his ears—warnings that he couldn't distinguish, that only made his pelt crawl and his tail fluff up with fear.

"I do," he replied.

"Then by the powers of StarClan I give you your true name as a medicine cat. Goosepaw, from this moment you will be known as Goosefeather. StarClan honors the power of your sight, and we welcome you as a full medicine cat of ThunderClan." Cloudberry rested her muzzle briefly on top of his head, then stepped back.

"Goosefeather! Goosefeather! Goosefeather!" whispered the unseen cats.

Goosefeather winced; then Sagepaw cheered, "Goose-feather!" The air in the cave instantly felt warmer. Goosefeather blinked gratefully at the white-furred Shadow-Clan apprentice.

"Welcome to life as a medicine cat, Goosefeather," meowed Chiveclaw of WindClan. His apprentice, Hawkheart, who had received his full name at the last half-moon, nodded.

Echosnout sniffed. "I hope he doesn't get any fancy ideas about knowing as much as the rest of us," she muttered.

Cloudberry raised her tail. "Goosefeather knows he'll never stop learning," she purred.

Goosefeather fought down a flash of anger. *I can already do more than any of you! I see all the cats that have gone before us, and things that have not yet happened. You have no idea what powers I have!*

The voices grew louder inside his head, as if the unseen cats knew what he was thinking.

"Blood will spill blood!"

"Darkness, air, water, and sky will come together!"

"He is a kittypet!"

"Water will destroy her!"

"Only fire will save the Clan!"

Shut up! Goosefeather screeched silently. *It's too much! I don't know what you're talking about!*

Sagepaw's mentor, Redthistle, shook her dark ginger pelt. "Time to go home," she mewed. "I'm so cold I can't feel my paws." She limped out of the cave with Sagepaw beside her.

Cloudberry nodded to Goosefeather, and he fled up the tunnel, pushing past the ShadowClan cats. The voices faded behind him, and he took deep breaths of the cold night air. He knew his gift was special, and that he had no choice but to serve his Clan as a medicine cat. But here, far underground, in the shimmering light of the moon-bathed crystal, Goose-feather's gift seemed more than he could possibly bear.

"Great StarClan! Are we out of borage already?" Cloud-berry stuck her head farther into the cleft in the rock, then withdrew it, sneezing. "Nothing but dust back there. You'll need to gather borage as well, Goosefeather."

He rolled his eyes. "At this rate I'll be bringing back half the forest," he meowed. "Can't I take one of the apprentices with me?"

Cloudberry shook a scrap of leaf off her ear and fixed him with her gaze. "As far as I'm concerned, you *are* an apprentice. It was Doestar's idea to give you your full name, not mine."

Goosefeather bristled. "I earned it! I saw the kittypets attacking our patrol!"

The old white cat turned back to her piles of leaves. "Your visions are a gift from StarClan. Everything else will have to be learned. Now go fetch those herbs while they're still green."

Goosefeather ducked through the ferns, which were turn-ing brown at the tips as the weather cooled and the days grew shorter. In the clearing, the apprentices had just returned from a border patrol with their mentors. Goosefeather nod-ded to them, but they just stared at him. Goosefeather felt a flash of annoyance. Why did they treat him like an outcast? Didn't they understand how important his powers were? Even

Moonpaw looked down at the ground as he walked past.

"Don't start thinking you're better than us just because you got your name!" hissed Rabbitpaw.

"I heard that," growled his mentor, Mumblefoot. But he didn't make Rabbitpaw apologize; on the contrary, Mumblefoot shook his head as Goosefeather padded by. *Do all my Clanmates resent my new name?* Goosefeather wondered.

Larksong, her belly swollen with kits, blinked sympathetically at him. "Don't let them bother you," she whispered. "It's just taking everyone a while to get used to the idea of such a young medicine cat."

Goosefeather shrugged. "Not my problem," he mewed.

He pushed into the gorse tunnel, wincing as a tuft of his gray fur got caught on a spike. He climbed out of the ravine and headed straight into the forest. There was a patch of comfrey halfway to Fourtrees that had still had several green plants last time he visited. The trees were silent, and the air was still except for occasional crisp brown leaves drifting down. One brushed against Goosefeather's nose, and he purred in amusement. At first it had been alarming to watch the forest fade and turn brittle, but Cloudberry had reassured him that it would come back to life in newleaf, after the long, cold moons of leaf-bare.

He reached the comfrey and started to pick the biggest leaves, nipping them low down on the stalk to make them easier to carry. He was just stacking them in a pile when he heard a crashing sound beside him. Goosefeather spun around just as a clump of bracken split apart and Stormtail burst through.

The blue-gray warrior paused when he saw Goosefeather, and bared his teeth. "Watch out!" he snarled. He sprang past Goosefeather and vanished into the brambles.

There was a single moment of stillness, and suddenly Goosefeather knew exactly what was about to happen. He had known about this since he was the tiniest kit, and in a way he had been waiting for it all his life. This had been his very first vision, and like all the rest, it was doomed to come true.

The forest drew breath around him, and a huge black-and-white shape loomed through the bracken, bellowing in rage. Goosefeather braced himself. The badger had found him.

It was far bigger than he had imagined, but the narrow, striped face was the same, and the sharp teeth dripping with saliva. The creature fixed beady black eyes on him and lunged toward him with a roar. There was no time to recall any of the battle moves Goosefeather had seen being practiced by the apprentices. He dropped to the ground and curled himself into a tiny ball. The terror he had felt as a tiny kit flooded through him, clamping his chest like talons. *"Daisytoe!"* he whispered.

The badger landed with a thud on all four paws, trapping Goosefeather under its belly. Its fur stank like rotting flesh, and its hair was coarse and bristly. Goosefeather tried to wriggle free, but the badger spun around far more quickly than its size suggested and held Goosefeather down with one massive paw. Huge sharp claws sank into Goosefeather's pelt, and he lay still, too scared even to shiver.

Is this how it ends? he wondered, his mind strangely clear. *If I see a dead cat now, will he be coming to take me to StarClan?*

The badger seemed puzzled by his lack of resistance. It rolled him roughly onto his side and lowered its head to sniff at him. Goosefeather retched as foul breath filled his nose. Then the badger curled back its lips, revealing cracked yellow teeth, and Goosefeather suddenly knew that he didn't want to die.

He let out a screech, bucking wildly under the badger's paw until he could tear himself free. With a snap, the badger shut its jaws and lunged for Goosefeather again. Goosefeather knew there had to be something he could do to defend himself, some clever twist of claws or teeth, but all he knew were herbs. And dead cats.

"Help me!" he yowled.

The badger grunted as if it liked the idea of prey that made a noise. It slapped Goosefeather to the ground with its front paw and loomed over him. A globule of drool fell into Goosefeather's eye.

"Get off him!" There was a shriek behind the badger, and the massive head jerked away from Goosefeather. Blinking away the drool, he spotted a small silver shape clinging to the badger's shoulders. "Leave him alone!"

"Moonpaw! What are you doing?" Goosefeather yowled.

His sister didn't look up from jabbing her claws into the badger's neck. "Saving you, mouse-brain. Get out of here while you can!"

The badger was twisting and snapping at the tormentor on its back. One of its flailing front paws almost knocked

Goosefeather off his feet, but he scrambled under brambles until he was out of reach. *I can't leave Moonpaw to fight it on her own,* he thought desperately. But he knew there was nothing he could do to help her. He had no fighting skills.

Suddenly there was a thrumming of paws, and a horde of blurry shapes flew at the badger. Yowls split the air, and the badger hunched under the warriors' attack. Goosefeather saw Daisytoe tear the badger's ear with her claws, while Windflight savaged its stumpy tail. Moonpaw sank her teeth once more into the badger's scruff; then the mighty animal let out a bark and started to shuffle away into the bracken. One by one, the warriors dropped to the ground and chased after it, still spitting and snarling.

Only Moonpaw remained, her sides heaving and blood welling from a scratch above her eye. "Goosefeather!" she panted. "Are you there?"

Goosefeather crawled out from beneath the brambles. "I'm here," he meowed. "You saved my life, Moonpaw! Thank you!" He stood up and tried to rub his muzzle against her head, but she ducked away.

"You shouldn't be out on your own if you can't defend yourself!" she hissed. "I can't believe you've been given your full name when you don't even know how to fight."

Goosefeather shook his head. "Wait, it's not my fault the badger attacked me. It was Stormtail—"

Moonpaw stared at him. "Really? You're going to blame Stormtail for this? Who do you think found the patrol and told them what was happening? I don't believe you, Goosefeather.

You put all our lives in danger today. I won't always be here to save you. Try living in the real world for a while, and learn how to look after yourself!"

She brushed past him and bounded into the bracken, following the trail left by the badger.

CHAPTER 7

❧

"I'd say you've been very lucky," purred a soft voice.

Goosefeather jumped. He hadn't noticed the tortoiseshell-and-white she-cat standing beside him. "You think?" he retorted. "I nearly get my fur clawed off by a badger, and even my sister thinks I'm a freak." He paused and studied the cat. "I've seen you before, haven't I? You were watching the attack by the kittypets. Who are you?"

The she-cat twitched one ear. "I'd be insulted that you don't know, except that I can hardly blame ThunderClan for wanting to forget about me. But I know all about you, Goosefeather, and what you can see. I can help you, if you like."

"Really? Are you going to show me another vision?" Goosefeather felt his energy returning.

The she-cat snorted. "Why are you so concerned about the future? You have to live in the real world too. You need to learn a few fighting moves, or any cat will be able to flay your pelt if they want to." She padded around him, and Goosefeather was aware of powerful muscles sliding beneath her thick fur. "In fact, there is no better warrior to teach you how to fight."

Goosefeather turned around to keep her in sight. "I could ask any of my Clanmates to teach me," he mewed. "I don't need your help."

The she-cat stopped and looked at him. "Oh, I think you do, Goosefeather," she mewed softly. "After all, not even your sister offered to help, even when she had just seen you being half eaten by a badger."

Goosefeather felt the hair rise along his spine. He didn't need a stranger to taunt him. "Leave me alone," he snarled, but without another word the she-cat sprang at him, claws unsheathed.

Goosefeather stumbled backward, tripping over his own tail, and landed in the leaf mulch. The tortoiseshell cat stood looking down at him, her lip curled in amusement. "Get up. When I do that again, duck sideways so you take my weight on one shoulder. If you keep your hind legs under you, you should be able to flick me off." She stepped back, letting Goosefeather scramble to his paws. "Ready?"

He nodded. She leaped forward, and this time Goosefeather lurched to the side. A frond of bracken jabbed him in the eye and he almost lost his footing, but he felt the she-cat strike him nothing more than a glancing blow as she crashed to her paws.

"Better!" she cried. "Now you try!"

Goosefeather shook his head. "I only want to defend myself. I won't be attacking anyone."

The she-cat hissed. "You'll be useless if you can't take the fight to your enemy. Attack is by far the best form of defense!

Now come to me, and watch what I do."

Reluctantly Goosefeather sprang at her, halfheartedly baring his teeth. The she-cat stepped to the side and wrapped one paw around his front leg, sending him sprawling to the ground. "You're making it too easy," she hissed. "Try again, and this time act like you mean it. Pretend I've just clawed out your mother's eyes."

Goosefeather pictured Daisytoe bleeding and blind, and lunged at the she-cat with real fury. She tried to step away again, but he kept his weight over his haunches and followed her. His front paws landed a satisfying blow on the back of her neck. The she-cat huffed and straightened up.

"Much better!" she purred, her eyes gleaming. "Now let's try some ground moves."

The shadows crept out from beneath the trees and the air turned chilly as they fought. The she-cat showed Goosefeather how to use his own weight against his opponent, how to anticipate a move by watching his enemy's paws, and how to pummel the soft parts of the belly and throat to cause the worst injuries. Sometimes Goosefeather flinched, and a small voice inside him asked if it was right that a medicine cat should know how to cause so much pain. Then he remembered Moonpaw blaming him because he couldn't defend himself against the badger, and he let his claws slide out as he raked his mentor's pelt.

She screeched and sprang away. "Careful, little one!" she spat. "You don't want me to fight for real, I promise you." She licked her ruffled chest fur. "I think we've done enough for today. I wouldn't say you're ready to take on another badger, but I think you could hold your own against a cat."

Goosefeather nodded, panting. "Thank you. Really. I can't believe I didn't know any of this before."

The she-cat glanced sideways at him. "Just don't go looking for an excuse to practice on Stormtail," she teased.

Goosefeather stiffed in surprise. "You know Stormtail?"

"Oh, I know every one of you." She started to walk into the bracken.

"What is your name?" Goosefeather called after her.

The she-cat carried on walking without looking back. "Mapleshade," she mewed.

Limping from a sore shoulder where Mapleshade had wrenched him off his paws, Goosefeather headed back to the ravine. Moonpaw was approaching from the other direction. She ran up when she saw him, her fur fluffed out in alarm.

"I've been looking for you! I'm really sorry for running off like that," she blurted out. "I was frightened for you, that's all. We drove the badger off the territory, so you'll be safe now."

Goosefeather shrugged. "You were right. I do need to learn how to take care of myself."

"But you're a medicine cat. It's the duty of the warriors to keep you safe." Moonpaw followed him as he started to walk down the path. "I could show you some moves, if you like. Windflight says I'm doing really well."

"Don't worry. I'll figure something out on my own," Goosefeather meowed without stopping.

"But you can't be on your own all the time!" Moonpaw protested. "Don't you get lonely? It's not normal, not having friends."

Goosefeather halted and spun around, hissing. "Don't you understand? This *is* my normal. Get used to it, because nothing's going to change." He turned and ran the rest of the way down to the gorse bushes.

Stormtail was standing beside the fresh-kill pile. Goosefeather walked up to him and put his mouth close to the warrior's ear. "I know what you did," he hissed. "You left me alone with that badger because you wanted me to get hurt."

Stormtail turned to him, bristling. "Don't be so absurd!" he meowed. "I ran to fetch help!"

"You brought it to me deliberately! If I had died, my blood would be on your paws! Moonpaw saved my life!"

"Thank StarClan for your brave sister, then," Stormtail purred. "She's a wonderful cat."

"Leave Moonpaw out of this!" Goosefeather snarled.

He was interrupted by Smallear racing up to him. "Cloudberry needs you in the nursery. Larksong is having her kits!"

Goosefeather glared at Stormtail. "This isn't over," he spat. He spun around and raced to the nursery. From inside, he could hear Larksong panting and Cloudberry talking quietly to her. Goosefeather slipped through the branches and crouched beside the medicine cat.

"Ah, good, you're here," she murmured in the same soothing tone. "Larksong, Goosefeather has arrived just in time to welcome your first kit. One more push!"

The tortoiseshell she-cat let out a gasp as a spasm rippled along her flank. Goosefeather stared, fascinated, as a tiny wet bundle slid from beneath Larksong's tail. Cloudberry drew the bundle toward her with one paw and nipped through the transparent layer that surrounded it. "Here you go," she mewed, nudging it toward Goosefeather. "Start cleaning him up." She turned to Larksong and ran one paw along the she-cat's flank. "You have a beautiful son," she purred. "But I think there's another to come. Don't give up now."

Goosefeather began to lick the tiny kit's damp fur, keeping one eye on Larksong. A heartbeat later there was a second bundle lying in the moss. Cloudberry pushed it toward Larksong's head. "Another tom," she meowed. The little cat opened its jaws in a high-pitched wail. "With a loud voice already," Cloudberry purred. "Come on, Larksong, clean him up so they can have their first feed."

Goosefeather felt his kit start to wriggle beneath his tongue. "I think this one's hungry," he mewed.

"Put him next to Larksong's belly," Cloudberry instructed. "He'll know what to do."

Goosefeather stared in awe as the kit nosed its way into Larksong's fur and latched onto a teat. "Amazing," he breathed.

"I agree," mewed Cloudberry softly. "I never get tired of this moment."

The second kit joined his brother, and Goosefeather watched them suckle. Larksong lay back and closed her eyes. Cloudberry started to pull away the stained moss. "We'll freshen up her nest and leave her in peace," she whispered.

Goosefeather rested one paw on the kit he had cleaned. At once, images burst into his head, tumbling and flashing in a blur of senses: the Moonstone, the strong smell of herbs, a gaping wound padded with thick white webs, glittering starlight full of voices. He looked up at Cloudberry. "He's going to be a medicine cat!" he breathed.

Quickly he placed his paw on the other kit. Now he saw the four giant oaks silhouetted against the night sky, felt the cool stone of the Great Rock beneath his paws, watched the Clans swirl in the hollow below. He heard the roar of battle and tasted the sweetness of victory, echoed in the cheers of his warriors. "And this one will be ThunderClan's leader," he declared. He stared at Cloudberry, his head whirling. "We have to tell Doestar! These kits are truly special!"

He jumped up, but Cloudberry blocked his way with her tail. "Every kit is special," she told him fiercely. "You may think you know what will happen, but StarClan knows better than any of us. Let these kits grow up like any other, without the burden of knowing their future."

Goosefeather frowned. "I didn't have a chance to grow up like other kits," he growled. "You knew I was going to be a medicine cat."

The old white cat sighed. "You were always different, Goosefeather. I know it's hard, but you have to keep what you have seen to yourself this time." She rested the tip of her tail on Goosefeather's shoulder. "You have a very precious gift, young one. Sometimes it will feel like a burden, but I believe that StarClan has given it to you for a reason, so you must always be grateful for it and treat it with care."

She glanced over her shoulder at the kits, who were snuf-fling at Larksong's belly with milky muzzles. "Now let's leave these perfect little bundles to get some rest. It's time to tell their Clanmates the good news."

CHAPTER 8

As the moons rolled into leaf-bare, more and more kits were born, until Goosefeather could hardly squeeze into the nursery. Harepounce gave birth to a pair of pale-furred she-cats, Specklekit and Whitekit, and Rainfur joined her soon after with Dapplekit, Tawnÿkit, and Thrushkit. Cloudberry insisted on dealing with the births on her own, sending Goosefeather to fetch soaked moss and fresh bedding instead. Goosefeather knew she didn't want him to touch the newborn kits for fear he would see their entire future unroll.

Meanwhile Larksong's brace of toms, Sunkit and Featherkit, grew into strong little cats, ready to nip Goosefeather's tail when he wasn't watching, or shred their freshly laid nest with their thorn-sharp teeth. As soon as their eyes were open, Larksong shooed them out of the nursery to give the other queens some peace. Her sons tottered about the clearing on sturdy legs, fur fluffed up against the cold. A tendril of ivy lay on the ground beside the half-tree, and the kits pounced on it with ferocious squeaks.

"Did you see Sunkit jump just then?" Goosefeather mewed to Cloudberry. They were at the fresh-kill pile, choosing a soft piece of prey for Nettlebreeze, who was complaining of tooth-ache. "He's already more powerful than his brother."

Cloudberry looked at Goosefeather, her yellow eyes wary. "Be careful," she murmured. "Don't let the kits hear you say that."

Goosefeather let out a hiss of irritation. "I was only making an observation!"

His mentor shook her head. "You see his future every time you look at him. Don't let that blind you to what is happening now, Goosefeather."

"I can't take away what I have seen," Goosefeather growled. "The fact that Sunkit is going to grow up to be our leader makes him special."

"*All* kits are special!" Cloudberry flashed. "To their mothers, they are the most perfect creatures that ever walked in the forest. But as medicine cats, we must treat our Clanmates as equals. None is more deserving of our care than another. You should know that by now."

She broke off as Doestar approached. The pale-furred leader looked at the fresh-kill pile. "Has every cat eaten yet?" she asked.

"Almost," Cloudberry meowed. "Here, you could take the remains of this squirrel." She pushed it toward Doestar, but the she-cat backed away.

"Save it for the queens. I'm not hungry."

"You have to eat," Cloudberry murmured. "Your warriors don't want to see you starve yourself."

Doestar flicked the tip of her tail. "There are too many

hungry mouths in ThunderClan," she mewed. "Three litters born at the start of leaf-bare! How will we feed them all?"

"Like we always do, with clever hunting," Cloudberry insisted. "Trust your warriors, Doestar. ThunderClan will survive."

Goosefeather looked down at the vole he had chosen. It was plump and thickly furred, and its unseeing eyes were bright. If StarClan continued to send them such healthy prey, they would hardly notice leaf-bare passing through the forest.

Goosefeather opened his eyes with a start. The air inside the medicine cats' den was bitterly cold, and there was just enough moonlight filtering through the cleft in the rock to show his breath hanging in clouds above his nest. Goosefeather stretched and felt the chill pierce his fur as he uncurled. Beside him, Cloudberry was snoring gently in her own nest, her thick tail over her nose.

Goosefeather felt too restless to go back to sleep. He slid out of his nest and padded out of the den. The ferns were crisp with frost, and the moon was barely a claw-scratch in the clear indigo sky. Goosefeather winced as he followed the path to the clearing. The ground was hard as stone beneath his paws, and he was so cold he could hardly breathe. The air was completely still, and the only sound came from an owl somewhere in the distance, calling to its mate. Goosefeather paused. That wasn't the only sound he could hear. A faint moaning was coming from one of the dens.

He ran into the clearing and stopped dead in horror. His

Clanmates staggered around him, ribs sticking out of scabby pelts, eyes bulging from sharp-edged faces. The air was thick with wails of pain and the low, steady keening of a cat lost in grief. Two cats, Squirrelwhisker and Rooktail, clawed at the place where the fresh-kill pile had been; it was nothing now but a few scraps of fur and a scattering of tiny bones. A ginger shape lay slumped in the middle of the clearing, eyes open and clouded. To Goosefeather's dismay, none of the other cats paid any attention to it. Instead they stepped over the dead cat's crumpled legs, blinded and numb from hunger.

A few cats watched from the edge of the clearing, their pelts sleek and glossy, their bellies plump with food. But their eyes were filled with sorrow, and Goosefeather knew that these were StarClan cats, the dead cats he saw every day among his Clanmates. Waves of grief came from them as they watched the living cats starve.

Goosefeather felt heavy wetness clinging to his belly fur and looked down to see that he was standing in thick snow. A bleak-eyed, hunch-shouldered cat lurched close to him. "Daisytoe?" Goosefeather whispered. The she-cat didn't hear him. She stumbled to the fresh-kill pile and leaned on Rooktail.

"You said you would go out hunting," she rasped. Her gaunt flanks heaved as she fought for breath.

The black tom flicked his tail. "I did," he growled. "But there's no prey in this snow."

"We're all going to die!" wailed Squirrelwhisker, grinding her paws into the remains of the fresh-kill pile.

"No!" Goosefeather yowled. "I won't let this happen!"

The cats vanished, and he was alone in the moonlit clearing. He whirled around and raced to the den beneath Highrock.

"Doestar! Wake up!"

He burst into the musty darkness and blinked. The leader sat up in her nest, her fur ruffled from sleep.

"Goosefeather! What's wrong?"

"The Clan is starving!" he wailed. "This leaf-bare is too harsh. There is no prey and we are all going to die!"

Doestar bounded across the den and pressed her shoulder against Goosefeather. She felt warm and solid, and he started to breathe more steadily. "Calm down," she told him. "Have you had a vision?"

Goosefeather nodded. "It was snowy and cold . . . more cold than it has ever been. The fresh-kill pile was empty, and there was nothing for hunting patrols to catch. Cats were dying from hunger . . ." He trailed off, picturing the dead ginger cat lying alone in the center of the camp.

There was a stir at the entrance to Doestar's den, and Pineheart appeared. "Is everything okay?" he meowed. "I was returning from the dirtplace and saw Goosefeather coming in."

"Goosefeather has had a vision," Doestar explained. "This is going to be a harder leaf-bare than usual, it seems." Her voice was even, but Goosefeather could feel her heart thudding beneath her fur.

Pineheart looked at Goosefeather. "Did your vision show you a way to survive what's coming?" There was an edge to his voice, and Goosefeather swallowed the urge to hiss at him.

One day Pineheart would be leader and Goosefeather would be his only medicine cat; he had to keep peace with the deputy now and win his trust.

"No," he admitted. "But we have a chance to do something, now that we have been warned."

Doestar nodded to Goosefeather. "I want Cloudberry to hear this as well. Fetch her, please."

Goosefeather ran into the icy air and woke the old medicine cat. She sat in the leader's den and listened quietly as Goosefeather explained what he had seen.

"We'll have to find a different source of prey," mewed Doestar, pacing across the cave and back again. "Should we expand the territory? Send cats into Twolegplace?"

Pineheart flicked his ears. "I can't see our warriors being happy about that. But perhaps we could set borders around the treecutplace. I don't think we'd be challenged if we wanted to hunt there."

Cloudberry was gazing into the distance. "There is something we could try," she murmured. "I remember a very cold leaf-bare when I was a kit in RiverClan. The river froze, trapping all the fish. Some warriors broke off a piece of ice at the edge of the river and brought it back to the camp. It contained a fish, stone-cold and dead. But when the warmth of the dens melted the ice around it, the fish was perfect fresh-kill. Somehow the ice had kept it fresh."

Goosefeather tipped his head on one side. "Are you saying we should wait for the river to freeze, and eat fish?"

"No. I think we should find a way to keep our own prey

fresh for when we have nothing else to eat," Cloudberry mewed.

"But we don't have enough water on our territory," Pine-heart pointed out.

"Maybe not," meowed Doestar, flicking her tail. "But what if the same thing happens in the ground? We know the earth freezes when it gets very cold. If we buried the fresh-kill, wouldn't it freeze too? Then we could dig it up when we need it."

Goosefeather nodded, his fur bristling with excitement. "If we send out extra hunting patrols for the next moon, we could store enough food to last until newleaf!"

"I'll split the dawn patrol and send half out to hunt," Pine-heart meowed. "And the apprentices can hunt instead of battle training later on."

"We don't want to risk the strength of our Clan in battle," Doestar warned.

Her deputy looked at her. "The greatest risk is starving to death, wouldn't you say?" he mewed softly.

Doestar nodded, her eyes troubled. "Goosefeather, tell no one else about your vision. I don't want any cat to panic. We can say that we are preparing for the chance of a hard leaf-bare, but no cat must know what you have foreseen."

Goosefeather dipped his head. *As usual,* he thought. Doestar and Cloudberry were always concerned about how his Clanmates might react to his powers. *What about me? Don't they worry about how I feel, carrying the weight of ThunderClan's future all by myself?*

* * *

Within three sunrises, the camp had been transformed. The clearing was dotted with large holes, each a full fox-length across, dug by the cats with sharpest claws and strongest front legs. As Goosefeather was weaving between the holes to the gorse tunnel, Stormtail looked up from his freshly turned pile of soil.

"Is this something to do with you?" he growled, flicking earth from his whiskers.

Goosefeather stepped out of the way as Adderfang staggered past with a dead squirrel, which he dropped into Stormtail's hole. "Doestar wants to be sure we are prepared for leaf-bare," Goosefeather meowed. "Have you forgotten how many kits have been born this moon?"

The gray warrior began scraping soil over the squirrel. "We've never done anything like this before. Have you been seeing things?" He glanced sideways at Goosefeather.

Goosefeather leaned close to him. "You'd better believe I can see the future, Stormtail. Aren't you curious about what's going to happen to *you*?" Without giving the warrior a chance to reply, he turned away.

He had to wait for a hunting patrol to bring in the latest catch before he could enter the gorse tunnel. He watched Flashnose and Rainfur deposit a pigeon and two mice into a hole dug by Rockfall and Heronpaw. The dark brown apprentice was dusted with earth, and one of his claws was bleeding. Goosefeather reminded himself to check all the apprentices' paws at the end of the day.

He slipped through the gorse and climbed out of the ravine. For a while, Beetail padded beside him, the StarClan cat keeping him silent company through the bracken. The air was dry and cold, with heavy yellow clouds looming over the tops of the trees. There was a light wind that rattled the bare branches and ruffled Goosefeather's fur.

Tucking his nose into his chest fur, he trotted along the path that led to Snakerocks, where one remaining patch of catmint grew. Cloudberry wanted to preserve some leaves before they were spoiled by frost. He could hear a hunting patrol near the border with Twolegplace; one of the apprentices was chasing a squirrel, cheered on by Moonpaw and Rabbitpaw. Goosefeather stayed away from the squirrel's route and padded into the grassy space at the foot of the smooth gray boulders known as Snakerocks.

As he looked at the deep cracks and clefts in the rocks, his ears started to buzz, and he felt the ground dip under his feet. Two she-cats were hissing at each other. Goosefeather recognized one of them as Mapleshade, the cat who had taught him how to fight after the badger attack. The other had speckled golden fur and sad, haunted eyes. She was accusing Mapleshade of betraying her brother. She lunged at Mapleshade; the tortoiseshell-and-white cat stepped back, sending the golden cat stumbling into a pile of stones. There was a flicker of movement as something long and sinuous rose up from behind the nearest rock. The golden she-cat leaped away with a shriek.

"Adder! It bit me! Help!"

Mapleshade let out a hiss. "Like you helped my kits?

Never! I hope you die in agony!"

Goosefeather watched in horror as the gold-furred cat writhed on the ground. Mapleshade turned and walked into the bracken. The golden cat faded away and the clearing was empty once more.

Goosefeather felt eyes burning into his pelt. He spun around. Mapleshade was watching him from on top of a rock. "What's the matter?" she asked. "You look like you just saw a fox eat your own mother."

"Did you really let that cat get bitten by an adder?" Goosefeather demanded. "And leave her here to die?"

Mapleshade looked surprised. "Of course. I hate every cat in ThunderClan, and will not rest until I have had vengeance on every last one."

"But—but you helped me," Goosefeather stammered. "You showed me how to fight after the badger attacked me, remember? That wasn't vengeance."

Mapleshade's eyes gleamed. "I have no need to punish you," she growled. "You are doomed already. StarClan has seen to that."

"What do you mean?" Goosefeather demanded. Mapleshade started to walk away. "Come back! Why do you think I'm doomed? You have to tell me!"

But the she-cat had vanished, and Goosefeather was standing alone in the clearing, shivering and breathless with fear. *All these visions,* he thought. *And yet I've never seen my own future. . . .*

CHAPTER 9

"I am proud to announce three new litters of kits in ThunderClan."
Doestar's voice rang through the hollow above the heads of
the listening cats. Behind her, the other leaders were outlined
in silver from frosty moonlight.

Houndstar, the ShadowClan leader, leaned over to Volestar of RiverClan. Goosefeather heard him mutter, "So close
to leaf-bare? Those warriors won't like having to catch prey
for so many hungry mouths!"

Doestar must have overheard, because she continued.
"ThunderClan is well prepared for leaf-bare. My Clan will
grow strong through the coldest moons, and I will bring you
our new apprentices when the warm weather returns!"

There were cheers from the ThunderClan cats, and Chiveclaw, the WindClan medicine cat, mewed to Cloudberry,
"You'll be busy with all those little ones!"

Cloudberry nodded. "Thank StarClan, they are all fit and
well. Noisy, though!"

Echosnout of RiverClan snorted. "In my day, kits knew
when to keep quiet."

Cloudberry flicked her ears. "In your day, Echosnout, I was

one of those kits under your care, and I don't remember being quiet at all!"

The old she-cat huffed and turned away. Above them on the Great Rock, the WindClan leader, Heatherstar, had stepped forward and was reporting a black-and-white dog loose on the moor. Her warriors had chased it down to the Thunderpath, where a Twoleg caught it.

"I gave it a scratch that it won't forget in a hurry," purred Dawnstripe, a cream-striped golden tabby.

A brisk wind rattled the branches of the giant oaks, sending a flurry of raindrops spattering into the hollow. Houndstar jumped to his paws. "We should get home before the rain starts," he called. "Come, ShadowClan!"

The tangle of cats parted smoothly in four directions, streaming up out of the hollow and plunging into the forest. Goosefeather ran beside his mother. Daisytoe was limping slightly from an ache in her haunches; with a shock, Goosefeather realized that his mother was growing old. He stayed close to her as they made their way through the trees. Thick clouds had blown in to cover the full moon, and raindrops pattered steadily onto the branches.

The ThunderClan cats raced down the side of the ravine and bounded into their camp. The cats who had stayed behind came out to hear the news from the Gathering, then retreated quickly into their dens as the rain pelted down. Goosefeather followed Cloudberry into their den beneath the rock. Their pelts steamed in the damp air. Cloudberry shook herself, sending drops flying onto Goosefeather's muzzle.

"I'd rather it was cold than wet," she complained. "This weather gets into my bones now." She climbed stiffly into her nest and curled up. Goosefeather pulled some feathers over her flanks to keep her warm.

"The wind is strong enough to blow the rain away," he meowed. "It will be dry by dawn."

But it wasn't. Goosefeather was woken by the thrumming of raindrops on the rock above his head. Outside, the browning ferns were half flattened, and the clearing was awash with rivulets. Warriors ran from den to den hunched against the windblown rain, and the fresh-kill pile was sitting in a brackish puddle.

Pineheart surveyed it with a frown. "We'll have to move it to higher ground," he meowed. "I'll get Mumblefoot and Rooktail to do that as soon as they return from the dawn patrol."

Mistpelt emerged from the elders' den on her way to the dirtplace and hissed as her paws sank into mud. "Whose bright idea was it to dig up half the clearing?" she muttered. "If it keeps raining, we'll all sink up to our necks!"

Goosefeather looked at the freshly turned soil that marked the storage places for fresh-kill. Each one bubbled with liquid brown sludge. He pictured the prey underneath, soaked through and festering. . . . "Pineheart!" he yowled. "The fresh-kill will be ruined! We have to dig it up and take it somewhere dry!"

The deputy stared at him. "But we've only just buried it! Where else can we put it? The ground will be soaked everywhere in the forest."

Goosefeather was already scraping at the nearest patch of mud. "We can't waste time thinking about that. We have to dig it up before it rots!"

He was dimly aware of Pineheart running to the warriors' den and summoning the cats still in their nests. Harepounce ran from the nursery and started digging alongside Goosefeather. Her light brown pelt was soon smothered in wet earth, and her whiskers were thick with sludge, but she kept scratching until their paws hit a lump of sodden fur.

"It's a vole," Harepounce panted. She crouched down and hauled at it with her teeth. Goosefeather scrabbled at the soil on the other side of the fresh-kill. With a squelch the vole was pulled free, and Harepounce sat back on her haunches.

Goosefeather gazed down at the vole in dismay. Its flanks had caved in, the flesh eaten away by fat white maggots, which writhed in the shriveled fur. The remains of the creature stank worse than crow-food, and greasy slime was oozing out of it, soaking Goosefeather's paws.

"It's ruined," Harepounce whispered.

All around them, warriors were digging up more rotten prey. Soaked, maggoty, and wasted away to nothing, their precious stores were useless. Goosefeather looked up and saw Doestar standing below Highrock, her eyes dark with fear. Pineheart was standing beside her, his tail lashing as he promised to send out more patrols, restock the stores. But there was a weight in Goosefeather's belly like cold stone. His vision was going to come true. There was nothing he could do to save his Clanmates from starvation.

* * *

Harepounce died first, refusing to eat a mouthful from the moment they dug up the rotten prey and instead giving all her meager share to her kits. The rain stopped and snow came, smothering the forest into silent whiteness, which was pierced by moans of pain and hunger. Pineheart kept sending out hunting patrols, but again and again they returned empty-pawed.

Goosefeather and Cloudberry turned their paws raw from scraping in the snow in search of leaves to soothe bellyache and ward off coughs and fever. Flashnose died from a bout of sickness that racked her body with terrible spasms, and Stagleap and Hollypelt faded soon after. By the time Nettle-breeze slipped into a slumber from which he couldn't awake, sprawled in the middle of the clearing on his way back from the dirtplace, none of the cats were strong enough to move his body. A circle of StarClan cats gathered around the dead tom, their pelts noticeably shiny amid the mangy, dull-eyed warriors.

Goosefeather stared down at the stiffening ginger cat softly being covered with snowflakes and felt a surge of molten fury in his belly. Swiftbreeze staggered past, almost tripping over one of Nettlebreeze's legs.

"Careful!" Goosefeather hissed.

The tabby-and-white she-cat turned to him with clouded, vacant eyes. A scrap of bark clung to her whiskers. Goose-feather knew that some of the warriors had started chewing twigs in an effort to fill their empty bellies.

"He can't feel anything now," Swiftbreeze rasped, sounding older than stone.

"He still deserves our respect," Goosefeather mewed. He was too weak to move Nettlebreeze himself, but he tried to tuck the dead cat's legs under his belly so that no one else would fall over him.

He heard paw steps crunching over the snow and looked up to see Cloudberry limping toward him. The medicine cat looked hollow beneath her white fur, and her teeth seemed too large for her mouth. "Rabbitpaw dug up some worms today," she croaked. "I'm sharing them with Rainfur and the kits. Do you want one?"

Goosefeather pictured the slimy, throbbing creature and gagged. "It's okay," he mewed. "Save them for yourself." He gently picked up Nettlebreeze's tail in his jaws and draped it over the ginger cat's back.

"We did everything we could," Cloudberry whispered close to his ear. Her breath smelled rotten. "It's not your fault we couldn't stop this happening. The rain spoiling all our prey was just bad luck."

Goosefeather lifted his head and looked at her. "There is no such thing as bad luck," he told her. "Only destiny. I knew this was coming. But everything I did just made it worse."

He turned and plunged through the snow toward the gorse tunnel. Churned slush showed where a patrol had gone out in the hope of finding something to eat. Goosefeather scrambled up the ravine and walked into the silent forest.

How had he ever thought his visions were a gift? StarClan

hadn't blessed him; they had cursed him instead. He would always know the worst that would happen, and be powerless to change it. Mapleshade was right: He was doomed.

"Goosefeather?"

A soft voice made him stop and look around. A familiar dark brown figure was waiting beneath a patch of bracken.

"Pearnose!"

The dead cat looked more alive than any of his Clanmates. Goosefeather padded up to her, inhaling her sweet, leaf-fresh scent.

"I have seen what is happening in ThunderClan," Pearnose murmured. "My heart is breaking for you all."

Goosefeather closed his eyes and fought down the urge to wail like a kit. "I can't believe there was nothing we could do to stop it. I knew what was coming!"

The she-cat licked the top of his head. "You walk a difficult path, my friend. You must learn that it is not your role to change the future. Instead, all you can do is shine a light through the darkness, like the tiniest flame. Your Clanmates must deal with their destinies as they unfold. You cannot be responsible for all of them."

Goosefeather let out a long sigh. "Then my gift is useless," he whispered. "Without power, everything I see, everything I know, will bring me nothing but pain." He lifted his head and opened his mouth in a yowl. "StarClan! Why have you done this to me?"

CHAPTER 10

❦

The snow did not last forever. The days lengthened, and the biting chill left the air. The forest echoed with the sound of dripping water, and tiny green buds appeared on the trees. The ThunderClan cats emerged, weak and blinking, from the moons of darkness and horror.

On the first day of sunshine, Doestar summoned her Clanmates to give the apprentices their warrior names. "They have fought hunger alongside us," she declared, "with the courage of lions and the loyalty of true warriors. Moonflower, Poppydawn, Heronwing, and Rabbitleap, your Clan welcomes you."

Goosefeather cheered his sister's new name with a burst of pride. She had never given up hope during the hungry moons, never stopped looking for food or caring for her Clanmates. Then Goosefeather saw Stormtail watching Moonflower with a light in his eyes that made Goosefeather's stomach clench. Of all the warriors, would Moonflower choose him as her mate? Goosefeather didn't need a vision of the future to know the answer.

Beside him, Cloudberry wheezed, breaking into his thoughts. Goosefeather turned to his mentor. "Go lie down in the sun," he urged. "I'm going to forage for catmint today. You should take some."

Cloudberry shook her head. "I'm fine," she rasped. "But it's a good idea to look for herbs. Specklekit was complaining of bellyache this morning. I think it's because she's had a good feed from Rainfur for the first time since her mother died, but we could give her something to ease the pain."

Rainfur had brought the kits into the clearing to watch the warrior ceremony. The queen had suckled all five since Harepounce's death, and she looked like a ragged pelt draped over empty bones. But the kits had survived, and Rainfur was given first choice of every piece of fresh-kill now that prey was returning to the forest.

"See if you can find some chervil, too," Cloudberry added.

Goosefeather looked at her in surprise. "Is there sickness in the camp?"

"It's always good to have some in stock," Cloudberry replied carefully, but Goosefeather saw her gaze flit to Doestar, who was climbing down from Highrock. The leader looked as thin as her Clanmates, her pelt ragged and her breath rasping in her chest. As she passed Goosefeather, he realized that her eyes were sore and oozing, and she smelled faintly of the dirt-place, as if she had made one visit too many.

"Is Doestar sick?" he whispered to Cloudberry.

The medicine cat was watching Doestar limp into her den. "I will care for her myself," she announced without directly answering. "Let no other cat into the den. Food and soaked moss must be left outside. And whatever herbs you can find, bring them straight to me." She paused and looked at Goosefeather. "Don't let any cat know that Doestar is ill. This is her last life, and it would panic them too much to think of losing their leader now." She rested her tail on Goosefeather's shoulder. "A medicine cat keeps many secrets," she murmured.

Goosefeather ran into the forest and gathered every medicine he could find, even alder bark, which was used for toothache, and blackberry leaves, which eased bee stings. He figured nothing could hurt Doestar now, and one of them might help unexpectedly. Back at the camp he sent Moonflower for soaked moss; the she-cat grew round-eyed with worry at the urgency in Goosefeather's tone, but he told her that Doestar was merely exhausted and needed to rest to regain her strength.

He chose the biggest mouse from the newly stocked fresh-kill pile and dragged the food and wet moss to the entrance to the den beneath Highrock. "Cloudberry!" he called softly.

The white cat peeked out. "Are you alone?" she rasped. Goosefeather nodded. "Good. Let no other cat come near." Cloudberry reached out and pulled the mouse toward her. Then she looked at Goosefeather. "Will you stay here tonight?" she asked quietly. "I . . . I'd like to know you are close by."

"Of course," Goosefeather whispered. He pushed the soaked moss into the mouth of the den, then circled to make a scoop in the earth that was comfortable enough for sleeping. He rested his chin on his paws and watched the stars strengthen in the darkening sky. *StarClan, watch over Doestar,* he prayed. *She has suffered so much. Let her live to see her Clan grow well again.*

He was woken at dawn by a stir of movement at the mouth of the den. Cloudberry stood there, her shoulders slumped with exhaustion. "She's gone."

Goosefeather swallowed the lump of grief that rose in his throat. "Shall I help you wash her?"

Cloudberry shook her head. "I'll do it. And no other cat must come near her during the vigil. Whatever Doestar had, we cannot let it spread. We are all too weak to fight this sickness."

What about you? Goosefeather wanted to wail. But he said nothing. He knew what Cloudberry was doing, and he could only honor her by following her wishes exactly.

As the sun began to slide behind the treetops, Cloudberry hauled Doestar out of the den. Goosefeather had already warned his Clanmates to stay back, so the cats watched in horrified silence as Cloudberry staggered across the clearing, her jaws clenched firmly in Doestar's creamy ruff. She stopped in the center of the clearing and looked around. "You can honor our leader without putting yourselves in danger from her sickness," she rasped. "Please, for your own sake, stay back." She lay down and rested her nose against Doestar's cheek. The leader's clouded eyes stared up at the sky.

One by one, the ThunderClan cats walked past at a careful distance. Fallowsong was coughing, and Goosefeather reminded himself to give her catmint. She didn't have greencough yet, but he wasn't prepared to wait. When he looked at

Doestar's unmoving body, he saw another cat stretched out beside her, cold and lifeless, thick white fur stirring faintly in the breeze. They would be sitting vigil for Cloudberry soon, leaving him as ThunderClan's only medicine cat. Lying down at the edge of the clearing, he dozed off, trying to recall all the herbs he needed to restock his stores.

Cloudberry woke him at dawn. "I will bury Doestar," she told him. "You must take Pineheart to the Moonstone for his nine lives ceremony. I am too weak to make the journey. You know what to do, don't you?"

Numb, Goosefeather nodded. He felt as if Cloudberry were being pulled away from him, growing more and more distant until she was only a claw-point of light in swirling darkness. As if she could read his thoughts, Cloudberry mewed, "You have been a good apprentice, Goosefeather, and you will be a good medicine cat. Trust your instincts and remember everything I have taught you." She leaned her forehead against him. "Good-bye, my friend."

Goosefeather struggled to speak around the lump in his throat. "I don't want to leave you," he whispered.

"But I must leave you," Cloudberry replied. "You are not the only cat who is powerless to change the future." She lifted her head and gazed at him. "I don't envy you what you can see, Goosefeather. You must learn to live with the most terrible knowledge. Put your Clan first in all things, and may StarClan light your path, always."

She turned away, leaving Goosefeather chilled with sorrow. Pineheart padded up to him. "Shall we go?" he asked softly. The red-brown tom's eyes were wet with grief. He glanced at Doestar's body. "I never thought this would happen so soon," he murmured. "I don't know if I will be half the leader she was."

"Doestar will watch over you from StarClan," mewed Goosefeather. "You'll be fine."

"Really?" There was a flicker of hope in Pineheart's eyes. "Have you had a vision?"

Distracted by the sight of Cloudberry bending over the dead leader once more, Goosefeather nodded. Then he braced himself. "Come, we have a long journey ahead of us." He led Pineheart out of the camp, feeling the gazes of his Clanmates burning into his fur. They were the new leader and medicine cat. The future lay on their shoulders.

They reached Mothermouth as night was falling. It had taken longer than usual to reach Highstones because both cats were still weak from the Great Hunger, yet unable to eat because of the ceremony that lay ahead. Pineheart hesitated at the mouth of the tunnel, but Goosefeather plunged into the shadows, the cold stone familiar beneath his paws. After a moment he heard Pineheart following him, his breath loud in the confines of the winding passage.

The Moonstone sparkled faintly when they entered the cavern. Without speaking, Goosefeather and Pineheart lay down with their muzzles touching the base of the crystal. Goosefeather felt eyes watching him from the edges of the cave, heard the whispers just beyond his hearing, but ignored them and concentrated on slipping into the darkness that waited for him.

He found himself standing in a clearing in the forest—not a place that he recognized, exactly, but filled with familiar scents and warmed by sunshine. Pinestar, the new leader of ThunderClan, stood in the middle of the grassy space, surrounded by nine cats with starlit fur and glowing eyes. Among them was Pearnose, who nodded to Goosefeather. One by one, the StarClan cats stepped forward and gave Pinestar a life: for courage, for loyalty, for knowing when to fight and when to pursue peace instead. Pearnose gave him a life for appreciating the work of a medicine cat and trusting the wisdom of this companion throughout his leadership.

As the ninth cat moved forward, a long-legged gray tom with piercing blue eyes, Goosefeather's ears started to buzz. The grassy clearing vanished and Goosefeather was standing in a sharply scented, too-colorful enclosure with a red stone Twoleg den looming over him. His heart pounded with fear, and he crouched down, ready to leap over the wooden border behind him and flee into the forest. Then he noticed a cat in front of him: sturdy, thick-furred, with a reddish-brown pelt. Pinestar!

A gap appeared in the side of the den, and a Twoleg stepped out. Pinestar trotted up and arched himself against the creature's legs, purring and pressing against the hairless pink paw that reached down to stroke him. Goosefeather staggered backward. He tried to call out to his leader, but no sound came out. Pinestar reared up on his hind legs and patted the

Twoleg's knees. Then he followed the Twoleg into the den, still purring, and the gap closed behind him with a snap.

Goosefeather stared after him in horror. The red stone den and the brightly colored flowers around him faded away, and he was back in the clearing. The starlit cats had vanished, and Pinestar stood in front of him, trembling with excitement.

"I received my nine lives!" he whispered.

Goosefeather nodded. Pearnose's words rang in his ears. *It is not your role to change the future*. Goosefeather knew that Pinestar was going to betray his Clanmates, Doestar, and every part of the warrior code by leaving the forest to become a kittypet. Every sunrise from now, Goosefeather would wake wondering if this was the day that his leader would abandon his Clan. He couldn't tell any cat, not even Pinestar, because that was not his duty. He could only wait, and watch. He was, as always, cursed to keep his knowledge a secret. He had seen the future.

And there was nothing he could do to change it.

WARRIORS

RAVENPAW'S
FAREWELL

ALLEGIANCES

CATS OUTSIDE CLANS

RAVENPAW—sleek black tom

BARLEY—sturdy black-and-white tom

VIOLET—pale orange tabby she-cat with dark orange stripes and white paws

RILEY—pale gray tabby with dark gray stripes and blue eyes

BELLA—pale orange she-cat with green eyes

LULU—pale sandy she-cat with long fur

PATCH—gray and pale orange tom

MADRIC—brown tabby tom

PASHA—very dark tabby tom

SKYCLAN

LEADER   **LEAFSTAR**—brown-and-cream tabby she-cat with amber eyes

DEPUTY   **SHARPCLAW**—dark ginger tom

MEDICINE CAT   **ECHOSONG**—silver tabby she-cat with green eyes

WARRIORS   (toms and she-cats without kits)

CHERRYTAIL—tortoiseshell-and-white she-cat

WASPWHISKER—gray-and-white tom
APPRENTICE, DUSKPAW

EBONYCLAW—striking black she-cat (daylight warrior)
APPRENTICE, HAWKPAW

BILLYSTORM—ginger-and-white tom
APPRENTICE, PEBBLEPAW

HARVEYMOON—white tom (daylight warrior)

MACGYVER—black-and-white tom (daylight warrior)

BOUNCEFIRE—ginger tom
APPRENTICE, BLOSSOMPAW

TINYCLOUD—small white she-cat

NETTLESPLASH—pale brown tom

RABBITLEAP—brown tom
APPRENTICE, PARSLEYPAW

PLUMWILLOW—dark gray she-cat
APPRENTICE, CLOUDPAW

FIREFERN—ginger she-cat

APPRENTICES

(more than six moons old, in training to become warriors)

DUSKPAW—ginger tabby tom

HAWKPAW—dark gray tom with yellow eyes

BLOSSOMPAW—ginger-and-white she-cat

CLOUDPAW—white she-cat

PEBBLEPAW—brown-speckled white she-cat with green eyes

PARSLEYPAW—dark brown tabby tom

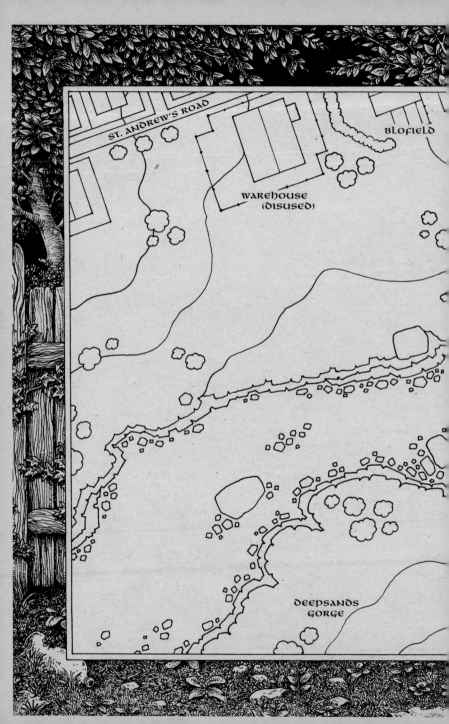

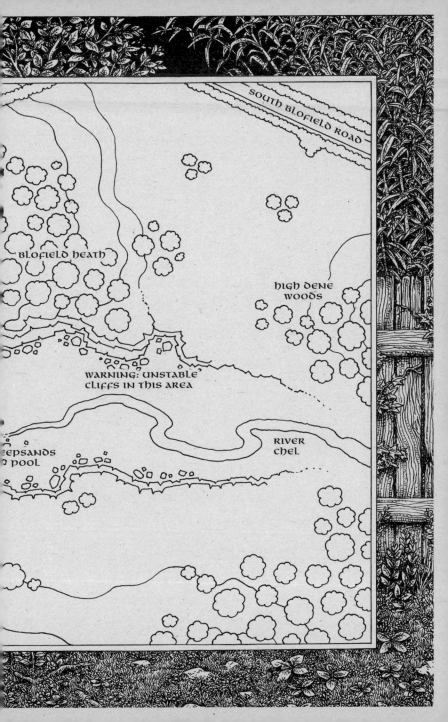

SOUTH BLOFIELD ROAD

BLOFIELD HEATH

HIGH DENE
WOODS

WARNING: UNSTABLE
CLIFFS IN THIS AREA

eepsands
pool

RIVER
CHEL

CHAPTER 1

❦

"Faster, Ravenpaw! Keep up!" Graypaw glanced over his shoulder before he plunged into a clump of ferns.

Ravenpaw dug his claws into the ground and picked up speed. He saw Graypaw's striped pelt vanish into the bracken, just behind the orange flash of Firepaw's fur. Ravenpaw burst through the ferns and raced after his Clanmates. They were running much faster now, so quickly that the colors of the forest were a blur of green, brown, and pale gold.

They whisked through the undergrowth, following paths that grew narrower and narrower, but even the densest clump of brambles didn't slow them down. Smooth gray shapes loomed up and vanished in a heartbeat. *I didn't know we were heading toward Snakerocks,* Ravenpaw thought in surprise. Then they were pelting next to the Thunderpath, monsters roaring alongside them, but the apprentices were too quick; they were leaving the howling yellow-eyed monsters behind.

Now they were beside the river, brown and churning and flecked with foam. The trail along the bank was little more than the thickness of a reed, slippery with wet green moss, but the cats didn't falter, not even when stiff green stalks lashed against their fur.

I wish we could run like this forever! thought Ravenpaw. His legs weren't tired at all, his paws were lighter than dried leaves, and he was breathing as easily as if he were lying in his nest.

In front of him, Firepaw had reached the base of Sunningrocks, the vast mound of stones that stood beside the river. Firepaw swarmed up the rocks without slowing down. Graypaw and Ravenpaw reached the top only a moment behind him, and all three cats stood side by side, looking out across the trees.

"There is no better place than ThunderClan!" Firepaw declared.

"ThunderClan!" Graypaw echoed.

Ravenpaw opened his mouth to join in, but a raindrop splashed onto his muzzle, making him jump. The sky was still blue and cloudless, and the sun blazed on his black fur, but out of nowhere rain was falling, heavier and heavier.

"You're getting wet!" grumbled a voice close to Ravenpaw's ear. A paw jabbed him in his flank, and he rolled over to see Barley standing over him. Behind his friend's head he could see pale gray sky through a crack in the barn roof. Another trickle of raindrops landed on the back of his neck, and Ravenpaw jumped out of his nest with a hiss.

"I thought you checked the roof before we made our nests last night," he muttered. His dream still tugged at the edges of his mind, and he was convinced he could smell the scent of his old friends close by.

"Don't be such a grouch," Barley teased. "Do you want me

to go climbing over the whole roof every night before you go to sleep, just to make sure you won't get wet? Come over here where it's dry."

He patted the hay where he was lying. Ravenpaw stayed where he was for a moment, halted by a sharp stabbing pain in his belly.

Barley pricked his ears. "Are you okay?"

"I'm fine," Ravenpaw mewed. "It's probably that mouse you caught two sunrises ago. I told you it didn't look right."

Barley squinted up at the gap in the roof. "I don't think this rain is going to last," he meowed. "Would you like to go to the forest today? Once the weather turns, it won't be so easy to get there, and we haven't been there in moons."

Ravenpaw tasted the air. He could smell leaf-bare approaching, cold and crisp like stone. "Yes, I'd like that," he mewed. He stretched out his front legs and arched his back, curling his tail until it brushed his ears. The pain in his belly had subsided to a dull ache, and Ravenpaw hoped that a walk to the forest would get rid of it completely.

They sprang down the stacked hay to where Barley had hidden the remains of the pigeon he had caught the day before. Ravenpaw wasn't hungry—his belly felt strangely full—but he picked at a wing when he felt Barley's gaze boring into his pelt. When Barley had finished cleaning his whiskers, they slipped through a hole in the wall and padded through the long grass that grew beside the barn. The rain had stopped, and the clouds were thinning to reveal slender strips of blue.

Barley paused at the edge of a stretch of pale stone. Faint

barks were coming from one of the fields beyond the Twoleg den, suggesting that the dogs were far away, so the cats trotted across the stone and plunged into the hedge. Barley led the way, his big paws leaving prints in the damp earth. Ravenpaw tried to put his feet into the same imprints, but Barley's legs were longer than his. He had to trot to keep up.

A few cows lifted their heads and watched as the cats crossed the field. Ravenpaw had been scared of the huge black-and-white creatures at first, but now he regarded them with a sort of affection. He was so used to seeing them around, they almost felt like his Clanmates.

For a moment he was back in his dream, standing on top of Sunningrocks and looking down over the forest where he had been born. *I wonder where Firestar and Graystripe are now?* It had been a long, long time since they were apprentices together. When Ravenpaw had first left ThunderClan, they had visited him sometimes, but then Firestar had led all four Clans out of the forest when the giant Thunderpath came. Graystripe had disappeared before that, stolen by Twolegs. After the Clans had gone, Ravenpaw had seen Graystripe once, escaped from the Twolegs and looking for ThunderClan, and he'd pointed him in the direction they had gone. He hoped Graystripe had found them.

Ravenpaw shivered. *Wherever you are, I hope you are safe, well fed, and at peace. May StarClan light your paths, always.*

"Come on!" Barley bounded back to him. "Let's check that the tunnel isn't flooded."

The Thunderpath was much broader than it had been

when Ravenpaw had first crossed it as an apprentice. The hill on the far side had been gouged out, leaving huge scars in the earth. Even this close to dawn, the Thunderpath teemed like a river of gleaming fish, with monsters growling up and down. It was too wide for cats to cross, so instead Barley and Ravenpaw used a narrow tunnel that ran underneath. It was dark and damp, and just big enough for a badger to squeeze through; mercifully Ravenpaw hadn't come face-to-face with one of those in the narrow space.

The tunnel did sometimes fill with water after heavy rain, but today there was nothing more than a muddy trickle running along the bottom. Taking a deep breath, Barley plunged in. Ravenpaw gritted his teeth and followed, hating the way the tunnel wrapped around him. The air thrummed with the noise of the monsters overhead, and it was impossible to think of anything but pressing forward to the cold, clean air on the other side.

Ravenpaw burst out at a run and almost crashed into Barley. They were at the edge of a wall of dense brambles. There was no way through; instead they had to creep along the edge, following the land as it rose steeply above the Thunderpath. The earth had been ripped away here to make way for the new stone path, and the broad sweep of moor had become a sheer cliff that echoed with the roar of monsters.

Ears flattened against his head, Ravenpaw set off up the slope. The noise faded a little as he scrambled to the top of the cliff, where a strip of short, windblown grass led down to the trees. The breeze was stronger up here, tugging at Ravenpaw's black fur. Familiar scents filled his mouth, bringing memories tumbling into his mind: the ravine, Gatherings, the scent of the medicine cat's den, training with Tigerclaw . . .

Ravenpaw shook himself. There was a reason he had left the forest.

He padded to the edge of a shallow dip surrounded by gorse and small boulders. Ravenpaw had a feeling this used to be the WindClan camp, but the images in his mind were hazy, and there was no trace of cats here now. Behind him, Barley growled as a gust of wind almost knocked him off his paws.

"Let's get into the shelter of the trees," he called. He ran across the stretch of grass, his black-and-white fur distinct against the green. Ravenpaw glanced into the dip once more before following. Had WindClan survived the journey? Had any of the Clans?

The bracken under the trees felt still and quiet after the open moor. Ravenpaw paused to catch his breath, listening to the tiny rustles of unseen prey. Above his head, tangled branches hid the sky. The cats pushed their way through the brittle fronds until new sounds assailed their ears: the rumble of monsters moving more slowly, as well as the shouts of Two-legs.

Ravenpaw reached the edge of the trees and looked down. It seemed a lifetime ago that he had stood here and seen four huge oaks in moonlight. The hollow had vanished, flattened out to make room for squat, silver dens and a broad expanse of black stone filled with rows of silent monsters. The air was thick with fumes and the stench of something hot and almost prey-like but unappealing, and Ravenpaw's stomach curdled.

Barley started pushing his way into the bracken along the top of the slope. Ravenpaw knew he was following an ancient path that had once led around the top of the hollow and down through the trees to the ThunderClan border. When the Clans had been here, Barley wouldn't have dreamed of walking confidently through this territory. Now that the Twolegs had taken it over, there were no borders left, no patrols for a loner to fear.

They left the silver dens behind and pushed deeper into the trees. The paths once used by ThunderClan were faint and overgrown. A huge mound of brambles covered pale gray boulders that jolted Ravenpaw back to his dream: This must be Snakerocks, though the snakes seemed long gone as well. A few pine trees began to appear among the oaks and beeches, and something about the curve of the almost invisible path felt achingly familiar beneath Ravenpaw's feet.

"Watch out!" yowled Barley, springing forward and blocking Ravenpaw with his shoulder. Ravenpaw blinked and looked down. The ground gave way a mouse-length in front of him, plunging into a narrow hollow filled with thorns and half-grown trees.

"It's the ravine," Ravenpaw whispered. "The place where I was born!"

CHAPTER 2

"Do you think we can get down?" mewed Barley. He started to push his way under the brambles.

"Wait," Ravenpaw ordered. "There should be a path." He trotted along the slope until he found a tiny gap between two bushes. "Here it is." He hesitated for a heartbeat, wondering what memories might be waiting for him below. *The past can't hurt me now.* He ducked and squeezed into the space, tucking in his tail to avoid catching it on brambles. He could hear Barley following.

The slope beneath Ravenpaw's paws felt instantly familiar. There was the half-buried flint with a sharp edge; here was the narrow trench worn by the flow of rainwater. *The ravine!* In all his visits to the forest since the Clans had left, Ravenpaw had never come back to this spot before. The noise of the monsters was so faint he could barely hear it, and for a moment Ravenpaw wondered why Firestar had abandoned his home. There was still room for ThunderClan to live here!

But Firestar had wanted to save all four Clans. *One Clan alone will always struggle,* he had told Ravenpaw in a quiet moment in the barn. Something in his words had made Ravenpaw question him; it was as if Firestar knew exactly how difficult it was for a single Clan to survive on its own. And that had led to one of the most extraordinary stories Ravenpaw had ever heard: about a vision that had sent Firestar and Sandstorm on a journey to save a long-forgotten fifth Clan. Ravenpaw wondered if SkyClan had survived without the protection of other Clans around it. In his mind's eye he could almost picture the sandy gorge as Firestar had described it all those moons ago.

Barley jolted Ravenpaw back to the present. The black-and-white tom had pushed ahead as they picked their way through the remains of a long-dead gorse bush—*I think this was the entrance,* Ravenpaw recalled with a thrill—and now he was standing in a tiny space, not much bigger than their combined nests.

"Was this your camp?" Barley asked in astonishment.

Ravenpaw looked at the densely packed brambles, the brittle ferns that surrounded a small gray boulder, and the larger rock that was half swallowed by ivy. "Yes," he breathed. "Yes, this was our home."

He spun around, the brambles disappearing in his mind, uncovering the expanse of the clearing fringed by tidy dens and the lush green ferns that led to Yellowfang's store of herbs. He saw Bluestar spring to the top of the Highrock, her blue-gray fur thick and lustrous in the sun, her voice clear and steady as she summoned the Clan.

"Let all cats old enough to catch their own prey join here for a Clan meeting!"

"What did you say?" Barley half turned from where he was

sniffing at a blackberry-studded thicket. Ravenpaw thought that might have been the nursery, but he couldn't be sure.

"I was just remembering," he meowed. To his relief, nothing about the camp reminded him of the troubles that had driven him out of the forest. Instead he felt excited, full of barely contained energy, the way he had felt when he had first been made an apprentice. "Did I tell you about my first hunting session? I tracked a scent all the way to Sunningrocks, but it turned out to be a Twoleg and his dog! Dustpaw dared me to attack them, but Graypaw said Tigerclaw would be furious if I filled the fresh-kill pile with my first-ever catch!"

Ravenpaw rolled a piece of moss under his paw as more memories surged inside him like leaves unfurling. "Once, I was cleaning out the elders' nests and I picked up a tick on my muzzle. Graypaw had to sit on me while Spottedleaf put mouse bile on it! That stuff was disgusting!"

He paused when he noticed that Barley was looking at him strangely. "What's wrong?"

Barley flicked the tip of his tail. "I'm happy that you have some good memories from your time with the Clan. But . . . but don't forget why you left. Tigerclaw would have murdered you if you'd stayed. He knew you had seen him killing Redtail."

Ravenpaw was startled by the emotion in Barley's voice. He ran over and pressed his shoulder against Barley's warm flank. "Don't ever think that I regret leaving the forest!" he hissed. "Firestar and Graystripe saved my life when they brought me to you. Since then, I've never wanted to be anywhere but by your side. It's just . . . I never expected to be able to come back and remember the good things about being in ThunderClan. If it helps block out some of the bad memories, then I'll be glad."

Barley licked the top of his head. "I'll be glad too. Where do you want to go next?"

"I don't know. Let's see where we end up!"

Ravenpaw cast one glance back at the Highrock, then scrambled back up the steep slope. A spatter of rain penetrated the branches, so he decided to stay under the trees rather than follow the trail that led out of the forest to Sunningrocks. Part of him didn't want to see if it had been swallowed up by greenery like the rest of the familiar landmarks; he preferred to remember it as it had been in his dream: a perfect, clear viewing point for the whole of the territory.

They trotted side by side along a path marked by deer hooves and the occasional sweep of a fox's tail. Pine trees took over the woods, and through the tidy lines of their trunks Ravenpaw glimpsed the pale swath of wooden fence that marked the boundary with Twolegplace. As they drew closer, pungent scents of Twoleg dens, monster fumes, and kittypets washed over them.

"They still don't come very far into the forest," Ravenpaw commented as he paused by a tree stump to sniff a kittypet mark.

Barley glanced over his shoulder at the dense tangle of trees. "I can't imagine it looks more inviting now than it did when the Clans were here. Kittypets have everything they want from their Twolegs, don't they? Food, shelter, company, all without having to make any effort."

Ravenpaw looked sideways at his friend. "Kind of like us, then," he teased.

Barley bristled. "At least we catch our own prey!"

Ravenpaw purred, though another jab of pain in his belly reminded him that he needed to be more careful about what he ate. The barn provided good hunting, but he couldn't assume that every catch would make good fresh-kill.

They padded side by side through the long grass at the base of the wooden fence. It felt cool and welcoming under Ravenpaw's feet, and he reflected that it had been a long time since he had walked this far. Life on the farm had made him soft!

Suddenly there was a hiss above their heads.

"Oi! You down there! What are you doing?"

Ravenpaw and Barley looked up. A ragged-furred brown tabby was crouched on top of the fence, glaring down at them. A scar across his muzzle and notches in his ears suggested that he wasn't afraid of a fight.

"We're just passing through," Barley called. "Don't worry."

In a flash the tabby tom sprang down from the fence and blocked their path. His tail lashed. "I'll decide what I worry about, thank you," he growled. He stretched out his neck and sniffed. "You're not from around here. You don't smell like kittypets, but you don't smell like the woods, either. Who are you?"

"We live on a farm," Barley began, but Ravenpaw cut him off.

"Calm down. We're not doing anyone any harm," he meowed.

The tabby curled his lip. "I don't like the look of you," he snarled. "This is my home"—he nodded to the Twoleg den on the other side of the fence—"and I claim all hunting rights in this part of the woods. You're not welcome."

And you're ridiculous, thought Ravenpaw. But he was tired and his belly hurt, and a fight was the last thing he wanted. "Come on," he muttered to Barley. "Let's go."

They started to walk around the kittypet, but he sprang after them, claws unsheathed. "You don't think you're getting away that easily, do you?" He let out a yowl, and in a heartbeat more faces popped up along the fence.

Ravenpaw scanned them in alarm. Kittypets, yes, but also one or two who looked too mean and scrawny to share Twoleg dens.

"I think we should get out of here," he whispered to Barley, who nodded.

"No need for a fight," Barley announced. "We're leaving."

Ravenpaw and Barley set off again, but the wooden fence rattled behind them as several cats jumped down into the forest.

"Run!" screeched Ravenpaw, and without looking back, he and Barley pelted along the edge of the trees. Ravenpaw felt his chest start to burn, and the ache in his belly sharpened with every footstep. From the noises behind them he could tell that some of the cats had given up, but enough stayed in pursuit to keep Ravenpaw in flight. His fighting days were long gone; all he wanted to do was get out of this place, back to the safety of the barn.

They followed the long curve of the fence until the woods fell away and the ground dropped down beside them to the vast, stench-filled Thunderpath. They were running along a narrow strip of earth now, trapped by the high fence on one side and a cliff on the other. The barn lay in the other direction, and Ravenpaw started to wonder if they would ever find their way back.

Ravenpaw felt his legs start to slow. Beside him, Barley slowed too. "Keep going, Ravenpaw!" he panted. There was a joyful yowl behind them, as if the tabby tom could tell his prey was weakening.

"What is going on?" The air was split with a shriek from the top of the fence, and an orange shape slammed onto the ground at Ravenpaw's heels. He stumbled to a halt and spun around to see a she-cat arching her back and hissing, her eyes furious slits. *Oh, great. Another angry kittypet.*

"Violet!" Barley gasped.

Ravenpaw blinked. *It's Barley's sister!*

"Barley!" cried the orange cat. In a heartbeat, she whipped around to face the cats in pursuit. "Stop right there, Madric!" she ordered.

To Ravenpaw's surprise, the brown tabby skidded to a stop. The two cats behind almost crashed into him. "Go away, Violet," he snarled. "These cats were trespassing!"

"Nonsense!" spat Violet. "This is my brother, Barley, and his friend Ravenpaw. They are welcome anywhere, do you understand?" She flattened her ears at the tabby tom. *"Any-where."*

The tabby hissed, but he flicked his tail at the cats who had kept pace with him. "Come on," he growled. "I don't think they'll bother us again." He narrowed his eyes at Ravenpaw. "You're way out of your depth here, old cat," he jeered. "Go back to your nest."

Violet stepped in front of him. "Enough," she snapped. With a final growl, the hostile cats turned and trotted away. Violet tipped her head to one side, studying Barley and Ravenpaw. "Well, you two looked better the last time I saw you."

Barley shrugged. "Our bones are getting a little old for this kind of thing," he admitted. His eyes brightened, and he rubbed his head against Violet's cheek. "It's been too long, sister! How are you?"

"I'm well!" she declared. "And I have something to show you!" She led the way to a hole at the foot of the fence. Before squeezing through, she glanced back at Ravenpaw. "Are you okay? Did one of those cats injure you?"

Ravenpaw shook his head, still breathless.

They ducked through the fence and emerged into an enclosed space of smooth green grass edged with strong-smelling bushes. Ravenpaw felt his skin prickle. A Twoleg den was the last place he wanted to be.

"It's okay," Violet mewed as if she sensed his hesitation. "We're not going inside, and my housefolk aren't home anyway."

She bounded across the grass and jumped onto a wooden

platform that stretched along the side of the red stone den. There was a bundle of soft, brightly colored pelts at one side. As Ravenpaw drew nearer, he saw the pelts quiver, and he picked up a scent he hadn't smelled in a long, long time . . .

"I'm back, poppets!" Violet called.

Several tiny faces burrowed out of the pelts. *Kits!* Ravenpaw was whisked back to memories of the nursery: the smell of milk clinging to his fur, the looming, gentle shape of his mother.

"Oh, wow," breathed Barley as sturdy little bodies swarmed around him, mewling and purring and tugging at his fur with tiny sharp teeth.

"This is my brother, Barley," Violet announced. "And his friend Ravenpaw. Be gentle, Bella!" she pleaded as a pale orange she-kit reached up and fastened her claws into Ravenpaw's ear.

Ravenpaw used his front paw to pry her off and placed her back on the ground. Huge green eyes stared up at him curiously. *She looks just like Firestar!*

"Do you and Barley have kits?" she mewed.

"Er, no," Ravenpaw answered.

She tipped her head to one side. "Where do you live? What are your housefolk like? Why haven't you come to see us before?"

"So many questions!" chided Violet, sweeping her tail around her daughter. "Ravenpaw, this is Bella. She started talking before any of the others, and I'm not sure when she'll stop." Her voice was warm and full of love as she gazed down at the little orange cat.

Ravenpaw felt something tugging at his tail. A gray tabby tom clutched the tip between his paws and grappled with it. Ravenpaw flicked his tail and the kit rolled away. He almost fell off the wooden platform, and Violet had to leap to stop him.

"Oh, Riley," she sighed. "Can you try to be a bit less clumsy, please?"

"It was my fault," Ravenpaw mewed quickly. "Good fighting," he commented to Riley, who was tottering back on sturdy legs to have another go at his tail. In his mind, Ravenpaw pictured Graystripe as a kit, almost exactly the same color, except that his eyes had been amber while Riley's were a clear, piercing blue.

Barley was trying to remove a pair of kits from the top of his head.

"Lulu, Patch, get down!" Violet ordered. She shot an exasperated glance at Ravenpaw. "I'm so sorry. I think they're a bit overexcited by your visit."

"We should be going anyway," meowed Barley. "It's a long way back to the farm."

"The farm?" echoed Bella. "What's that?"

"It's where we live," mewed Ravenpaw. "Far away, on the other side of the Thunderpath. It's a place with sheep and cows, and lots of fields."

Riley screwed up his face. "What is a sheep and cow? And a field?"

"We'll visit them one day," Violet promised, touching the

tip of her tail to his dark gray ear. "Now go lie down for your nap." She herded the kits back to the pile of pelts.

"I'm not even the tiniest bit sleepy," Ravenpaw heard Bella declare.

Violet shooed them into a huddle of furry bodies, then returned to Barley and Ravenpaw. "It was really good to see you," she meowed. "Please, come again any time. Or maybe we'll visit you!"

Barley purred. "You would be very welcome." He reached out and touched his chin to the top of his sister's head. "You're a wonderful mother. I'm so pleased for you."

"Thank you." Violet glanced at her kits, squirming and snuffling among the pelts. "They mean the world to me. Now go safely, and try to stay out of Madric's way. I'd like to say that he's all snarl and no bite, but I don't trust him."

"We won't go back that way," Ravenpaw promised. He stroked Violet's flank with the tip of his tail. "Good-bye, and don't let those kits wear you out!" Then he turned to Barley. His paws ached with tiredness and his belly was still sore, but the thought of returning to the barn gave him energy. "We've had enough adventures for a lifetime today! Let's go home."

CHAPTER 3

❧

Leaf-bare rattled the last dry leaves from the trees and hedges and covered the fields in a thick pelt of snow. Ravenpaw and Barley peeped out at the dense white flakes tumbling silently from the sky. There were still plenty of mice to eat inside the barn, and as the stock of hay shrank, hunting became easier, with fewer places for prey to hide.

The pain in Ravenpaw's belly became a familiar throb, worse if he ate too much or slept in a cold draft. He could forget about it most of the time. A wrench to his shoulder, from an overzealous game of chase up and down the hay with Barley, was more of a nuisance. Ravenpaw had missed his footing and fallen several fox-lengths onto the stone floor. Barley was beside him in a heartbeat, licking his flank, urging him to keep still.

Ravenpaw flexed each paw in turn and opened his eyes. "I'll live," he grunted. But when he stood up, his shoulder burned, and he could hardly put his paw to the ground. Barley helped him to their nest and curled his body around him, soft and hay-scented and comforting.

Ravenpaw sighed. "I'm getting old."

"Mouse-brain," Barley purred affectionately. "I've seen at least two more leaf-bares than you, and I'm not old!"

Ravenpaw let his eyes close. "Stay with me while I sleep?"

"I'm not going anywhere," Barley promised, settling his chin more comfortably into Ravenpaw's black fur.

Neither am I, Ravenpaw thought.

Leaf-bare passed, the snow melted, and the days grew almost imperceptibly longer, bringing the hint of new green leaves along the hedgerows. Ravenpaw's shoulder healed, and he and Barley started to hunt outside again, prowling the fields at twilight as huge brown-and-white owls swooped over their heads.

One evening, as they were making the most of the first genuinely warm day of sunshine, they were startled by a muffled yowl.

"Barley! Ravenpaw!"

Ravenpaw looked around. The cry seemed to come from farther up the hedgerow. He crouched down and prowled along the edge of the field, mouth open to scent the air. There were cats up ahead, definitely. Soft-furred, with a hint of kittypet . . .

"It's us!" Two fluffed-up shapes sprang out of the hedge in front of Ravenpaw, one pale ginger and the other a dove-gray tabby.

Ravenpaw blinked in surprise. "Riley? Bella? What are you doing here?"

A taller shape emerged behind them. "They insisted on

coming to see you," Violet explained, sounding weary. "I hope you don't mind."

Barley bounded up to touch noses with his sister. "Mind? Of course not! It's great to see you!" He looked at Riley and Bella, who were sniffing a tall blade of grass. "But . . . weren't there more of them last time?"

Violet's eyes clouded. "Lulu and Patch have gone to a new home." She blinked. "But we still see them sometimes, and they are very happy. At least I know they are together."

Bella bounced up to Ravenpaw. She had grown a lot since their first meeting; her head was up to his shoulder. She was taller than her brother, more angular, and her chin tapered to a point that suggested a strong will. Riley still had traces of his fluffy kit pelt, but he had broad shoulders and sturdy legs.

"Can we go to the farm?" Bella pleaded. "It's taken ages to get here, and I want to catch a mouse!"

"I'm so hungry I could die!" Riley mewed.

"Of course you can come to our home," Barley purred. "You're welcome to stay as long as you want. We have plenty of food, and warm places for you to sleep."

Violet's nostrils flared. "It's all right; we won't trouble you for more than a night. I don't want our housefolk to worry about us too much."

They headed to the barn, Riley and Bella racing ahead and stopping every time they saw something new. At the sight of their first cow, their eyes bugged out so much that Ravenpaw had to hide a laugh.

"It's huge!" Bella gasped.

"Are you sure it's friendly?" Riley whispered, gazing at the animal at the other side of the field.

"Well, it won't want to talk to you," meowed Ravenpaw. "But I'm fairly certain they don't eat cats. What do you think, Barley?"

The black-and-white tom pretended to ponder for a moment. "There was that one time you nearly got your tail bitten off . . . ," he mewed.

"What?" Violet shrieked.

"That sounds amazing!" mewed Bella. "Tell us about it, Ravenpaw! Did you use your warrior moves to fight the cow?"

Violet looked flustered. "I'm sorry, they're obsessed with stories about the Clans that used to live in the forest. One of the other kittypets talks about them—I think he met you once, actually. His name is Smudge. Black-and-white, thick fur?"

Ravenpaw nodded, memories pooling around him once more. "Yes, he was a friend of Firestar's from before he joined ThunderClan."

"We want to join ThunderClan too!" Riley announced. "We're really brave, and good at fighting, and I can creep so quietly that Bella doesn't even know I'm there!"

"I do too!" Bella snorted. "You're as loud as . . . as . . ."

A volley of barking split the air, making all the cats jump.

"As those dogs!" Bella declared.

Violet crouched down, ready to flee, but Barley rested his tail on her shoulder. "It's all right; they're tied up. They like the sound of their own voices, that's all."

The dogs continued to bark until a Twoleg hollered from inside the red stone den. Then they fell quiet.

"Come on, let's show you the barn," meowed Ravenpaw. The kits were quiet and wide-eyed when they first entered the huge wooden den. Nearly all the hay was gone now, and the far end of the barn was thick with shadows.

Violet shuddered. "It's a bit creepy."

Barley purred. "Don't worry; you're safe with us. Those ferocious mice won't attack you while we're here."

"Ferocious mice?" Bella echoed, looking delighted.

"Not really," Ravenpaw meowed. "But they can be tough to catch sometimes. Would you like to watch me hunt?"

"Yes, please!" Riley and Bella mewed.

"I'll show you our nest," Barley told Violet. "You can rest there while Ravenpaw finds you something to eat."

Ravenpaw led the kits to the back of the barn, where the shadows were so thick he could almost feel them pressing down on his fur. Both young cats did their best to tread quietly; Bella was very light on her paws, and Riley did better than Ravenpaw was expecting, given his bulkier frame. The scent of mice hung on the air. Ravenpaw picked out a trail that seemed fresh and followed it into a corner.

"Keep still," he whispered to Riley and Bella as he crept forward. He dropped into a hunter's crouch and stalked toward the tiny hole where the mouse scent was strongest. His recently injured shoulder twinged, so he shifted his weight onto his other three legs. There was a tiny scrabble at the very edge of his hearing. A pointed nose appeared, whiskers twitching. Then the mouse shot out of the hole.

Ravenpaw pounced and killed the mouse with a bite to its neck. *I thank StarClan for sending this prey,* he thought.

"What did you say?" Riley called. He was standing on tip-toe, craning his neck to see if Ravenpaw had made the catch.

Ravenpaw straightened up with the mouse at his feet. He hadn't realized he had spoken out loud. He couldn't remember the last time he had thanked StarClan for prey. "Nothing," he meowed. "Would you like to carry it back?"

Bouncing with excitement, Riley and Bella dragged the mouse back to the pile of hay. Violet looked astonished.

"Did you catch that yourself?"

Bella let go of her end of the mouse. "No," she panted. "But we watched Ravenpaw do it! He was brilliant!"

"He hunts like a real warrior!" Riley declared. Ravenpaw purred with amusement. When had this kittypet ever seen a warrior hunt?

"Good catch," Barley remarked.

"When I'm a warrior, I'm going to hunt just like Raven-paw," Bella vowed.

"Not this again, Bella." Violet sighed. "There aren't any warriors now, remember?" She glanced at Ravenpaw. "I know you used to be one, of course, but you aren't anymore, right?"

Ravenpaw shook his head. "No, no, I'm not a warrior."

Riley glared. "But that doesn't mean we can't be! You could train us, Ravenpaw! We'd work really hard, I promise!"

Bella nodded. "We'd do everything you said, practice all the battle tactics and the hunting moves. I wouldn't even mind doing dawn patrols!"

Ravenpaw blinked. "Wow. Smudge has told you a lot."

"Oh, yes," mewed Riley. "He said we could be warriors just like Firestar."

"Except that ThunderClan is gone," Violet put in. "Smudge has no right to encourage these silly daydreams. I don't mind you practicing your hunting and fighting with each other, as long as no one gets hurt. But you're going to find good homes and be kittypets, just like me, and there's nothing wrong with that."

But there is! Ravenpaw found himself wanting to reply. *Why would any cat want to be a kittypet when they could live outside, hunting for themselves, keeping themselves safe, seeing so much more than the confines of a Twoleg den?*

Barley was tugging pieces of loose hay into piles. "Come on, you should eat while the mouse is still warm. Then you can sleep here with us tonight."

"We'll leave at dawn," Violet meowed firmly. "We need to get home before our housefolk think we've gone forever."

"But we don't want to go home," whispered Bella.

"It's your home, not ours," Riley muttered. "We want to be warriors!"

CHAPTER 4

Ravenpaw and Barley traveled as far as the Thunderpath with Violet and the kits. Riley and Bella dragged their paws, insisting on stopping to sniff every stalk of grass and every rabbit hole. "Come on, you two!" Violet meowed. "If you don't hurry up, I'll leave you behind!"

"I wish you would," Riley muttered.

"Don't say that," Ravenpaw chided. "She's your mother and she loves you very much. Of course she wants you to go home with her."

The young tom fixed his clear blue gaze on Ravenpaw. "There's nothing wrong with being a kittypet. But Bella and I were born to be warriors. Please help us, Ravenpaw! You're the only warrior left in the forest!"

"I'm not a warrior, and I don't live in the forest," Ravenpaw mewed. "My home is with Barley now."

"But you could train us! We could start our own Clan!" Bella pleaded.

Violet bounded over to them and licked the top of Bella's head. "Stop pestering Ravenpaw. Look, we've reached the tunnel. We need to let Ravenpaw and Barley go home now."

She ushered them away.

Bella glanced back at Ravenpaw. "Please!" she begged. "Just think about it!"

Then she ducked into the tunnel and vanished behind her brother. Violet followed, her orange tail whisking out of sight.

"Think about what?" Barley mewed in Ravenpaw's ear.

"Oh, nothing. Just their crazy idea about becoming warriors. They think I could train them."

Barley let out a huff of amusement. "Ah, kits. Did we have such mouse-brained ideas at that age?"

"Well, I certainly wanted to be a warrior," Ravenpaw commented.

"That's different. You were born in ThunderClan." Barley pushed his way through the hedge and waited for Ravenpaw to join him. "Should we hunt out here?" He sniffed the air. "I think it's going to rain later." Before Ravenpaw could reply, he bounded along the edge of the field, his black-and-white tail sticking up in the air.

Ravenpaw watched him, his head whirling. Was it really such a crazy idea, that he should train Riley and Bella to be warriors? His memories had never seemed more vivid than they were now. Returning to the ravine before leaf-bare had brought back so much of his former life: hunting techniques, the best way to tackle an enemy in battle, how to mark out a territory. And last night he had found himself thanking StarClan after catching that mouse. Were his warrior ancestors watching over him even now? Surely they would have followed the four Clans to their new home.

Ravenpaw shivered, suddenly feeling very alone. His Clan-mates had vanished, and he wasn't a warrior anymore. Yet he remembered so much about hunting and fighting and going on patrol. He was happy with Barley—happier than he had ever been in the forest—but he didn't regret being Clanborn for a moment. Who was he to tell Riley and Bella that they shouldn't dream of becoming warriors?

Ravenpaw slept badly that night. His belly hurt, and he had only just dropped off when he was woken by an owl hooting. He wriggled deeper into the hay, burying his muzzle in Bar-ley's soft fur. But sleep seemed far out of reach, and instead his mind spun with thoughts of Riley and Bella. From what he had seen, Ravenpaw thought that any Clan would be fortu-nate to have them. They were brave, quick, and eager to learn. He wished he could send them to ThunderClan, but he had no idea where his former Clanmates were.

"You're right," breathed a voice in his ear. "They are too far away now."

Ravenpaw sat bolt upright. "Who's there?"

A sweet, slightly watery scent wreathed around him. "Don't be alarmed. It's Silverstream."

"Silverstream?" Ravenpaw whipped his head around. A sil-ver tabby she-cat sat beside him, her tail curled neatly over her paws. Her blue eyes gleamed in the half-light. "From River-Clan?"

"Yes, a long time ago," came the reply.

Ravenpaw glanced down at Barley. He was still sleeping,

his flank rising and falling evenly.

"You are dreaming. We won't disturb him."

Ravenpaw strained to see the she-cat more clearly, but her pelt shimmered against the hay behind her, and he felt that if he tried to touch her, his paw would slip right through. "Why are you in my dream?" he asked.

"Because StarClan has not forgotten you. Not all of us left the forest. I have been watching you with Riley and Bella, and I can see that they would make good warriors. But they need your help, Ravenpaw."

"You really think so?"

The she-cat blinked at him, her eyes like shining blue moons. "Of course. You changed the course of your life once. There is no better cat to help Riley and Bella follow their hearts. Every cat deserves to choose their own path."

"But what can I do? There are no Clans left in the forest."

Silverstream paused and stared into the shadows at the edge of the barn. "There is another Clan close by. Do you remember Firestar telling you about it?"

"SkyClan!" Ravenpaw nodded. "He and Sandstorm went there after the battle with BloodClan. But I don't know where it is, only that they followed the river past Highstones. I don't even know if SkyClan has survived this long."

"They have survived, and they can help these young cats find their destiny. Go with them, Ravenpaw. Show them that they can become warriors."

"What if SkyClan doesn't want any more warriors?" Ravenpaw argued. "What if we get lost? I'm not the right cat for something like this."

"A true warrior will do anything for his Clanmates." Silverstream was growing fainter now, little more than a wash of glittering light against the shadows.

"I'm not a warrior!" Ravenpaw protested. But it was too late. Silverstream had vanished.

Barley stirred. "Wha's wrong?" he mumbled.

"Go back to sleep," Ravenpaw whispered, stroking his paw along Barley's flank. "All is well." He lay down and closed his eyes. "I am not a warrior," he repeated under his breath.

The newleaf sun was so strong the following morning that the barn felt hot and stuffy. The cats made their way outside to a sheltered spot on top of a stack of logs. Barley stretched out flat on his side, the tip of his tail twitching as a fly buzzed around him.

Ravenpaw couldn't settle. His mind was too full of his dream, of Riley and Bella, of the possibility of finding SkyClan somewhere upriver.

"Stop fidgeting!" Barley grunted. "Or go do something useful and fetch me a thrush. I'm bored of eating mice."

Ravenpaw ran his paw over a piece of bark. "I want to take Riley and Bella to SkyClan."

"Huh? What are you talking about?"

"Do you remember me telling you about the Clan that Firestar and Sandstorm found upriver? It was driven out of the forest a long time ago, but StarClan sent them to restore it and teach the cats how to live like warriors again."

"SkyClan. I remember."

"Well, I think that's Riley's and Bella's best chance of becoming warriors."

Barley sat up. "But you've never been to SkyClan."

"I know where it is," Ravenpaw argued. "Roughly. And there's something else about SkyClan. Firestar told me that they have warriors who are also kittypets, who spend half their time in a Twolegplace. Don't you think that might make them more welcoming to Riley and Bella?"

Barley stared at him. "Have you got dandelion fluff in your brain? You want to go on a journey who-knows-where because my sister's kits have decided they don't want to be kittypets? You're joking, right?"

Ravenpaw felt his heart beat faster. "I'm not joking. I . . . I have to do this. For Riley and Bella, and for myself. I owe it to ThunderClan."

Barley flattened his ears. "You owe ThunderClan nothing. ThunderClan has nothing to do with Riley and Bella! Anyway, Violet will never agree to it."

"I don't think it's Violet's decision to make," Ravenpaw meowed.

"Good luck changing her mind," Barley grunted. "Look, I like those youngsters as much as you do. But they're not forestborn; they're kittypets. It's not fair to encourage them in these crazy ideas."

"It's not a crazy idea."

Barley stood up and narrowed his eyes. "It's far too dangerous. Riley and Bella know nothing about surviving outside their Twoleg den. And your shoulder has only just healed!"

"My shoulder is fine," Ravenpaw hissed.

"But I thought you were happy here," Barley whispered.

The hurt in his old friend's eyes was too much for Ravenpaw to bear. He looked away. "I am happy. I have been since the moment I first arrived. But by taking me in, you gave me the chance to make a choice, don't you see? Riley and Bella want to choose their own paths, too. I am the only cat who can help them. I . . . I hoped you'd come with us."

Barley walked to the edge of the woodpile. "I think you're a fool," he growled. "You're putting all three of you in danger because of some stupid kits' dreams. I won't come with you, and I don't want to hear another word about it."

He jumped down into the long grass, leaving Ravenpaw staring after him in dismay.

"We're going to be warriors!" Bella squeaked. "Thank you, Ravenpaw!" She flung herself at him, almost knocking him off the wooden platform. Riley bounced on his paws, purring loudly.

Behind them, Violet's eyes were wide with horror. "What do you mean, you know of a Clan that will take them? I thought you didn't know where the Clans had gone."

"This is a different Clan," Ravenpaw explained. "One that's much closer, and friendlier to kittypets." His pelt burned under the force of Violet's gaze. "It will be up to SkyClan to decide if they want to train Riley and Bella as warriors. If they don't, then I'll bring them home again."

It sounded so simple, but Ravenpaw couldn't help wondering if Barley was right and his brain had turned to fluff. He winced when he thought of his old friend. They had hardly spoken since their quarrel on the woodpile, and at night Barley had even made a separate nest to sleep in. Ravenpaw hadn't imagined he could feel so much pain without being physically wounded.

He dragged his thoughts back to Violet. He had to convince her that this was the best thing for her kits. Silverstream would never have visited him if she didn't believe it, too.

"You and Barley have lived in the wild," Ravenpaw reminded her. "There is a part of you that knows what it is to be free, to hunt for yourself, to find your own shelter. Why shouldn't Bella and Riley know that too?"

"Because I want to keep them safe!"

"Wait!" Ravenpaw and Violet turned to see Bella staring at them, her green eyes huge. "Riley and I will never be happy as kittypets. You know that. Please, let us go."

Riley nodded. "It's what we want."

Violet's tail drooped. "Oh, my precious kits," she murmured. She rested her chin on Bella's head and met Ravenpaw's gaze. "You're right. I chose to be a kittypet having known the alternative. How can I deny the same choice to my kits?"

"You mean we can go?" Bella gasped.

Violet nodded. "I will think of you every day, my loves. Be the best warriors you can. And if you ever come by this way again, please remember me."

"We'll never forget you!" Bella's voice trembled. "You're

the best mother a cat could ever have! I . . . I don't want to go if I'll never see you again."

Violet stepped back. "Courage, little one!" Ravenpaw saw the sadness in her eyes and marveled at how strong her voice sounded. "Partings are always hard, but endings are just the start of something else!" She looked at Ravenpaw. "I'm not a fool. I have seen how they hunt and play fight. I know that, with training, they could be great warriors. But please, until then, keep them safe."

"I will," Ravenpaw promised. He curled his tail at Riley and Bella. "Come on. We have a long journey ahead of us."

He jumped down onto the short green grass. Bella followed, but Riley paused, looking back at his mother. "I will think of you every day," he meowed.

"And I of you," Violet replied. Her eyes were liquid with sadness. "Go well, my darlings. Make me proud."

"We will!" Bella called.

They trotted across the grass and squeezed through the hole in the fence. A gust of wind struck their faces on the other side, flattening their fur and filling their muzzles with the scent of monsters, trees, and distant hills. For a moment Ravenpaw was tempted to push the kits back through the hole. What was he doing, taking them on a journey to an unknown Clan?

Then Riley raced ahead, shouting, "We're going to be warriors!" Bella sprinted after him, and Ravenpaw followed. These young cats had chosen their destiny, and he had promised Silverstream he'd help them.

CHAPTER 5

❧

"You're really not coming with us?" Ravenpaw spoke quietly so that he wouldn't disturb Riley and Bella, who were still sleeping. Tendrils of dawn light pierced the walls of the barn, and the air was already warm.

Barley shook his head. "We've been over this already," he mewed. "I think you're making a massive mistake."

"And I thought you trusted me!" Ravenpaw retorted. "I'll come straight back, as soon as I've delivered Riley and Bella to SkyClan. Firestar and Sandstorm made this journey safely. There's no reason I won't, too."

"They were warriors," Barley hissed. He sounded angry, but Ravenpaw could hear the pain beneath his words. "Is that what this is all about? You want to prove that you're as good as a Clan cat, even though you were only ever an apprentice?"

Ravenpaw flinched. "What are you talking about?"

"I don't believe you're doing this for Riley and Bella. I think you're doing it for yourself, because you want to be in a Clan again."

"You're wrong!" Ravenpaw gasped.

"Am I? Ever since we went back to the forest, you haven't

stopped going on about what it was like when you lived there. I bet you wish you'd never left!"

Ravenpaw felt his shoulders sag. "You're being ridiculous. Is this really how it's going to end, Barley? With us at each other's throats?"

"You're the one who's leaving," Barley growled.

"Well, you're making it easier!"

"Is it time to go?"

Both cats spun around. A small orange face was looking down at them from the top of the stack of hay. Bella was quickly joined by her brother, who had a wisp of dried grass stuck to one ear.

"We're awake!" Riley announced. He bounced down the hay and landed beside Ravenpaw. "Should we hunt first?"

Barley twitched his ears. "No need," he meowed gruffly. "I caught extra for you last night." He moved a pile of hay to reveal two mice and a young pigeon.

Ravenpaw blinked at him. "Thanks."

"I didn't do it for you. I did it for them." Raising his voice, Barley added, "I'm going for a walk. If you're not here when I get back, well, I hope you find what you're looking for."

Bella looked up, her cheeks bulging with pigeon. "Aren't you going to see us off?" she mumbled.

"Ravenpaw knows the way out," Barley replied. The tip of his tail twitched. "Don't do anything stupid. Make your mother proud." He stalked out of the barn with a final sideways glare at Ravenpaw.

"Eat as much as you want," Ravenpaw told the young cats,

forcing himself to sound cheerful. *I can't believe he didn't say good-bye.* "But not so much that it's uncomfortable to walk. We have a long way to go"—the thought struck him yet again that he had no idea how long—"so we'll be able to stop and hunt on the way."

His belly was churning too much to leave room for food, but he munched down a few bites of mouse. He wished he could remember the traveling herbs that Spottedleaf had given him before the journey to the Moonstone, but it was too long ago, and he could only remember curling his lip at the bitter taste.

They finished eating and pushed the rest of the prey back under the hay. Ravenpaw looked at the cats in front of him, so similar to his old friends Firestar and Graystripe. *But these cats know nothing about living in the wild,* he reminded himself. *You will have to teach them everything.*

Riley and Bella stared back at him expectantly, pelts groomed, eyes dazzling bright. They had made their choice, and they couldn't imagine that anything might go wrong.

Ravenpaw lifted his head. "Come on, you two. Let's go find SkyClan!"

He led them through the fields—one covered in lush grass, the other filled with springy green cornstalks—until they reached the river. It was broad and lazy here, flowing idly toward the gorge at the edge of the moor. Riley and Bella opened their eyes wide when they saw the water.

"We don't have to swim across, do we?" Bella hissed,

fluffing up her orange fur.

Ravenpaw thought for a moment. Firestar had described following the river all the way to the gorge, but had said nothing about crossing it. "No," he replied.

"Phew," puffed Bella.

They padded along the path that ran beside the river. It was broad and flat, and full of the scents of Twolegs and dogs. Riley and Bella stopped to sniff every stalk, every paw print, every tiny trail. Even a leaf blowing in the breeze had to be pounced on and shredded.

"How's my pounce?" Riley called, scraps of beech leaf clinging to his muzzle.

"Keep your weight on your hind legs right until you spring," Ravenpaw told him. "If you lean on your front paws, you'll put yourself off balance." Riley crouched down again, practicing. "But you'll wear yourself out if you don't stick to walking for a while," Ravenpaw added. He noticed Bella staring into a clump of reeds. "We'll hunt later, I promise," he told her.

"I'm not hunting. I'm watching that green stone with eyes."

Ravenpaw padded over to her. "That's a frog. Not good for prey, unless you're starving. Or in ShadowClan."

"Ooh, we've heard about ShadowClan!" mewed Riley. "Tell us a story about them!"

Ravenpaw sighed. "If it means you'll keep walking, okay." He didn't want to frighten them with how vicious Clan life could be, so he made up a story about ShadowClan queens teaching their kits how to jump like frogs. It kept Riley and Bella distracted enough that they covered a decent stretch before Ravenpaw realized it was sunhigh and time to rest. He sank down under the hedgerow at the side of the path and licked his haunches. His legs were aching, and his belly felt as if he had swallowed a stone.

There was a loud scrabbling noise in the scrubby grass behind him. Ravenpaw turned to see Bella stepping proudly through the brittle stalks with a shrew in her jaws. She dropped it in front of him. "Fresh-kill!" she declared with her tail curled high above her back.

"Great catch!" Ravenpaw purred.

There was a crack and a thud on the other side of the hedge, and Riley pushed his head through the branches. "Oops!" he panted. "I was chasing a sparrow, but it got away."

"Don't worry; Bella's caught enough for all of us," Ravenpaw meowed. "And I'm not surprised that sparrow escaped. You sounded like a herd of cows thundering through the hedge!"

Riley scrambled through the hedge and rubbed his muzzle on his sister's head. He had to stretch up to reach her. "You're practically a warrior already!" he mewed.

"There's still a lot to learn," Ravenpaw warned.

At that moment a storm of barking sounded farther along the river. Ravenpaw sprang up, his fur bristling.

"We're used to dogs," Riley boasted. "There was a fluffy white one in the garden next to ours. Bella and I used to scratch its nose whenever it looked under the fence." Huge paws thundered along the path toward them, and Riley's eyes grew huge. "But it wasn't as big as this dog!" he yowled.

He leaped into the hedge as if he had grown wings. Bella followed, and Ravenpaw scrambled after them, giving Bella's rump a shove with his nose to boost her into the higher branches. They clung to the swaying twigs and looked down at the massive brown beast, which was snuffling up the remains of the shrew. When it finished, it looked up, its long pink tongue lolling, its hot breath stinking of prey.

"Is it going to eat us next?" Bella whimpered.

"Let's hope not," Ravenpaw muttered. He sank his claws into the branch and tried to wriggle deeper into the hedge.

A Twoleg bellowed close by, making all the cats jump. The dog looked around; then its ears drooped and it trotted away. Ravenpaw let out a long breath. *That was way too close.* He waited until the sound of paw steps had faded, then slid down to the ground. Riley landed behind him, but Bella stayed where she was, clinging to a branch at the top of the hedge.

"Come on, Bella!" Ravenpaw meowed. "It's safe now!"

"What if that dog comes back?" Bella squeaked.

"It won't," Ravenpaw replied.

"You don't know that!"

Ravenpaw sighed. "Well, not for sure, but I can't see it along the riverbank, and I can't hear it anymore. We're going in the opposite direction, so we have time to get away."

"I'm scared," Bella mewed in a tiny voice. "I want my mother."

Riley crumpled a dead leaf under his paw. "Maybe this wasn't such a good idea," he mumbled.

For a moment Ravenpaw wanted to agree with him. Then

he remembered Silverstream telling him that he was these cats' only chance of choosing their own path. "All warriors get scared sometimes," he told them. "It's the only way to tell if you're being brave. You kept yourselves safe from that dog, didn't you? You did well, both of you. Violet would be very proud of you. But we need to keep going, before the dog comes back."

Above his head there was a faint whimper. Ravenpaw looked up. "You can't stay up there forever, Bella! A hedge is no place for a cat, kittypet or warrior!"

"Do you promise the dog won't get me?" Bella mewed.

"I promise."

There was a crackle of twigs and a few tumbling leaves; then Bella squeezed out from the bottom of the hedge. Her fur was full of scraps, and her eyes were wide with fear. Ravenpaw licked the top of her head. "Well done. You're doing great."

He padded onto the path and looked up and down. There was no trace of life, Twoleg or dog, in either direction. "Let's go!" he called, and set off at a trot. Riley and Bella fell in behind him. Ravenpaw tried not to show that the incident with the dog had rattled him, too.

They had to dodge a few more Twolegs and dogs as they traveled on, but it was easy to spot them from a long way off and hide in the hedgerow. Bella was unusually quiet, and Riley stayed close to her, giving her encouraging licks. When it started to get too dark to see the edge of the riverbank, Ravenpaw looked for a place to spend the night. He found a squat, angular, gray stone den at the edge of a field just on the other side of the hedge. The floor was damp earth, and it smelled sharply of cows, but there were no other animals in the field and no scents of foxes or badgers.

Ravenpaw led Riley and Bella into the den and waited while they lay down. They looked exhausted, their flanks heaving, and their pelts were dusty and matted. "Stay here and clean yourselves," Ravenpaw told them before hauling his weary legs back outside and heading for the hedgerow. He found a nest of eggs halfway along the field and carried them one at a time under his chin to his companions. Bella made a face at the slimy texture of the eggs, but Riley ate more enthusiastically.

"I'm so hungry, I could eat grass!"

Ravenpaw clawed some moss from a log that lay at the entrance to the den and shaped it into a nest for all of them. Riley and Bella curled up together in a pool of gray and orange fur and fell asleep at once. Ravenpaw lay down beside them, feeling the warmth of their fur against his belly. Moonlight filtered through a small hole in the wall of the den, and Ravenpaw twisted around to look up at the glowing orb. *Is Barley looking up at the moon too?* he wondered. They had hardly spent a night apart since he'd first come to the barn. But in spite of his sadness, exhaustion dragged Ravenpaw into sleep.

Riley and Bella were still subdued the next day. Bella refused to eat the thrush that Ravenpaw had caught, saying it smelled funny. For a moment Ravenpaw was tempted to snap at her for being ungrateful, but he reminded himself that they were a long way from everything they had ever known and must be missing their mother. He let Riley finish the thrush, then led them back to the riverbank.

They traveled faster now that Riley and Bella were less interested in stopping to sniff every new scent. Ravenpaw stayed in front, keeping watch for dogs or Twolegs. The sun warmed his black fur, and although his legs were still tired, he found himself looking forward to rounding each new corner, seeing the river and fields and hedges roll out before him. His whiskers quivered at every fresh sound or smell, and he felt younger than he had in a while. Even the ache in his belly seemed to have faded. Ravenpaw wished that Barley were with him, sharing the adventure.

A small copse of trees appeared on the bank. Ravenpaw decided to hunt, hopefully for something that Bella would eat.

"We'll stop here for a while," he announced. Riley plunged into the trees, gray tail waving. Bella lay at the edge of the path and scraped at the grass with her paw.

"I'm too tired to hunt," she mewed.

"Then wait here until we come back," Ravenpaw told her, trying not to show his annoyance. He whirled around and followed Riley into the trees. There were few scents of prey in the copse, but he managed to track down a mouse in a clump of bracken.

Ravenpaw hauled his catch back to where he had left Bella. The patch of grass was empty.

"Bella?" he called softly.

No reply. Then Ravenpaw heard the rumbling voice of a Twoleg farther up the river. He turned to see a full-grown male crouching on the edge of the bank beside a long pole, which hung out over the water. Bella was arching her back and purring in delight as she ate something from the Twoleg's hairless front paw.

Ravenpaw flung down the mouse and raced along the bank. "What do you think you're doing?" he screeched. "Get away from there!"

Bella spun around and glared at Ravenpaw. "He's giving me something to eat!" she hissed. "I was hungry!"

Ravenpaw leaped forward and grabbed her by the scruff of her neck. It was tricky, as Bella was almost as tall as him. He was aware of the Twoleg stumbling away to the far side of the bank, making noises of alarm.

"Come with me!" Ravenpaw ordered through a mouthful of orange fur. He dragged Bella along the bank and into the shelter of the trees.

"What's going on?" gasped Riley, who was heading through the bushes toward them.

"Bella was taking food from a Twoleg!" Ravenpaw spat.

"What's wrong with that?" Bella yowled.

"You're supposed to be a wild cat now!" Ravenpaw snarled. "Twolegs are not your friends! And they are never a source of food!" He took a deep breath and tried to make his fur lie flat. "If you're going to be a warrior, then Twolegs must be your enemies."

Bella flattened her ears at him. "That's mouse-brained! He

was being friendly and giving me treats!"

"You can't trust Twolegs," Ravenpaw insisted. "They don't like warriors."

Riley flicked his tail. "She didn't do anything wrong, Ravenpaw. She didn't know she wasn't supposed to take his food."

"Look, these are the rules now," Ravenpaw growled. "If you aren't going to listen to me, we may as well turn back." He tipped his head to one side. "Is that what you want?"

Riley and Bella stared at him, frozen.

Ravenpaw nodded. "Come on, then. And don't stop for *anything.*"

He stomped out of the trees and headed along the riverbank once more. The Twoleg had gone, leaving behind a strong scent that made Ravenpaw's nose twitch. He could hear Riley and Bella trotting behind him, both still bristling at the way he had spoken to them.

That's not my problem, Ravenpaw told himself. *They have to respect their mentor, or SkyClan won't have anything to do with them. I will have to start teaching them the warrior code.* The vastness of his task struck him again.

Do Riley and Bella have any chance of becoming warriors?

CHAPTER 6

❦

After another uncomfortable night's sleep, this time under a bush on the riverbank, where they were disturbed by the sound of voles plopping into the river, Ravenpaw woke at dawn and managed to catch a fat young pigeon. Riley and Bella tucked in, Bella with her eyes narrowed as if she was making a point of showing Ravenpaw that she understood the rules about food.

Watching the young cats eat, Ravenpaw felt a pang of compassion. They were so far from home, and they were being very brave considering they were barely out of kithood. Perhaps there was a way he could get the day off to a good start.

"Would you like to learn a few battle moves before we set off?" *I hope I can remember a few!*

Both cats' eyes lit up. "Yes, please!" mewed Bella, jumping to her paws.

"Real warrior moves?" Riley asked, and he purred when Ravenpaw nodded.

The path was wide and flat enough to make a good training ground.

"We'll start with the hunter's crouch," Ravenpaw explained.

He dropped to his belly, keeping his hind paws tucked under him.

"We know about that already," Riley meowed. "That's what we do when we're going to pounce on something."

Ravenpaw looked up at him. "That something doesn't have to be prey, does it? It can be a useful way to attack an enemy, especially if you're lying in wait. Find your balance, breathe out, then go!" He sprang forward and landed almost on top of Bella.

"Awesome!" purred Riley.

"Now you try," Ravenpaw puffed, trying to ignore the stabbing pain in his belly.

The young cats settled down onto their haunches and leaped forward one by one. Bella nearly fell over and Riley didn't cover much distance, but it was a decent start. Ravenpaw dragged a stick out of the hedge.

"Pretend that this is your enemy," he panted. "I want you to land with your front paws on the back of its neck, here." He indicated a lump on the stick.

Bella did well this time, dropping down with her paws lightly on her imaginary enemy's neck. Riley stumbled as he took off and ended up breaking the stick in two.

"Well, at least you wounded your enemy," Ravenpaw commented, looking down at the splintered wood.

"Teach us something else!" Bella pleaded.

"Just one more; then we need to set off. Let's try a front-paw blow." Ravenpaw beckoned to Riley with the tip of his tail. "Imagine we're face-to-face in battle. I'll reach up with my front paw like this, fast as I can, and bring it down straight on top of your head. If I can't reach, I can rear up on my hind legs, but see how this leaves my belly exposed? You have to be quick for this move!"

Bella took Ravenpaw's place and lightly patted her brother's head. "Too slow," Ravenpaw warned. "He would have known exactly what you were going to do. Riley, you can use the duck-and-twist move to get out of Bella's reach. Drop sideways, tuck your legs under you, and roll out of the way. Excellent!" he praised as Riley folded himself into a ball and tumbled to the edge of the path. "But don't fall in the river," Ravenpaw added.

Riley and Bella took turns practicing the front-paw blow and duck-and-twist. Bella had good reach with her long legs, but Riley's broad shoulders gave him more power, and he was surprisingly fast given his sturdy build.

"We'll make warriors of you yet!" Ravenpaw exclaimed. "Good work!"

Riley looked at him, his flanks heaving. "That was fun!"

"I can't wait for our first battle!" Bella mewed.

Ravenpaw shook his head. "Never wish yourself into a fight," he murmured. "It will come soon enough." For a moment he thought of Violet, how terrified she would be to know that her kits were preparing for danger. *It's better to be prepared,* Ravenpaw told himself. "Come on, you two. Let's keep going." He flicked his tail, and the two cats fell in behind him.

Farther along the river, they reached an abandoned Two-leg den made from crumbling red stones. There was no trace of Twoleg scent in the air, and the den was completely silent. Ravenpaw glanced at his companions.

"Want to explore?" he suggested.

"Yes, please!" Riley meowed.

Ravenpaw followed them inside. The floor was strewn with broken stones and dotted with large Twoleg relics. A jagged wooden slope led up to another level, and above that Ravenpaw could see glimpses of sky through holes in the roof.

"Watch this!" yowled Riley. He sprang onto the nearest Twoleg relic, then bounced onto the wooden slope. It creaked under his weight, so he leaped down onto the floor, sending up a puff of dust. "That was fun!" he gasped.

"I'll chase you!" Bella mewed, bounding toward him. Riley skidded around and set off at a sprint, hurtling past Ravenpaw so fast that his fur was flattened.

Ravenpaw started to worry that something would overhear them. He opened his mouth to warn them to be quiet, when a shadow filled the doorway behind him. Ravenpaw whirled around, claws out, ready to fight. He stared in astonishment.

"Barley!"

Ravenpaw's first thought was to fling himself at his old friend and cover him with joyous licks. But he held back, remembering their bitter words the last time they had seen each other.

Barley spoke first. "I'm so sorry," he blurted out. "I should never have tried to stop you from helping Violet's kits. You are brave, and generous, and I don't deserve you. . . ."

Ravenpaw bounded forward and pressed his muzzle against

Barley's cheek. "Don't be such a mouse-brain. You were right to be concerned. It's been hard, but we're okay." He felt a lump in his throat. "Even better now that you're here."

Barley nuzzled the top of his head. "I left not long after you did. I thought that the barn was my home, but my home is wherever you are." He took a step back and blinked at Raven-paw. "I . . . I thought you were leaving because you didn't want to be with me anymore."

"That will never happen!" Ravenpaw meowed. "I'm sorry I left without you. I've missed you every step of the way."

"Whoa! It's Barley!" Bella came tearing down the wooden slope. Her brother's paw steps thudded overhead, and Raven-paw glanced nervously at the trembling ceiling.

With a clatter, Riley rushed down to join them. "Are you going to come with us to SkyClan?"

Barley nodded. "I couldn't let you have this great adventure without me, could I?"

"It's been amazing!" Bella mewed, to Ravenpaw's surprise. "There was this really fierce dog, and we had to hide in the hedge!"

Barley looked alarmed.

"It's okay," Riley put in. "We stayed super quiet until the dog went away. Ravenpaw made sure we didn't come out till it was safe."

"And he's taught us great battle moves!" Bella exclaimed. "We can do the hunter's crouch, the front-paw blow, and the duck-and-twist!"

Barley glanced at Ravenpaw. "I'm glad to hear he's been

looking after you," he purred.

Bella nodded. "Yes, but he's *really* bossy," she added.

"As he should be!" Barley meowed. "He knows all about living in a Clan, so you must listen to everything he says." He looked around the abandoned den. "Now, are you planning to make a camp here, or should we keep going?"

"Let's go!" yowled Riley, racing out the door with Bella on his heels.

Ravenpaw blinked affectionately at Barley. "You certainly know how to motivate them!"

The black-and-white tom ran his tail over Ravenpaw's flank. "I'm so proud of you for doing this. You're right; they deserve to choose the life they lead. Just as we did, a long time ago."

Side by side, they padded into the sunshine. Ravenpaw forgot the tiredness in his legs as he trotted beside Barley. Riley and Bella took the lead, calling back to let the older cats know about every new scent, every ripple in the river, every crushed leaf.

"They're certainly observant," Barley commented as they all stopped to look at a dragonfly that Bella had spotted on a reed.

As dusk fell, they reached a shallow pool fed by a low waterfall. Ravenpaw and Barley settled onto warm, flat boulders and basked in the final rays of the sun while the young cats played at the edge of the water, chasing rainbows in the spray. Riley ventured too far from the shore with one leap and vanished into the pool with a splash. Bella squeaked in horror, but a moment later her brother emerged, scattering drops of water, with a wriggling fish in his jaws. He scrambled out and dropped it triumphantly beside Ravenpaw and Barley.

"Look what I caught!" he announced.

"Caught? Or did it land in your mouth when you fell?" Barley teased.

"Whatever happened, it's the best fresh-kill we've had in a while," Ravenpaw purred. "Well done, Riley!"

The gray tabby shook his fur, making Bella spring away with a yelp as water spattered her pelt. Ravenpaw let them start eating first. He was conscious of Barley standing very close to him as they watched the young cats tuck in.

"I can't believe how well they've settled into living wild," Barley murmured. "You've done a great job."

"They've been very brave," Ravenpaw replied. "I'm proud of them."

Barley leaned against him, smelling warm and soft and familiar. "You should be," he whispered.

CHAPTER 7

They slept in the long grass beside the waterfall, lulled by the soft splash of water, and woke as the first rays of sun crested the trees. Barley caught a squirrel, and Ravenpaw was relieved to see Bella eating as eagerly as her brother once more.

The river grew steadily narrower and shallower beside them until it was tumbling between steep sandy banks, with barely enough room for the cats to squeeze through beside the water. They walked in single file, Ravenpaw in the lead and Barley bringing up the rear. Riley and Bella were full of chatter, competing to spot minnows beneath the glittering surface. Ravenpaw only listened with half an ear; he knew they were approaching the end of the river, and that meant they could cross SkyClan's boundary at any moment.

"I'm as hot as a fox on fire!" Barley panted. "Can we find somewhere shady to stop?"

Ravenpaw narrowed his eyes. There seemed to be nothing but the stream and its sandy banks ahead of them. There were trees at the top of the banks, but he doubted they could scramble up the sheer slope. Then Riley squeezed past him.

"I'll take a look!" The gray tom ran a short distance along

the bank to some gorse bushes. He paused to sniff them, then vanished from sight.

When the others caught up to him, Riley was peeking smugly from a small cave sheltered by the gorse. It was cozy but shallow, with just enough room for the four cats to lie down.

"I'm hungry," Bella mewed.

"We'll rest here for a moment, then find somewhere to hunt," Ravenpaw promised. His paws were sore from the scorching sand, and his belly was aching. As the others settled around him, he closed his eyes.

Suddenly his nose filled with powerfully familiar scents. He heard soft whispers, not from his companions but from two other cats. These were voices he hadn't heard in a long time, and Ravenpaw's heart leaped. Although he couldn't make out the words, he knew he was listening to Firestar and Sandstorm. He could feel them all around him, nervous and excited. They had sheltered here too, knowing that their journey was close to its end.

I've done it! Ravenpaw thought. *I have followed their paw steps to SkyClan!*

He opened his eyes to see Bella standing at the entrance to the little cave, gazing out.

"I think I heard something!" she mewed. "Another cat!"

Ravenpaw took a deep breath. "We are close to SkyClan territory now," he meowed. Three pairs of eyes stared at him in the dim light. "I don't think we've crossed their border, but we must tread carefully from now on. No Clan welcomes trespassers."

Riley licked his chest. "What if they don't like us?" he muttered.

"What if they think we're just dumb kittypets?" Bella added.

Barley rested his tail on her flank. "If you're not welcome, we'll take you home. We won't abandon you, I promise."

Ravenpaw met his friend's gaze over the heads of the young cats and nodded.

They crept out of the cave and padded quietly along the stream. There was no sign of the cat that Bella thought she had seen, but Ravenpaw kept his mouth open to taste the air. The gorge widened, and the banks sloped downward until they were walking through trees beside the sparkling stream. Barley caught a young rabbit, and they ate quickly, with the older cats keeping a wary eye out for signs of the Clan.

The sky had filled with clouds, bringing an early dusk. Ravenpaw decided that they should spend the night here and enter SkyClan in the morning. Barley found a heap of dry leaves under a hazel tree, which would make a decent enough nest. Riley and Bella settled down obediently; they were much quieter than usual, as if they knew that the real adventure was about to begin. Ravenpaw asked Barley to stay with them while he scouted around the immediate area.

"We don't want SkyClan to find us sleeping a mouse-length from their border!" he pointed out, and Barley nodded.

Ravenpaw left the stream and slipped through the trees, pausing every few steps to sniff bushes and taste the air. There was a strong smell of cats here, though he hadn't found any border marks yet. There were tangs of kittypet scent too, sometimes almost hidden beneath the wild-cat traces, at other times clear and sharp and unexpected so far from any Twoleg dens. Ravenpaw hadn't been anticipating such a mix of scents, even knowing that SkyClan had some warriors who lived as kittypets part of the time.

He returned to the hazel bush and lay down. Barley was fast asleep, snoring, but Riley and Bella were still awake.

"We're not sleepy!" Bella whispered.

"Tell us some more about the warrior code!" Riley begged.

Ravenpaw sighed. "Okay, but after that you must go to sleep. Who can remember the rules we've talked about so far?"

"You must be ready to die for your Clan," Riley began. "And you can't be friends with cats from other Clans."

"Don't trespass on another Clan's territory," Bella mewed. She put her head to one side. "But if SkyClan is the only Clan around here, that doesn't matter, does it?"

Ravenpaw flicked his ears. "There could be loners in the woods who won't welcome visitors. Go on."

"Elders and kits must eat first," Riley meowed. "And you only kill something if you're going to eat it."

"That's two rules!" Bella protested.

"You're both doing very well," Ravenpaw told them. "Right, here are some more." For a moment he was back in the training hollow, listening to Whitestorm addressing all the new apprentices. Kind, patient Whitestorm, who had tried so hard to make Ravenpaw's apprenticeship bearable. "A new warrior keeps vigil for the whole Clan on their first night. A warrior must mentor at least one apprentice before they can become deputy." Ravenpaw paused, racking his brain. "When the Clan leader dies, the deputy takes over."

He stopped. Riley and Bella were very quiet, and their flanks rose and fell steadily. They had drifted off already. Ravenpaw curled up and tucked his chin into Barley's belly fur. Riley and Bella were trying so hard to learn about the life of a warrior; he just hoped SkyClan would give them a chance to try it for real.

"Ooh, what do we have here? Four little warriors lost in the woods?"

A shrill voice and a blast of hot breath jolted Ravenpaw awake. In a heartbeat he sprang to his feet, growling. Five cats circled the nest, eyes narrowed and ears flat back. These weren't warriors, though; they had the stench of kittypet about them, cloying and unwelcome among the leaves. Their fur was sleek and glossy, and they looked plump and overfed rather than well muscled. But their eyes were mean, and there was no mistaking the challenge in the first cat's voice.

"Swallowed your tongue?" he jeered. He was a dark tabby, almost black, with piercing green eyes. "I didn't think patrols were allowed to go to sleep!"

Ravenpaw heard the other cats stir beside him. "Leave us alone," he snarled. "We're doing no harm." He was confident that these weren't SkyClan warriors. They were too scornful of patrols, for a start. He took a step forward and let his fur rise along his spine.

"You're so scary," gasped the tabby, pretending to fall back. Then he leaned forward. "I'm joking. I don't like the look of you. You don't smell like those SkyClan fools, but you're scrawny enough to be wild. Go back to where you came from!"

"You'll have to make us," rumbled Barley, stepping up alongside Ravenpaw.

For a moment the tabby looked less certain. Barley was broad-shouldered and tall, and there was menace in his growl.

"You heard what Pasha said," meowed another kittypet. Her pelt was ginger and white. "Go away." The other three cats took a pace forward so that they were looming over the nest.

Bella squeezed in between Barley and Ravenpaw. "And you heard what we said. We're not going unless you make us! We're warriors, so we know how to fight!"

"Warriors?" spat Pasha. "Ha, they don't scare us." He twitched his ears at Ravenpaw. "Run along, squirrel-breath."

Slam!

Quick as lightning, Ravenpaw raised his front leg and clouted the tabby between his ears. The kittypet staggered backward with a yowl.

"You'll regret that!" he hissed. He stalked toward Ravenpaw, his thick tail lashing.

One of his companions, a she-cat with silver and black patches, interrupted. "This is boring, Pasha. I'm getting cold. Can't we run through the gorge like we did last night? That was way more fun."

"This bunch of weasels will be too easy to fight," agreed the ginger-and-white she-cat.

Pasha glared once more at Ravenpaw. "If I see you again, you'll regret it," he snarled. Then he whirled around and bounded into the trees. "Come on! Let's give SkyClan another surprise!"

Ravenpaw watched them vanish into the shadows. His heart was pounding, and his paw throbbed where he had struck the tabby.

"Well, they weren't very nice!" Bella exclaimed.

"It sounds like they're not that nice to SkyClan, either," Barley commented. He arched an eyebrow at Ravenpaw. "Do you think they're going to invade the camp?"

Ravenpaw shrugged. "I think they're more hot air than action," he meowed. "Otherwise they'd have shredded us while we were asleep. But I don't think they'll trouble us again tonight. Their Twolegs will expect them home before dawn."

He lay down again and licked his sore paw. The others settled around him.

"I'll stay awake to make sure they don't come back," Barley murmured in Ravenpaw's ear.

Ravenpaw nodded his thanks. They must be close to the border with SkyClan, judging by what those cats had said. Tomorrow Riley and Bella would see their new home for the first time.

If SkyClan will have them.

CHAPTER 8

Ravenpaw didn't expect to go back to sleep after the excitement of their night visitors, but he woke to find himself alone in the nest with sunbeams reaching under the edge of the branches.

"Barley?" he meowed.

"Right here," came the reply, and Barley's black-and-white rump appeared, dragging a squirrel through the leaves. "We caught you something to eat," he announced.

Riley and Bella's faces appeared at the edge of the bush. "We climbed a tree and chased it down to Barley!" Riley meowed.

"Wow," mewed Ravenpaw, impressed. He recalled Firestar telling him about SkyClan's unusual skill in hunting above the ground. Perhaps Riley and Bella would fit in even better than he had imagined.

They shared the squirrel and buried the remains a little way from the bush. Then Riley found the way back to the stream, and they carried on, all of them alert to noises and scents from the trees around them.

Even so, Ravenpaw jumped when there was a blur of movement from behind a holly tree and three cats leaped out to block their path. All were she-cats: A long-legged ginger warrior was flanked by a gray warrior and a smaller white cat who looked like an apprentice, judging by her trembling paws and huge eyes.

"What are you doing here?" growled the ginger cat. "This is SkyClan territory!"

Ravenpaw caught a strong scent from the holly bush, and he realized they were less than a fox-length from a border mark.

"You're not welcome here!" hissed the gray warrior.

"Yeah! You should make like a tree and *leave*!" chimed the little white cat. The gray cat looked down at her in surprise.

"But we've come a long way," Riley began.

"Then you'll have a long walk home," snarled the ginger cat.

"Wait," Ravenpaw pleaded, stepping forward alongside Riley. "We come in peace. I am a friend of Firestar, who saved your Clan. Do you know him?"

The three cats looked blankly at him. Ravenpaw felt his heart sink. He hadn't anticipated that SkyClan might have forgotten all about the ThunderClan cats who helped them moons ago.

Then the ginger cat stirred. "My mother has talked about a cat of that name. What do you want? Is he here?"

Ravenpaw shook his head. "No, but he was once my closest friend, and I hoped that his friends in SkyClan would be prepared to speak to me."

The ginger she-cat looked him up and down. "You don't smell like a Clan cat," she commented. "You smell of cows."

"I'm not a Clan cat," Ravenpaw admitted. "At least, not

anymore. Look, is Leafstar still your leader? Please, may we speak with her? Tell her . . . tell her that Firestar's friend Ravenpaw is here."

The warrior studied him for another heartbeat, then turned to the small white cat. "Cloudpaw, fetch my mother." Cloudpaw nodded and scampered off.

Barley came up to join Ravenpaw. "I'm Barley," he announced, dipping his head. "And these are Riley and Bella."

The ginger she-cat twitched her tail. "I'm Firefern, and this is Plumwillow."

"Er . . . nice territory," Ravenpaw stammered, trying to break the strained silence.

"How would you know? You haven't seen it," Plumwillow pointed out.

Barley caught Ravenpaw's eye and shook his head. It looked as if they weren't going to make friends with these warriors today.

Riley and Bella were just starting to fidget when Ravenpaw heard the sound of paw steps. Cloudpaw raced back along the stream, followed by a brown-and-cream tabby. She was not young, but she moved gracefully and her amber eyes were bright. She stood beside Firefern and studied the visitors.

"I am Leafstar, leader of SkyClan." Her gaze met Ravenpaw's. "I remember Firestar talking about you. You left ThunderClan, didn't you?"

"Yes, I did," Ravenpaw admitted. "I live with Barley now"— the black-and-white cat bowed—"and we have come here with Barley's kin Riley and Bella."

"Do you still live near the Clans?" Leafstar asked. Ravenpaw nodded and was about to explain that the Clans had moved away when Leafstar went on. "Then you have come a long way. It must be important, whatever it is."

Ravenpaw felt suddenly unprepared. How could he ask this cool, powerful leader if two complete strangers could join her Clan?

He hesitated for too long. Barley lifted his head and blurted out, "My sister Violet's kits want to become warriors. Please, could they join SkyClan? They've already started their training, and they're really good."

Leafstar's eyes opened very wide. Beside her, Firefern and Plumwillow bristled. Cloudpaw leaned forward and sniffed Bella's fur. "That one smells funny," she mewed, recoiling. "She can't be a warrior!"

"Do we look like we take in strays?" Firefern growled.

"I'm not a stray!" puffed Riley.

"Hush!" Leafstar ordered, raising her tail. "SkyClan is honored by your request. I appreciate that you have traveled a long way. But it's not that simple. SkyClan is strong and thriving as it is. We don't need to recruit warriors from outside, as we have done in the past. We have enough loyal warriors already."

Ravenpaw felt as if the ground were opening under his paws. *She didn't even give Riley and Bella a chance!* He had imagined Leafstar being reluctant, of course, but he had hoped he'd be able to persuade her when she saw how determined the young cats were, and how much they had learned so far.

"Is it because we used to be kittypets?" Bella meowed.

"Because Ravenpaw told us that some of your warriors are still kittypets. We'd be warriors all the time, I promise!"

Leafstar blinked. "It's true that SkyClan has daylight warriors, but they have trained with us for many seasons, and I trust their loyalty to their Clanmates."

"We could train too!" Riley argued; Barley hushed him with a sweep of his tail across the young cat's muzzle.

"I cannot fault their enthusiasm," Leafstar commented to Ravenpaw. She tipped her head to one side. "But why have you come all this way to ask if they can join SkyClan? Why couldn't Firestar take Riley and Bella into ThunderClan?"

Ravenpaw blinked. "Because ThunderClan has gone," he managed to say, feeling grief choke him afresh. "All the Clans have left the forest. The forest was torn up to make room for a Thunderpath, and there was nowhere for the warriors to stay. I watched them leave, but I . . . I don't know where they are now."

Leafstar's eyes clouded. "Poor Firestar and Sandstorm, having to leave their home! I hope that they are safe, wherever they are."

"I believe that they are," Ravenpaw meowed. "StarClan would have told me if something terrible had happened, I think." He noticed Barley shoot a sideways glance at him, and Ravenpaw felt a twinge of guilt. He rarely spoke of StarClan to his friend, and perhaps Barley had assumed that his warrior ancestors no longer meant anything to him.

Leafstar sighed. "I have tried to keep the memory of Firestar and Sandstorm alive in my Clan," she murmured. "SkyClan owes everything to them. But many seasons have passed, and not all my warriors were there in the beginning." She drew herself up again. "Any friend of Firestar's is welcome to visit my Clan, but only as our guest. We will always be grateful for what Firestar and Sandstorm did. But we cannot accept unknown cats to train as warriors. I am sorry."

She turned to leave, making it clear that her welcome to Firestar's friends began and ended at the border to her Clan. The other cats followed, except for Plumwillow, who paused to hiss, "Don't steal any of our prey!" before trotting after her Clanmates.

Ravenpaw stared at the disappearing warriors in dismay.

"They were *mean!*" Bella growled.

"They didn't even give us a chance to show off our battle moves!" Riley muttered.

"I'm sorry," Ravenpaw mewed. "I didn't think she'd be like that."

"Let's go back to that cave in the gorge," Barley suggested. "I don't think we should hang around too close to the border." He padded over to Bella, whose tail was drooping. "I'm still very proud of you," he told her. "And you, Riley. You've learned so much on this journey! You're brave and strong and smart. You'd be great warriors. Wouldn't they, Ravenpaw?"

"Yes, of course." Ravenpaw started to walk back down the stream. His pelt burned. Why had he raised the hopes of these young cats, all for nothing but sore paws and travel-stained fur? A sharp pain jabbed in his belly, and he stumbled.

In a heartbeat Barley was beside him, propping him up. "Are you okay?"

"Just tired," Ravenpaw rasped. "I'll be okay once we get to the cave."

Barley stayed beside him, fussing, until he was settled on the dusty orange floor. Riley and Bella slumped down beside him with their chins on their paws.

"I'll go hunt," Barley meowed. "You stay here and rest."

Ravenpaw slept deeply until something prodded him in his side, sending a spasm through his belly. Riley and Bella were standing in the cave beside him, their eyes huge. It was dark—Ravenpaw had slept for longer than he thought—and Barley was curled at his back.

"Something's happening!" Bella squeaked.

Ravenpaw pricked his ears. Faint yowls and shrieks echoed along the banks of the gorge.

"Do you think SkyClan is being attacked?" whispered Riley.

"I don't know. Whatever it is, it doesn't sound good." Ravenpaw stood up and walked to the mouth of the cave.

"Where are you going?" Barley rumbled, sitting up.

"To see what's going on."

"Not without me," meowed Barley.

"Or us!" Riley and Bella put in.

Ravenpaw sighed. "Okay. But you'll have to be quiet."

"We'll be quiet as mice," Riley promised.

Bella put her head to one side. "Actually, mice are noisy.

Always squeaking and rustling around."

"Quieter than dead mice, then!" her brother hissed.

They padded along the stream to where the banks flattened out among the trees. The sounds of cats in distress grew louder. Ravenpaw passed the holly bush with the border mark and glanced back at the others, nodding to show that they should follow. Now they were inside SkyClan's territory. Ravenpaw felt his fur stand on end, but he kept going, still treading quietly even though any noise they might make would be drowned out by the screeches coming from in front of them.

He reached the edge of the trees and paused. In the starlight, Ravenpaw made out a huge, dark shape looming over the stream. A rock, perhaps? Beyond it, cats flashed back and forth between sandy cliffs, shrieking in alarm and fury. Ravenpaw twitched his tail to get the others' attention, then raced to the nearest cliff, which sloped up gently at first, then more steeply, to a huge expanse of scrubby grass. On the far side, bright yellow lights twinkled; that must be a Twolegplace, Ravenpaw guessed.

He padded to the edge of the cliff and looked down. He felt very exposed, but none of the cats in the gorge below noticed him. Barley, Riley, and Bella crept up beside him and stared in horror. Amid the crisscrossing paths that lined the valley, cats were charging back and forth, yowling in anger. A heap of soft, dark shapes went flying; from the scents that drifted up to the top of the cliff, Ravenpaw guessed that the fresh-kill pile had been scattered.

As Ravenpaw's eyes grew used to the starlight, he realized that five or six cats were chasing the others, rousting them with shrieks and hisses. More and more cats spilled from dens in the side of the cliff, including some tiny kits who looked barely able to walk.

"Get them back to the nursery!" screeched a she-cat.

"Poor little kits, too small to be away from their mother," jeered a familiar voice.

Ravenpaw looked at Barley. That was Pasha! He peered into the gorge again and made out the shapes of the other cats who had terrorized them the previous night. Were they taking on the whole of SkyClan?

"Warriors, to me!" yowled Leafstar, her cream patches glowing in the half-light. At last a more or less orderly line of cats formed up, and they charged at the intruders, hissing and spitting. With a chorus of mocking screeches, the kittypets whirled around and scrambled back up the cliff.

"We'll be back!" Pasha yowled, so close to Ravenpaw that he almost stepped on him.

Ravenpaw and his companions crouched in the grass without breathing until the kittypets had thundered away. Below, the SkyClan camp fell silent apart from the whimpering of kits as they were ushered back to their nest, and the angry muttering from elders who had been disturbed from sleep.

"Three nights in a row!" hissed one of them.

Leafstar spoke soothingly. "We'll find a way to stop them, I promise. Go back to your dens and get some rest."

"Whoa!" breathed Bella. "Those kittypets are giving

SkyClan a lot of trouble!"

Ravenpaw backed away from the edge of the cliff. His pelt smelled strongly of SkyClan, and he realized he had been lying on top of a border mark.

"Imagine having to put up with that every night!" Barley remarked.

They started to walk back down the slope to the stream.

"I don't understand why they let those kittypets get into their camp," Riley mewed. "SkyClan cats are warriors! They should be able to defend themselves!"

Ravenpaw shook his head. "I don't think the kittypets were there for any real purpose. They just wanted to wake everyone up and cause trouble."

"Thankfully, it's their trouble, not ours," meowed Barley. "Look, here's the cave. Come on, you two, get some sleep. We'll start for home tomorrow. Leafstar has made it clear that there's nothing to keep us here." He shooed Riley and Bella inside and curled around them.

Ravenpaw lay down near the entrance, his chin on his paws. Barley was right; if Leafstar wanted them to go, there was no reason to stay here any longer. But he couldn't forget the image of the warriors shrieking in dismay as their camp was invaded. Surely there was something SkyClan could do to stop it?

CHAPTER 9

❧

Ravenpaw opened his eyes to find that he was lying on smooth stone beside a still, star-filled pool. He sat up and looked around. Behind him, a pock-marked slope spiraled up to the top of the hollow. The stone beneath him was cool, but his fur felt warm. He padded to the edge of the pool and drank, feeling the water surge through him like light. He became aware of a cat standing beside him with her tail resting lightly on his back.

"Come sit with me, Ravenpaw," Silverstream purred. She positioned herself neatly on the rock with her tail folded over her paws and waited while Ravenpaw settled himself more slowly, wincing at the ache in his belly.

Ravenpaw noticed her watching him with concern. "I'm getting old!" he joked.

Silverstream just looked at him with huge blue eyes.

Ravenpaw felt a chill creep over his pelt. "I . . . I'm not going to see my home again, am I?"

"No," Silverstream admitted. "But you must not be afraid of dying somewhere else." There was a catch in her voice. "All that matters is that you are not alone, and that you know you are loved."

Ravenpaw felt a painful lump rise in his throat. "I'm afraid for Barley," he whispered.

"Barley knows that you don't want to leave him. He understands, and he will not love you less if he cannot see you."

Two more cats approached the edge of the pool: one dark gray tom with glowing blue eyes, the other a broad-shouldered tom with gray-and-white fur. Silverstream stood up and nodded to them, then padded away up the spiraling path.

The dark gray tom spoke first. "My name is Skywatcher," he meowed. "I was the last of the SkyClan warriors, until Firestar and Sandstorm came to save my Clan. There is a place for Riley and Bella in SkyClan, I promise. Be patient and you will help them find it."

"And I am Cloudstar, leader of SkyClan when we first came to the gorge," rasped the gray and white cat. "And before, when we lived in the forest with the other Clans."

Ravenpaw dipped his head. "I am honored to meet you both."

"I made the same journey as Firestar and Sandstorm, and now you and your friends," Cloudstar meowed. "I am grateful to you for bringing new warriors to my Clan."

"But they don't want them!" Ravenpaw burst out. "Leafstar wouldn't even let us cross the border!"

"Give them a chance to see what these cats can bring to the Clan," Cloudstar countered. "SkyClan needs your help. You saw that tonight."

Ravenpaw lashed his tail. "But SkyClan has its own strong warriors! Leafstar was quick to make that clear. What can we do that they can't?"

Without speaking, Skywatcher moved to the edge of the pool and flicked a pebble into the water. It landed with a splash and sent starry ripples out in circles, rolling all the way to the sides of the hollow.

"Look," Skywatcher ordered. "The stone reaches much farther than you might expect. Do you see?"

Ravenpaw watched the trembling waves and pictured SkyClan, scared and defensive inside the gorge, waiting for the kittypets to storm across the empty ground and invade their camp again. His mind cleared and he nodded. "I see," he replied.

Cloudstar rested his muzzle on top of Ravenpaw's head. "Please help us," he murmured. "In the name of the Clans, and the warrior code."

"I will," Ravenpaw promised.

He woke as the first gray light of dawn spilled into the cave. Outside, the air was cool and scented with leaves. Ravenpaw nudged Barley. "Wake up!"

"Is it time to go home?" Bella mewed sleepily. Beside her, Riley yawned.

"We're not going home," Ravenpaw announced. "We're going back to SkyClan."

Barley stopped mid-stretch. "What? They wouldn't even let us across the border yesterday." He narrowed his eyes. "And you need to get back to the barn for some rest."

"I'm okay," Ravenpaw told him. "I dreamed of StarClan

last night, and I saw something that can help deal with the kittypets."

"Let's go!" mewed Riley, running to the mouth of the cave. "Those fox-brained kittypets need to respect SkyClan!"

Ravenpaw felt a flash of pride at Riley's loyalty to a Clan that had treated him like a trespasser.

Bella nodded. "If there's anything we can do to help, then we have to go back."

Barley sighed. "I can see I'm outnumbered," he mewed. He brushed the tip of his tail along Ravenpaw's spine. "But if you need to stop and rest, tell me, okay? I know something's hurting you."

"I will."

Ravenpaw led them up the stream once more. They paused among the trees to hunt; Barley made Ravenpaw lie on some comfy moss while he and the young cats cornered a pigeon that was pecking at the foot of a beech tree. As soon as they had eaten and cleaned their muzzles, they continued to the edge of the woods.

In daylight, Ravenpaw could clearly see the huge, gray-brown boulder that hung over the stream. The water vanished beneath the rock, and sun-dappled ripples cast patterns of light onto the bottom of the stone. They had hardly gone past the holly bush when several figures appeared, running toward them. Plumwillow was in the lead.

"We told you to stay away!" she growled.

A ginger tom bounded beside her, his hackles raised.

"Get out of here!"

"Plumwillow, Bouncefire, wait!" A silver tabby she-cat with clear green eyes sprang down from a path near the foot of the cliff and blocked their way. "Enough! These cats mean no harm."

"We don't know that," Bouncefire muttered, but he stayed where he was and watched as the silver-gray cat approached Ravenpaw and his companions. Ravenpaw picked up the clean scent of herbs on her pelt and spotted a scrap of cobweb clinging to her ear.

"My name is Echosong," she meowed. "I am SkyClan's medicine cat. Leafstar told me about you."

Her voice was gentle, and Ravenpaw let the fur on his spine relax. "I need to speak with Leafstar. Please, it's important."

Echosong studied him for a moment, then turned, her fluffy silver tail straight up. "Follow me." She led them past Plumwillow and Bouncefire, who hissed under his breath, and up one of the narrow paths. She paused and looked back. "I'm sorry," she mewed. "There isn't much room in Leafstar's den. I can take Ravenpaw to her, but would the rest of you mind staying down here?"

Barley glanced at the warriors who had started to emerge from dens and behind rocks at the bottom of the valley.

"Don't worry, you're quite safe," Echosong told him. "Hawkpaw will look after you."

A sturdy little cat with sleek gray fur and piercing yellow eyes who had just come out of a den nodded. "Absolutely," he promised.

"Thank you," Echosong meowed. "Let me know if Ebonyclaw arrives and needs you to do something else." She went on to Ravenpaw, "Ebonyclaw is a daylight warrior, so she's not here yet. Hawkpaw is her apprentice."

"He seems very committed," Ravenpaw remarked.

Echosong nodded. "He is. As long as we keep him away from Billystorm's apprentice, Pebblepaw. The two of them do not get along!"

They left Barley, Riley, and Bella standing rather awkwardly with the gray apprentice and continued up the path. It led past several small caves—warrior dens, Ravenpaw guessed from the scents that wafted out—to a ledge where three cats sat: Leafstar, a ginger-and-white tom with a broad, handsome face, and a dark ginger tom whose gaze raked Ravenpaw's pelt as he approached.

Leafstar dipped her head. "Ravenpaw. I wasn't expecting to see you again." She indicated the cats beside her, the scowling dark ginger tom first. "This is Sharpclaw, my deputy. And this is Billystorm. Whatever you have to tell me, you can say in front of them."

Ravenpaw took a deep breath and hoped the warriors couldn't hear his heart pounding. "I want to help you with the kittypet, er . . . problem. We saw what happened last night, and I think there's a way you could stop it."

Sharpclaw stood up, hackles raised. "So you were trespassing?" he growled.

"We were on the cliff top, on the other side of your border marks," Ravenpaw replied, trying not to let his paws shake.

"Sit down, Sharpclaw," Leafstar mewed.

The ginger tom slowly folded his hind legs beneath him. "Those kittypets are a nuisance, nothing more," he rasped. "We're not afraid of them."

"But they must be taught to respect your boundaries," Ravenpaw meowed. "You cannot let them come into the heart of your camp!"

"We're hardly welcoming them in!" Billystorm pointed out.

Leafstar raised one paw. "Do you think you know a way to keep them out of the camp, Ravenpaw?" Her tone was light, as if she was prepared to listen to him out of politeness.

Ravenpaw stood up and unsheathed his front claws to mark a shape on the sandy ledge. With a few swift lines he made a circle with ripples spreading outward, just like the pattern in the moonlit pool in his dream.

"This is your camp," he explained, pointing to the circle in the center. "But the boundaries need to be much farther out, to keep trespassers at a safe distance." He rested his paw on the outermost ripple. "This is the point that you need to defend, halfway across the empty ground between your camp and the Twoleg dens. If you make that your boundary, and prove to the kittypets that you will not let them cross, then your home will be safe."

"Who are you to tell us about boundaries?" Sharpclaw huffed. "You're not even a Clan cat."

But Leafstar nodded, staring down at the marks in the sand. "You mean we should move our boundary back from the edge of the gorge? Yes, I can see there is sense in that. It will be harder to patrol because there are so few points to place markers out there, but it would certainly protect the gorge." She looked up at Ravenpaw. "How would you teach the kittypets to stay away from the new boundary?"

Ravenpaw gulped. Memories of his time in ThunderClan whirled in his head: patrols, checking border marks, training with Tigerclaw . . . "Constant patrols along the new border, all night, until the kittypets learn exactly where it lies," he meowed. "Your warriors will need to rest during the day, but perhaps the daylight cats can take over duties then? You might only need a constant patrol for one night, if you fight hard enough."

"We always fight hard enough!" Sharpclaw snarled.

Ravenpaw blinked. "Before sunhigh today, you must set markers along the new boundary. Build places to mark, if you must, from branches or piles of stones. Then rest until dusk, when every warrior and apprentice must take their place along the border. The kittypets must not be allowed to set one paw across the line." He stopped, panting. His belly was gripped by a spasm, and he tried hard not to curl into a ball to ease it.

Leafstar studied Ravenpaw with a thoughtful gleam in her eyes. "Once again, ThunderClan comes to help us," she mewed.

"Oh, I'm not ThunderClan anymore," Ravenpaw replied.

Leafstar didn't say anything. Instead she stood up and padded down the path to the bottom of the gorge, then leaped gracefully onto the boulder. "SkyClan, gather here!" she yowled.

Ravenpaw limped down behind Sharpclaw and Billystorm to join Barley. The black-and-white cat regarded him with concern, but Ravenpaw just nodded toward Leafstar, who was explaining the plan to expand the Clan's boundaries. Her Clanmates listened in silence, with frequent glances at the visitors. When Leafstar had finished, she beckoned to Ravenpaw with her tail. Ravenpaw gulped.

"Go on!" Bella squeaked, bouncing on her paws with excitement.

Ravenpaw stayed where he was—he didn't think he could jump anywhere with this pain in his belly—and turned to face the crowd of cats. "You are stronger than you realize," he began, raising his voice in spite of the throbbing inside him.

There were a few indignant murmurs.

"You know nothing about how strong we are!"

"Come here and fight if you think we're so weak!"

Ravenpaw carried on. "Unlike kittypets, you have your warrior ancestors on your side, and your faith in the warrior code to keep you strong. You have to make an invisible boundary visible—and *painful*—to the kittypets who show you no respect." He drew another breath. "They are not warriors! They will not win!"

"They are not warriors! They will not win!" echoed the cats, and Ravenpaw sagged with relief. Leafstar met his gaze and nodded.

Sharpclaw bounded onto the rock and began dividing the cats into patrols to trace out the boundary and create new markers far back from the edge of the cliff. To Ravenpaw's surprise, he paused and growled at Riley and Bella, "I suppose you want to help too?"

The young cats nodded so hard their ears flapped.

Sharpclaw flicked his tail at Riley. "You go with Cherry-tail, Waspwhisker, and Dustpaw to pile up stones for the new markers." Riley ran over to join the patrol. Sharpclaw gestured to Bella. "You can help Bouncefire and Blossompaw fetch sticks from the woods."

"What about the daylight warriors?" Plumwillow called from the middle of the crowd. "Are they going to do all the regular duties so we can rest before the fight?"

A slender black-and-white tom popped his head up. "We'll do all that, *and* stay to fight," he declared. Around him, several cats nodded. "We are SkyClan as much as you are! This is our battle too!"

"Thank you, Macgyver," Sharpclaw meowed.

"I've been invited to join a hunting patrol," Barley murmured in Ravenpaw's ear. "But you need to get some rest."

Ravenpaw opened his mouth to object, but Barley went on. "I can see you're in pain. Don't lie to me, please. Just look after yourself while I help with the fresh-kill pile."

Ravenpaw nodded. "I'll be here when you get back," he promised.

He watched the black-and-white cat trot over to a patrol that included Firefern. The ginger she-cat greeted him frostily, but a brown tom seemed more welcoming and fell in beside Barley as they padded out of the camp.

Echosong appeared beside Ravenpaw. "Are you feeling up

to a climb?" she asked. "It's not far, and I promise it will be worth it."

"Of course," Ravenpaw meowed. He followed her along the gorge and up a path that wound back and forth at tight angles until it reached the top of the cliff. Ravenpaw scrambled onto the flat ground with a grunt of relief.

"It gets easier," Echosong told him, hardly out of breath. She pointed with her tail to a rocky slab that jutted out over the gorge. "This is a very special place for SkyClan," she explained. "It's where we gather at the full moon, and where I come to speak with StarClan." She padded onto the rock and gestured to Ravenpaw to lie down beside her.

"I love it up here," Echosong murmured, gazing out at the gorge and the woods beyond. "It's so peaceful, and yet you can see everything that's going on."

Ravenpaw nodded. He could see Barley's black-and-white shape leaping through the trees; farther along the cliff, Riley was rolling a stone with his paws. Then he heard footsteps behind him and turned to see three cats approaching. He was faintly aware that Echosong had vanished and he was alone on the rock.

The figures were so familiar that his heart ached and he had to blink to see clearly. Bluestar, Whitestorm, and Lionheart stepped onto the rock and stood in front of him, each one dipping their head in respect.

"We are honored to see you again," Bluestar mewed. "Don't stand up," she added as Ravenpaw struggled to get his hind legs under him.

"I am the one who is honored," Ravenpaw purred.

"We have never forgotten you," Whitestorm told him. "We have watched over you, and rejoiced in the happiness you have found with Barley." He dropped his head. "I am only sorry we could not spare you the pain you suffered in ThunderClan."

"I wouldn't change a thing," Ravenpaw promised. "If anything had been different, I might not have had my life with Barley. I have been happier than I ever imagined a cat could be."

Lionheart gazed at him, and Ravenpaw felt his pelt glow with warmth. "We have come to do something we should have done a long time ago," the golden tabby explained. "We would like to give you your warrior name. You have more than earned it, with the courage, fairness, and loyalty you have shown to these cats, and to every cat who has crossed your path."

Ravenpaw took a deep breath. How often he had dreamed of this moment when he had been an apprentice, wondering what his warrior name would be! But he was no longer an apprentice, no longer part of ThunderClan or the forest. He looked at the noble cats in front of him.

"Thank you," he purred. "But I already have a name. I am proud to have been Ravenpaw all my life, and I see no reason to change it now."

Bluestar nodded. "I thought you might feel that way." She traced her paw across the stone. "You know that your time is drawing to an end, I think. Would you like to join us in StarClan? You would be very welcome."

Ravenpaw turned and looked down at the gorge. He could

see Barley standing at the edge of the woods, looking up at him. The black-and-white cat kinked his tail in greeting, and Ravenpaw waved his tail in reply. Then he turned back to the StarClan cats.

"I cannot join you," he mewed softly. "There is someone I need to wait for. I hope there is a place where we can be together, even though he is not a Clan cat."

Lionheart nodded. "We understand. And rest assured, there is a place waiting for you both. But you are welcome to visit us in StarClan whenever you wish. You will find a way, I promise."

He reached forward and rested his muzzle on Ravenpaw's head. Ravenpaw felt his soft breath against his fur, and slipped gratefully into painless sleep.

CHAPTER 10

♣

When Ravenpaw woke, Echosong was sitting beside him, her tail twitching.

"Ah, you're awake," she mewed.

The sun was sliding behind the trees, and dusky shadows were gathering in the gorge. The bare, scrubby grass that led to the Twolegplace was empty and quiet, but Ravenpaw scented fresh border marks drifting on the breeze. Cats circled restlessly in the SkyClan camp below.

"The new boundary is in place," Echosong told him as they made their way down the cliff. "My Clanmates are ready to defend it with their lives."

"I hope it doesn't come to that," Ravenpaw meowed with a stir of alarm.

Riley and Bella bounded up to him as he approached the boulder. "We've had such a great day!" Riley announced. "I was totally the best at pushing stones. Cherrytail told me!"

"And I found the longest stick!" Bella mewed. "Blossompaw helped me carry it."

A brown tom called to them.

"That's Rabbitleap," Riley explained. "We're in his patrol

tonight. See you later, Ravenpaw!"

The young cats whirled around and raced off.

Barley padded up to Ravenpaw, the scent of fresh-kill clinging to his pelt. "They've made friends already," he observed.

"There are some good cats in SkyClan," Ravenpaw agreed.
"How was the hunting?"

"Not bad at all. I caught two mice and a squirrel, which
silenced a few comments." There was a note of amusement in
Barley's voice. "Have you eaten yet?"

Ravenpaw's stomach churned at the thought of food. A
spasm of pain racked his body, and shadows swam behind his
eyes. He felt Barley press against him, holding him up.

"You need to lie down," his friend told him. He steered
Ravenpaw to a soft patch of sand at the edge of the gorge.
Ravenpaw sank down with a hiss of pain.

"You can't fight tonight," Barley mewed. His eyes were
huge with alarm. "You're not strong enough."

Ravenpaw gazed at his friend. "Oh, Barley. You know me
so well. Better than any cat ever has." He nudged Barley's
cheek with his nose. "But there is a secret that I have kept
from you without meaning to: I have always been a warrior. I
have a loyalty to these cats, and I must fight alongside them,
whatever happens."

Barley's eyes filled with water. "You're so stubborn," he
murmured. "I really can't stop you, can I?"

"No. But you can be at my side," Ravenpaw replied. "Please."

Barley leaned his head against Ravenpaw's. "Always."

Ravenpaw stood up with effort, and they joined the other

cats as they trekked in silence up the gorge and onto the plain of rustling grass. Sharpclaw signaled with his tail to send them out along the new border, the marks fresh and pungent on newly built heaps of stones and sticks. *They've worked hard today*, Ravenpaw thought.

On either side of him, the SkyClan warriors moved quickly and efficiently. It was impossible to tell which cats were the daylight warriors, apart from the faintest hint of a different scent on their fur. It was clear that, no matter where SkyClan found its warriors, this was a well-trained and deeply loyal Clan.

Ravenpaw and Barley crouched down in the grass alongside Billystorm and his apprentice, Pebblepaw. Her white fur was dusted with brown speckles, which kept her well hidden among the moonlit grass. Ravenpaw had lost sight of Riley and Bella farther along the line. He hoped they remembered everything he had taught them. *StarClan, keep them safe!*

Sharpclaw's quiet hiss traveled along the row of cats in the still air: "At my signal, *fight!*"

It seemed as if a whole moon passed before they heard paws thudding over the ground toward them. Ravenpaw tensed. There were more kittypets this time, and they were already shrieking with excitement. *They have no idea we are waiting for them!*

Beside Ravenpaw, Billystorm unsheathed his claws and gathered his haunches under him, ready to spring. Closer, closer, closer the kittypets thundered . . .

"Fight!" yowled Sharpclaw, and the SkyClan cats leaped forward in a single, hissing wave.

The kittypets scrambled to a halt, yowling in terror. They were vastly outnumbered but still put up a fight, taking on two or three SkyClan warriors each in a whirling fury of teeth and claws. All at once Ravenpaw was an apprentice again, remembering everything Tigerclaw had taught him. He leaped and dodged and lashed out with his claws. At his side, Barley fought like his shadow, matching him step for step, the equal of any warrior.

In the half-light, Ravenpaw found himself crashing into a she-cat with distinctive silver-and-black fur. It was one of the kittypets who had tormented them on their first night.

"*You're* still here?" she spat.

"We're more welcome here than you are!" puffed Barley, slamming into her flank.

The she-cat sprang away and launched herself at them, claws out. Ravenpaw folded his legs and ducked out of the way; as the she-cat skidded past, he reared up and brought his front paws down on her haunches. She dropped to the ground with a snarl, then gathered her hind legs and kicked straight back into Ravenpaw's exposed belly.

A white-hot pain seared through him. He was aware of Barley charging at the kittypet, raking his claws down her back and sending her shrieking across the grass. Ravenpaw fell backward and lay still, panting, waiting for the spasm to ease. He heard Barley thudding after the kittypet. The ground thrummed with the sound of fleeing paws, the kittypets being chased away by gleeful, hissing warriors.

Gradually silence fell over the plain. Cats came padding

back, a few of them limping. Ravenpaw heard a cheer: "We won! They're gone!"

The warriors started to move more quickly, running back to the gorge, to the camp they had kept safe, in order to celebrate.

Barley's face loomed over Ravenpaw. "Are you all right? Have you been injured?"

Ravenpaw shook his head and heaved himself up. Barley started to fuss, but Ravenpaw shot him a glare. There would be time for that later; now he wanted to share in SkyClan's victory. He stumbled back down to the gorge, leaning heavily on Barley's shoulder. Leafstar was standing on top of the rock, her cream patches of fur glowing in the moonlight.

"Ravenpaw, there you are!" she called. "SkyClan thanks you for helping us tonight! Without you, those kittypets might never have respected our borders."

The cats around the rock turned to look at Ravenpaw, their eyes gleaming like tiny stars, and yowled in triumph. Ravenpaw closed his eyes in relief. *We did it!*

There was a stir beside him, and Riley and Bella appeared from the throng. Their pelts were ruffled, and Bella had a claw mark on one ear, but they were quivering with excitement.

"Oh, wow!" Riley gasped. "That was amazing!"

"We did everything you showed us!" Bella mewed. "I did a front-paw blow that made a kittypet fall over!"

"Well done," Ravenpaw purred, trying not to show his pain. "I'm so proud of you!"

"We both are," Barley meowed.

"Riley, Bella, are you there?" Leafstar called from the rock. "I have something important to ask you."

The young cats glanced at each other, then pushed their way to the front of the cats. "We're here!" Bella mewed.

Leafstar beckoned to them with her tail. "Come, join me."

Riley and Bella scrambled up the boulder and stood on top. Leafstar faced them. "You fought well tonight," she praised. "As bravely as any of my Clanmates, in fact. I was wrong to think that I needed to know a cat from kithood before I could trust them. You have proved that you belong here."

Bella let out a tiny squeak.

Leafstar dipped her head. "Riley, Bella, will you do Sky-Clan the honor of joining us?"

Ravenpaw felt his heart flip over. Beside him, Barley purred so loudly his whiskers trembled.

The SkyClan leader nodded to two of her warriors. "Tinycloud, Nettlesplash, will you be their mentors?"

"With pleasure," meowed Tinycloud, a slight-framed white she-cat. Beside her, a sturdy brown tom nodded.

"Rileypaw, Bellapaw, StarClan welcomes you to SkyClan as apprentices." Leafstar began the ceremony, and Ravenpaw was plunged back to the clearing at the bottom of the ravine, listening to Bluestar announce his apprentice name for the first time.

"You need to rest," Barley whispered in his ear. Without arguing, Ravenpaw allowed his friend to usher him along the path that led to Echosong's den. His head was buzzing, but he could hear the SkyClan cats cheering, "Rileypaw! Bellapaw!" behind him.

A pale silver shape met them on the path. *Silverstream?* Ravenpaw wondered blurrily.

"Ah, Ravenpaw," murmured Echosong. "Come with me."

She turned to go into her den, but Ravenpaw hesitated. "Not inside, please," he rasped. "I'd rather be under the trees."

Echosong nodded, and she nudged him gently around until they were padding toward the woods.

"Wait!" Barley mewed, trotting alongside. "He's very sick! Shouldn't you take him to your den and treat him?"

"It is too late for that, Barley," Echosong murmured. "We must do what Ravenpaw wishes now."

They reached the rustling trees, and Ravenpaw sank down onto a patch of soft, cool grass. He felt shadows gathering around him, tugging at his limbs. He wasn't afraid; he knew it was time. Rileypaw and Bellapaw would live as warriors now, thanks to him. But Barley . . .

His old friend curled around him, just as he had always done when they slept. Ravenpaw could feel him trembling, and he wished there were something he could do to comfort him.

"It's all right," Barley whispered, his voice breaking. "I know you have to leave me. I will never forget you, I promise."

Ravenpaw gasped for one more breath. "I will wait for you. Wherever you are, I will find you." He let his head fall onto Barley's front paw. Everything was starting to feel very far away.

Somewhere in the distance, he heard cats approaching.

"We will give him a warrior's farewell," Leafstar meowed. "He may be far from home, but SkyClan will be honored to sit vigil for him."

There was a gulp from Barley.

I'm sorry, my friend, Ravenpaw thought. He let the shadows fill his mind. Around him, the trees shimmered with starlight, and his legs felt young and strong again. The pain in his belly had gone. Ravenpaw stood up and looked down at Barley. *I will always watch over you,* he vowed. Then he turned and walked into the woods. His heart cried out to stay with his friend, but he knew he had to keep walking. The shadows closed around him, but somewhere ahead there was warm sunshine creeping through the trees, and the scent of prey.

Farewell, Barley. I will see you again one day.

ERIN HUNTER

is inspired by a love of cats and a fascination with the ferocity of the natural world. As well as having great respect for nature in all its forms, Erin enjoys creating rich mythical explanations for animal behavior. She is also the author of the bestselling Seekers and Survivors series.

Download the free Warriors app and chat on Warriors message boards at www.warriorcats.com.

A new adventure begins for the warrior Clans.

Read on for a sneak peek at

A VISION OF SHADOWS

WARRIORS

BOOK ONE:
THE APPRENTICE'S
QUEST

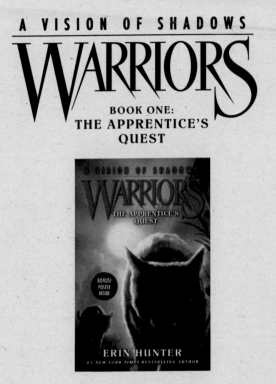

For many moons, the warrior cats have lived in peace in their territories around the lake. But a dark shadow looms on the horizon, and the time has come for Alderpaw—son of the ThunderClan leader, Bramblestar, and his deputy, Squirrelflight—to shape his destiny . . . and the fate of all the warrior Clans.

CHAPTER 1

❧

Alderkit stood in front of the nursery, nervously shifting his weight. He unsheathed his claws, digging them into the beaten earth of the stone hollow, then sheathed them again and shook dust from his paws.

Now what happens? he asked himself, his belly churning as he thought about his apprentice ceremony that was only moments away. *What if there's some sort of an assessment before I can be an apprentice?*

Alderkit thought he had heard something about an assessment once. Perhaps it had been a few moons ago when Hollytuft, Fernsong, and Sorrelstripe were made warriors. *But I can't really remember . . . I was so little then.*

His heart started to pound faster and faster. He tried to convince himself that some cat would have told him if he was supposed to prove that he was ready. *Because I'm not sure that I am ready to become an apprentice. Not sure at all. What if I can't do it?*

Deep in his own thoughts, Alderkit jumped in surprise as some cat nudged him hard from behind. Spinning around, he saw his sister Sparkkit, her orange tabby fur bushing out in all directions.

"Aren't you excited?" she asked with an enthusiastic bounce. "Don't you want to know who your mentor will be? I hope I get someone *fun*! Not a bossy cat like Berrynose, or one like Whitewing. She sticks so close to the rules I think she must recite the warrior code in her sleep!"

"That's enough." The kits' mother, Squirrelflight, emerged from the nursery in time to hear Sparkkit's last words. "You're not supposed to *have fun* with your mentor," she added, licking one paw and smoothing it over Sparkkit's pelt. "You're supposed to *learn* from them. Berrynose and Whitewing are both fine warriors. You'd be very lucky to have either of them as your mentor."

Though Squirrelflight's voice was sharp, her green gaze shone with love for her kits. Alderkit knew how much his mother adored him and his sister. He was only a kit, but he knew that Squirrelflight was old to have her first litter, and he remembered their shared grief for his lost littermates: Juniperkit, who had barely taken a breath before he died, and Dandelionkit, who had never been strong and who had slowly weakened until she also died two moons later.

Sparkkit and I have to be the best cats we can be for Squirrelflight and Bramblestar.

Sparkkit, meanwhile, wasn't at all cowed by her mother's scolding. She twitched her tail and cheerfully shook her pelt until her fur fluffed up again.

Alderkit wished he had her confidence. He hadn't wondered until now who his mentor would be, and he gazed around the clearing at the other cats with new and curious eyes. *Ivypool would be an okay mentor,* he thought, spotting the silver-and-white tabby she-cat returning from a hunting patrol with Lionblaze and Blossomfall. *She's friendly and a good hunter. Lionblaze is a bit scary, though.* Alderkit suppressed a shiver at the sight of the muscles rippling beneath the golden warrior's pelt. *And it won't be Blossomfall, because she was just mentor for Hollytuft. Or Brackenfur or Rosepetal, because they mentored Sorrelstripe and Fernsong.*

Lost in thought, Alderkit watched Thornclaw, who had paused in the middle of the clearing to give himself a good scratch behind one ear. *He'd probably be okay, though he's sort of short-tempered. . . .*

"Hey, wake up!" Sparkkit trod down hard on Alderkit's paw. "It's starting!"

Alderkit realized that Bramblestar had appeared on the Highledge outside his den, way above their heads on the wall of the stone hollow.

"Let every cat old enough to catch their own prey join here beneath the Highledge for a Clan meeting!" Bramblestar yowled.

Alderkit gazed at his father admiringly as all the cats in the clearing turned their attention to him and began to gather together. *He's so confident and strong. I'm so lucky to be the son of such an amazing cat.*

Bramblestar ran lightly down the tumbled rocks and took his place in the center of the ragged circle of cats that was forming at the foot of the rock wall. Squirrelflight gently nudged her two kits forward until they too stood in the circle.

Alderkit's belly began to churn even harder, and he tightened all his muscles to stop himself from trembling. *I can't do this!* he thought, struggling not to panic.

Then he caught sight of his father's gaze on him: such a warm, proud look that Alderkit instantly felt comforted. He took a few deep breaths, forcing himself to relax.

"Cats of ThunderClan," Bramblestar began, "this is a good day for us, because it's time to make two new apprentices. Sparkkit, come here, please."

Instantly Sparkkit bounced into the center of the circle, her tail standing straight up and her fur bristling with excitement. She gazed confidently at her leader.

"From this day forward," Bramblestar meowed, touching Sparkkit on her shoulder with his tail-tip, "this apprentice will be known as Sparkpaw. Cherryfall, you will be her mentor. I trust that you will pass on to her your dedication to your Clan, your quick mind, and your excellent hunting skills."

Sparkpaw dashed across the circle to Cherryfall, bouncing with happiness, and the ginger she-cat bent her head to touch noses with her.

"Sparkpaw! Sparkpaw!" the Clan began to yowl.

Sparkpaw gave a pleased little hop as her Clanmates chanted her new name, her eyes shining as she stood beside her mentor.

Alderkit joined in the acclamation, pleased to see how happy his sister looked. *Thank StarClan! There wasn't any kind of test to prove that she was ready.*

As the yowling died away, Bramblestar beckoned to Alderkit with his tail. "Your turn," he meowed, his gaze encouraging Alderkit on.

Alderkit's legs suddenly felt wobbly as he staggered into the center of the circle. His chest felt tight, as if he couldn't breathe properly. But as he halted in front of Bramblestar, his father gave him a slight nod to steady him, and he stood with his head raised as Bramblestar rested the tip of his tail on his shoulder.

"From this day forward, this apprentice will be known as Alderpaw," Bramblestar announced. "Molewhisker, you will be his mentor. You are loyal, determined, and brave, and I know that you will do your best to pass on these qualities to your apprentice."

As he padded across the clearing to join his mentor, Alderpaw wasn't sure how he felt. He knew that Molewhisker was Cherryfall's littermate, but the big cream-and-brown tom was much quieter than his sister, and had never shown much interest in the kits. His gaze was solemn as he bent to touch noses with Alderpaw.

I hope I can make you proud of me, Alderpaw thought. *I'm going to try my hardest!*

"Alderpaw! Alderpaw!"

Alderpaw ducked his head and gave his chest fur a few embarrassed licks as he heard his Clan caterwauling his name. At the same time, he thought he would burst with happiness.

At last the chanting died away and the crowd of cats began to disperse, heading toward their dens or the fresh-kill pile. Squirrelflight and Bramblestar padded over to join their kits.

"Well done," Bramblestar meowed. "It wasn't so scary, was it?"

"It was great!" Sparkpaw responded, her tail waving in the air. "I can't wait to go hunting!"

"We're so proud of both of you," Squirrelflight purred, giving Sparkpaw and then Alderpaw a lick around their ears. "I'm sure you'll both be wonderful warriors one day."

Bramblestar dipped his head in agreement. "I know you both have so much to give your Clan." He stepped back as he finished speaking, and waved his tail to draw Molewhisker and Cherryfall closer. "Listen to your mentors," he told the two new apprentices. "I'm looking forward to hearing good things about your progress."

With an affectionate nuzzle he turned away and headed toward his den. Squirrelflight too gave her kits a quick cuddle, and then followed him. Alderpaw and Sparkpaw were left alone with Molewhisker and Cherryfall.

Molewhisker faced Alderpaw, blinking solemnly. "It's a big responsibility, being an apprentice," he meowed. "You must pay close attention to everything you're taught, because one day your Clan may depend on your fighting or hunting skills."

Alderpaw nodded; his anxiety was returning. A hard lump of worry was lodged in his throat like an indigestible piece of fresh-kill.

"You'll have to work hard to prove you have what it takes to be a proper warrior," Molewhisker went on.

His head held high, Alderpaw tried to look worthy, but was afraid he wasn't making a very good job of it. Hearing Cherryfall talking to Sparkpaw just behind him didn't help at all.

". . . and we'll have such fun exploring the territory!" the ginger she-cat mewed enthusiastically. "And now you'll get to go to Gatherings."

Alderpaw couldn't help wishing that his own mentor was a little more like his littermate's, instead of being so serious.

"Can we start learning to hunt now?" Sparkpaw asked eagerly.

It was Molewhisker who replied. "Not right now. As well as learning to be warriors, apprentices have special duties for the well-being of the whole Clan."

"What do we have to do?" Alderpaw asked, hoping to impress his mentor and show that he was ready for anything.

There was a guilty look on Cherryfall's face as she meowed, "Today you're going to make the elders more comfortable by getting rid of their ticks."

Molewhisker waved his tail in the direction of the medicine cats' den. "Go and ask Leafpool or Jayfeather for some mouse bile. They'll tell you how to use it."

"Mouse bile!" Sparkpaw wrinkled her nose in disgust. "Yuck!"

Alderpaw's heart sank still further. *If this is being an apprentice, I'm not sure I'm going to like it.*

Sunlight shone into the den beneath the hazel bushes where the elders lived. Alderpaw wished that he could curl up in the warmth and take a nap. Instead, he combed his claws painstakingly through Graystripe's long pelt, searching for ticks. Sparkpaw was doing the same for Purdy, while Sandstorm and Millie looked on, patiently waiting their turn.

"Wow, there's a massive tick here!" Sparkpaw exclaimed. "Hold still, Purdy, and I'll get it off."

With clenched teeth she picked up the twig Jayfeather had given her, a ball of moss soaked in mouse bile stuck on one end, and awkwardly maneuvered it until she could dab the moss onto Purdy's tick.

The old tabby shook his pelt and sighed with relief as the tick fell off. "That's much better, young 'un," he purred.

"But this stuff smells *horrible*!" Sparkpaw mumbled around the twig. "I don't know how you elders can stand it." Suppressing a sigh, she began parting Purdy's matted, untidy fur in search of more ticks.

"Now you listen to me, youngster," Purdy meowed. "There's not a cat in ThunderClan who wasn't an apprentice once, takin' off ticks, just like you."

"Even Bramblestar?" Alderpaw asked, pausing with one paw sunk deep in Graystripe's pelt.

"Even *Firestar*," Graystripe responded. "He and I were apprentices together, and I've lost count of the number of ticks we shifted. Hey!" he added, giving Alderpaw a prod. "Watch what you're doing. Your claws are digging into my shoulder!"

"Sorry!" Alderpaw replied.

In spite of being scolded, he felt quite content. Cleaning off ticks was a messy job, but there were worse things than sitting in the sun and listening to the elders. He looked up briefly to see Sandstorm's green gaze resting lovingly on him and his sister as she settled herself more comfortably in the bracken of her nest.

"I remember when your mother was first made an apprentice," she mewed. "Dustpelt was her mentor. You won't remember him—he died in the Great Storm—but he was one of our best warriors, and he didn't put up with any nonsense. Even so, Squirrelflight was a match for him!"

"What did she do?" Alderpaw asked, intrigued to think of his serious, businesslike mother as a difficult young apprentice. "Go on, tell us!"

Sandstorm sighed. "What *didn't* she do? Slipping out of camp to hunt on her own . . . getting stuck in bushes or falling into streams . . . I remember Dustpelt said to me once, 'If that kit of yours doesn't shape up, I'm going to claw her pelt off and hang it on a bush to frighten the foxes!'"

Sparkpaw stared at Sandstorm with her mouth gaping. "He wouldn't!"

"No, of course he wouldn't," Sandstorm responded, her green eyes alight with amusement. "But Dustpelt had to be tough with her. He saw how much she had to offer her Clan, but he knew she wouldn't live up to her potential unless she learned discipline."

"She sure did that," Alderpaw meowed.

"Hey!" Graystripe gave Alderpaw another prod. "What about my ticks, huh?"

"And ours," Millie put in, with a glance at Sandstorm. "We've been waiting *moons*!"

"Sorry . . ."

Alderpaw began rapidly searching through Graystripe's fur, and almost at once came across a huge swollen tick. *That must be making Graystripe really uncomfortable.*

Picking up his stick with the bile-soaked moss, he dabbed at the tick. At the same moment, he happened to glance up, and spotted Leafpool and Jayfeather talking intently to each other just outside the medicine cats' den.

As Alderpaw wondered vaguely what was so important, both medicine cats turned toward him. Suddenly he felt trapped by Jayfeather's blind gaze and Leafpool's searching one.

A worm of uneasiness began to gnaw at Alderpaw's belly. *Great StarClan! Are they talking about* me? *Have I messed something up already?*

CHAPTER 2

♣

Alderpaw scarcely slept at all on his first night in the apprentices'
den. He missed the warm scents of the nursery and the familiar shapes of his mother and Daisy sleeping beside him. The
hollow beneath the ferns seemed empty with only him and his
sister occupying it.

Sparkpaw had curled up at once with her tail wrapped over
her nose, but Alderpaw dozed uneasily, caught between excitement and apprehension at what the new day would bring. He
was fully awake again by the time the first pale light of dawn
began to filter through the ferns.

He sprang up as the arching fronds parted and a head
appeared, gazing down at him, but he relaxed when he recognized Cherryfall.

"Hi!" the ginger she-cat meowed. "Give Sparkpaw a prod.
It's time for our tour of the territory!"

"Me too?" Alderpaw asked.

"Yes, of course. Molewhisker is here waiting. Hurry!"

Alderpaw poked one paw into his sister's side; and her
soft, rhythmic snoring broke off with a squeak of alarm. "Is

it foxes?" she asked, sitting up and shaking scraps of moss off her pelt. "Badgers?"

"No, it's our mentors," Alderpaw told her. "They're going to show us the territory."

"Great!" Sparkpaw shot upward, scrabbling hard with her hind paws as she pushed her way out through the ferns. "Let's go!"

Alderpaw followed more slowly, shivering in the chilly air of dawn. Outside the den Molewhisker and Cherryfall stood waiting side by side. Beyond them, he spotted Bumblestripe, Rosepetal, and Cloudtail emerging from the warriors' den. After a few heartbeats for a quick grooming, they set off with Cloudtail in the lead, and vanished through the thorn tunnel.

"There goes the dawn patrol," Molewhisker meowed. "We'll wait a few moments to let them get away. If you want, you can take something from the fresh-kill pile."

Alderpaw suddenly realized how hungry he was. With Sparkpaw at his side he raced across the camp.

"There's not much here," Sparkpaw complained, prodding with one paw at a scrawny mouse.

"The hunting patrols haven't gone out yet," Alderpaw meowed. He took a blackbird from the scanty prey that remained and began gulping it down.

"Wait till *we're* hunters!" Sparkpaw mumbled around a mouthful of mouse. "Then the fresh-kill pile will *always* be full."

Alderpaw hoped that she was right.

Molewhisker waved his tail from the opposite side of the

camp. Swallowing the last of their prey, the two apprentices bounded back to join him and Cherryfall, who took the lead as they pushed their way through the tunnel in the barrier of thorns that blocked the entrance to the camp.

Alderpaw's pads tingled with anticipation as he slid through the narrow space and set his paws for the first time in the forest.

By this time a gleam of reddish light through the trees showed where the sun would rise. Ragged scraps of mist still floated among the trees, and the grass was heavy with dew.

Sparkpaw's eyes stretched wide as she gazed around her. "It's so big!" she squealed.

Alderpaw was silent, unable to find words for what he could see. Except for the thorn barrier behind him, and the walls of the stone hollow beyond, trees stretched away in every direction, until they faded into a shadowy distance. Their trunks rose many fox-lengths above his head, their branches intertwining. The air was full of tantalizing prey-scents, and he could hear the scuffling of small creatures in the thick undergrowth among the trees.

"Can we hunt?" Sparkpaw asked eagerly.

"Maybe later," Cherryfall told her. "To begin with, we're going to tour the territory. By the time you're made warriors, you'll need to know every paw step of it."

Molewhisker nodded seriously. "Every tree, every rock, every stream . . ."

Alderpaw blinked. *All of it? Surely no cat could ever know* all *of it?*

"This way," Cherryfall meowed briskly. "We'll start by heading for the ShadowClan border."

"Will we meet ShadowClan cats?" Sparkpaw asked. "What happens if we do?"

"Nothing happens," Molewhisker replied sternly. "They stay on their side; we stay on ours."

Cherryfall set out at a good pace, with Sparkpaw bouncing along beside her. Alderpaw followed, and Molewhisker brought up the rear.

Before they had taken many paw steps, they came to a spot where a wide path led away into the forest, covered only with short grass and small creeping plants. Longer grass and ferns bordered it on either side.

"Where does that lead?" Alderpaw asked, angling his ears toward the path. "And why isn't there much growing there?"

"Good question," Molewhisker responded. Alderpaw was pleased at his mentor's approving tone. "That path was made by Twolegs, many, many seasons ago. The same Twolegs who cut out the stone to make the hollow where we camp. It leads to the old Twoleg den, where Leafpool and Jayfeather grow their herbs."

"But we aren't going that way today," Cherryfall added.

Heading farther away from the camp, Alderpaw noticed that the trees ahead seemed to be thinning out. A bright silvery light was shining through them.

"What's that?" Sparkpaw asked.

Before either of the mentors could reply, they came to the edge of the trees and pushed through a thick barrier of holly bushes. Alderpaw emerged onto a stretch of short, soft grass. Beyond it was a strip of pebbles and sandy soil, and beyond that . . .

"Wow!" Sparkpaw gasped. "Is that the lake?"

Alderpaw blinked at the shining expanse of water that lay in front of him. He had heard his Clanmates back in the camp talking about the lake, and he had imagined something a bit bigger than the puddles that formed on the floor of the hollow when it rained. He would never have believed that there was this much water in the whole world.

"There's no end to it!" he exclaimed.

"Oh, yes, there is," Molewhisker assured him. "Some cats have traveled all the way around it. Look over there," he continued, pointing with his tail. "Can you see those trees and bushes? That's RiverClan territory."

Alderpaw narrowed his eyes and could just make out the trees his mentor was talking about, hazy with the distance.

"RiverClan cats love the lake," Cherryfall mewed. "They swim in it and catch fish."

"Weird!" Sparkpaw responded. Giving a little bounce, she added, "Can I catch a fish?" Without waiting for her mentor to reply, she dashed across the pebbles and skidded to a halt with her forepaws splashing at the edge of the water. "Cold!" she yowled, leaping backward with her neck fur bristling. Then she let out a little huff of laughter and bounced back to the edge, her tail waving excitedly. "I can't see any fish," she meowed.

Molewhisker heaved a sigh. "You won't, if you go on like

that. Or anything else, for that matter. Yowling and prancing about, you'll scare away all the prey in the forest."

Sparkpaw backed away from the water again and joined her Clanmates beside the bushes, her tail drooping. "Sorry," she muttered.

"That's okay." Cherryfall rested her tail briefly on her apprentice's shoulders. "We're not hunting right now. And I know how exciting it is to see the lake for the first time."

Molewhisker flicked his ears. "Let's get on."

He took the lead as the cats padded along the lakeshore. Soon they came to a stream that emerged from the forest and flowed into the lake.

"This is the ShadowClan border," Cherryfall announced.

Alderpaw wrinkled his nose at a strong, unfamiliar reek that came from the opposite side of the stream.

"Yuck! What's that?" Sparkpaw asked, taking a pace back and passing her tongue over her jaws as if she could taste something nasty.

"That's the scent of ShadowClan," Molewhisker answered.

"That's *cat* scent?" Sparkpaw sounded outraged. "I thought only foxes stank like that."

"It only smells bad because we're not used to it," Molewhisker pointed out, beginning to lead the way upstream, back into the shelter of the trees. "We probably smell just as bad to them."

"Do not!" Sparkpaw muttered under her breath.

"You know that all the Clans scent-mark their boundaries," Cherryfall explained as they continued to follow the stream. "Of course, we all know where the borders are, but marking them reminds every cat that they aren't supposed to enter another Clan's territory without permission."

"You should be able to pick up the ThunderClan scent markers, too," Molewhisker mewed. "We'll show you how to set them. Before long, you'll be doing it as part of a border patrol."

"Cool!" Alderpaw exclaimed. For the first time he imagined himself as a warrior, maybe even leading a patrol, and setting scent markers to protect his Clan's territory. *I'm learning so much today! I feel like I'm becoming a real part of my Clan.*

After they had traveled some distance into the forest the stream veered sharply away, but the line of ShadowClan and ThunderClan scent markers continued in the same direction across the ground. On the ShadowClan side the leafy trees and thick undergrowth soon gave way to dark pines, the ground covered by a thick layer of needles.

"Now we'll show you something really different," Cherryfall promised. She beckoned the two apprentices into a hazel thicket, signaling with her tail for them to keep quiet. "What do you think of that?"

Alderpaw gazed out into a clearing. Several weird structures were dotted around, like little dens made of green pelts. Tasting the air, he realized they were right on the border between the two Clans. As well as the scent markings, he managed to pick up another scent he had never encountered before.

"Is this some sort of Twoleg stuff?" he asked. "I've never seen a Twoleg, but Squirrelflight says they come into the forest sometimes."

"Exactly right," Molewhisker purred, giving Alderpaw a light flick over his ear with his tail. Alderpaw felt his chest swelling with pride. "In greenleaf, Twolegs come and live here in these little dens."

"Why do they do that?" Sparkpaw asked, sounding as if she didn't believe him.

Molewhisker shrugged. "StarClan knows."

"Are they here now?" Alderpaw asked, glancing around nervously in case a Twoleg was looming up behind him.

"They're probably still asleep in there," Cherryfall mewed. "Lazy lot. Anyway, this clearing is in ShadowClan territory, so they're ShadowClan's problem. Let's be on our way."

THE TIME HAS COME
FOR DOGS TO RULE THE WILD

SURVIVORS

BOOK ONE:
THE EMPTY CITY

Lucky is a golden-haired mutt with a nose for survival. Other dogs have Packs, but Lucky stands on his own . . . until the Big Growl strikes. Suddenly the ground splits wide open. The longpaws disappear. And enemies threaten Lucky at every turn. For the first time in his life, Lucky needs to rely on other dogs to survive. But can he ever be a true Pack dog?

DON'T MISS

RETURN TO THE WILD

SEEKERS

BOOK ONE:
ISLAND OF SHADOWS

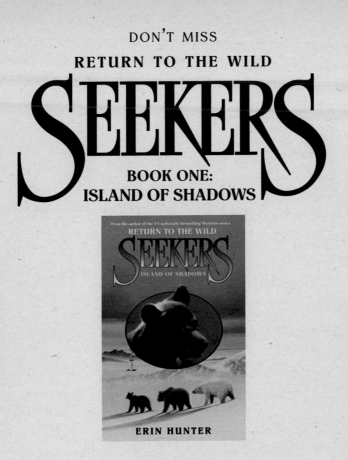

Toklo, Kallik, and Lusa survived the perilous mission that brought them together, and now it's time for them to find their way home. When the group reaches a shadowy island covered in mountains and ice, Kallik is sure they're almost back to the Frozen Sea. But a terrifying accident leads them into a maze of abandoned tunnels, unlike anything they've ever seen before—making them question their path once again.

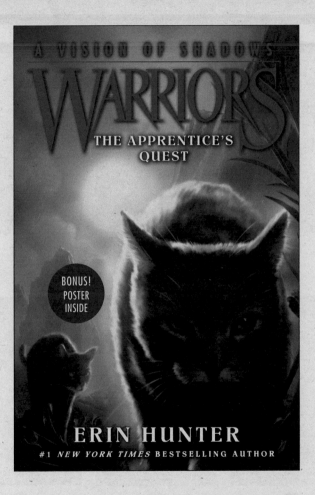

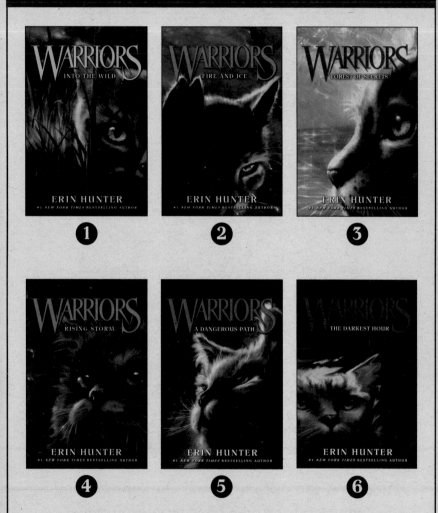

FOLLOW THE ADVENTURES!

WARRIORS: THE PROPHECIES BEGIN

In the first series, sinister perils threaten the four warrior Clans. Into the midst of this turmoil comes Rusty, an ordinary housecat, who may just be the bravest of them all.

HARPER
An Imprint of HarperCollinsPublishers

www.warriorcats.com

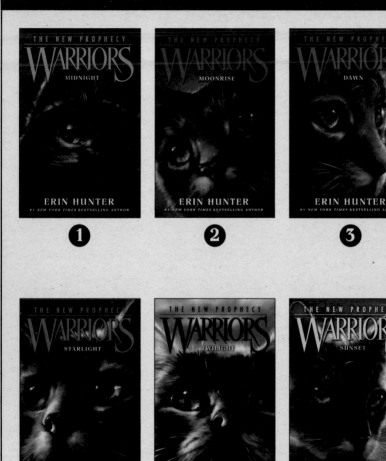

WARRIORS: THE NEW PROPHECY

In the second series, follow the next generation of heroic cats as they set off on a quest to save the Clans from destruction.

HARPER
An Imprint of HarperCollinsPublishers

www.warriorcats.com

WARRIORS: POWER OF THREE

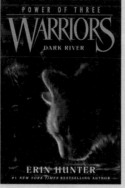

1

2

3

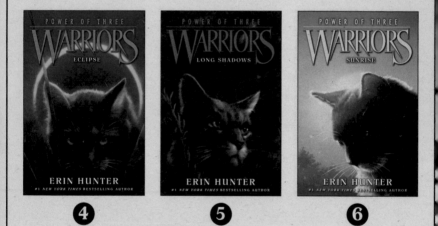

4

5

6

In the third series, Firestar's grandchildren begin their
training as warrior cats. Prophecy foretells that they will
hold more power than any cats before them.

HARPER
An Imprint of HarperCollinsPublishers

www.warriorcats.com

WARRIORS: OMEN OF THE STARS

In the fourth series, find out which ThunderClan apprentice will complete the prophecy.

HARPER
An Imprint of HarperCollins*Publishers*

www.warriorcats.com

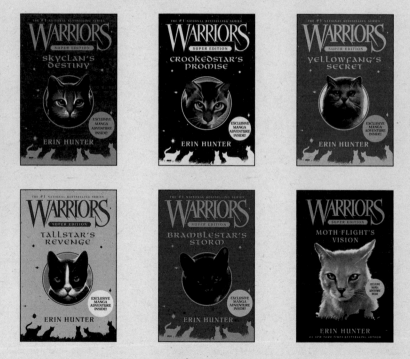

WARRIORS: BONUS STORIES

Discover the untold stories of the warrior cats and Clans when you download the separate ebook novellas—or read them in two paperback bind-ups!

HARPER
An Imprint of HarperCollinsPublishers

www.warriorcats.com

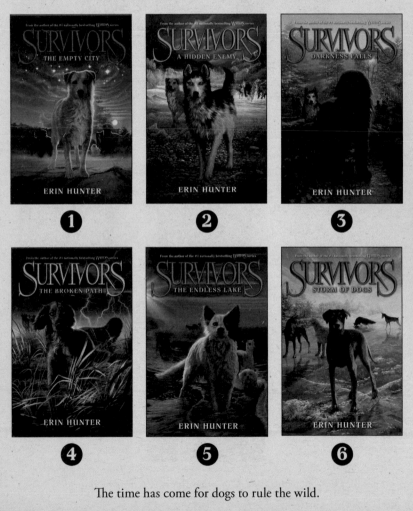